PRAISE FOR NINA LAURIN

"This addicting thriller rachets up the suspense until the very last page."

—*Woman's World* on *The Starter Wife*

"Laurin, with her knack for psychological suspense, here portrays the effects of obsession in chilling detail as the facts of Claire's life are revealed. A spine-tingler."

—*Booklist* on *The Starter Wife*

"*The Starter Wife* reminded me of the powerful novel *Girl on the Train* by Paula Hawkins."

—*Missourian*

"Nina Laurin's psychological suspense thrill ride will have you ripping through its pages at warp speed as you dig for the truth about a fateful event that drove two twin siblings apart."

—PopSugar.com on *What My Sister Knew*

"*What My Sister Knew* is a thriller built on shifting sands; just as one feels solid ground under his feet, the earth cracks open, and the reader falls into the abyss where nothing and no one is trustworthy. No suspense fan should miss this book."

—NYJournalofBooks.com

A WOMAN ALONE

A WOMAN ALONE

NINA LAURIN

GRAND CENTRAL
PUBLISHING

NEW YORK   BOSTON

Copyright © 2020 by Ioulia Zaitchik
Excerpt from *The Starter Wife* copyright © 2019 by Ioulia Zaitchik

Cover design by Lisa Amoroso
Cover photos: window © Jill Ferry /Arcangel; woman © Stanislav Solntsev / Trevillion Images
Cover copyright © 2020 by Hachette Book Group, Inc.

Grand Central Publishing
Hachette Book Group
1290 Avenue of the Americas, New York, NY 10104
grandcentralpublishing.com
twitter.com/grandcentralpub

First Edition: June 2020

Grand Central Publishing is a division of Hachette Book Group, Inc. The Grand Central Publishing name and logo is a trademark of Hachette Book Group, Inc.

The publisher is not responsible for websites (or their content) that are not owned by the publisher.

The Hachette Speakers Bureau provides a wide range of authors for speaking events. To find out more, go to www.hachettespeakersbureau.com or call (866) 376-6591.

Library of Congress Control Number: 2020932490

ISBN: 978-1-5387-1576-5 (trade paperback), 978-1-5387-1575-8 (ebook)

Printed in the United States of America

LSC-C

10 9 8 7 6 5 4 3

CHAPTER ONE

As I make my way downstairs, I hear the coffee machine whir to life. Even before the smell of expensive, exotic beans reaches me halfway up the stairs, I know it's making one long double espresso and one skim latte. The former for me, the latter for Scott.

It's only one of the many perks. When I went to take my shower, all I had to do was touch the sensor-laden handle. Detecting my signature, the water blasted from the showerhead at a precise pressure and temperature. No more cringing while the stream warms up, goose bumps racing up my arms and legs. Like the water, the floor is heated, exact to one-tenth of a degree.

As soon as I left the bathroom and Scott went in, more sensors detected the change, and imperceptibly, the air shifted. Silent, invisible fans started up in all corners of the bathroom, drawing the humidity out and cooling the air to the perfect breezy temperature he prefers.

Now I drop two sliced bagels into the toaster. One will come out barely warmed, and the other browned to a crisp and slathered with butter. It's nice not having to think about it but it also anchors one in one's habits, good or not-so-good. Lately, the tap in the bar has been pouring cocktails the second Scott comes through the front door at 6:30.

I don't have to worry about waking Taryn. At exactly 7:35, the curtains of her room upstairs will open and the tablet by her bed will flicker on, distracting her with morning cartoons while I prepare her oatmeal and come to get her.

Right now, I'm deliberately stalling. I want this moment with Scott, nice and quiet, without oatmeal flying in all directions and boisterous requests for the Pop-Tarts Taryn knows she's not going to get. She will be absorbed in her shows or interactive games or whatever the AI decides best fits her mood this morning. She won't notice if I take fifteen minutes longer.

I feel a brief flash of guilt that dissolves as soon as I pick up my coffee and breathe in the luxurious smell. Scott is coming down the stairs, his own tablet in hand. He gets his cup from the machine, deposits a quick kiss on my cheek as he passes me, and sits down at the counter.

"Where's Taryn?" he asks.

I tell him she's still upstairs.

"But I want to say bye to her before I go to work."

He looks a tiny bit vexed. I've become more attuned to shifts in his moods since we moved here, and I fear that he might have become more aware of mine as well. "And won't she be late for day care?"

I feel my face color slightly. Yes, she will be a few minutes late. I can't see the harm, although I know it's motivated by pure selfishness.

Scott misinterprets the blushing. "She's refusing to go again?"

"No," I reassure him with a laugh. "If anything, she likes it there a bit too much. The other day, she asked me if she could stay in the overtime group. Can you believe it? That's because all her friends do. I think she doesn't like that they're playing and... I don't know, bonding? Without her there."

Scott shakes his head and chuckles in turn. "It's good that she's making friends though. Maybe you can leave her in the overtime group once or twice a week so she doesn't feel left out."

"That's not a bad idea."

Deep down, I'm a tiny bit horrified by the suggestion. I know exactly why Taryn is one of the few children at the local day care to get picked up on time. Other parents work long hours to pay for living in SmartBlock. Many work right there at IntelTech, which gives employees discounts, but not quite as nice as the deal we got, since we got to be part of the trial program. I get the luxury to be a housewife—if you can call it that, considering that machines and futuristic gadgets do everything for me.

As if in response to my thoughts, the moment I set my empty coffee cup on the designated metal stripe on the counter, its surface opens up seamlessly and swallows up the cup, which will be washed and dried somewhere deep in the bowels of a concealed dishwasher. All designed to save time on busy mornings. For people who are hurrying to be somewhere. Who have something to do.

"Doesn't it make you feel kind of useless?" Scott jokes.

My laugh comes too soon, before he even finishes the question that's supposed to be rhetorical, I'm sure. It's sharp, tinny, and hollow.

He finishes his coffee, stuffs the last of his undertoasted plain bagel into his mouth, and the dishes disappear in turn. When he gets up to leave, it's exactly five minutes past eight. The house has memorized how long we take to do each and every insignificant task: eat a bagel, four minutes; check the news, five minutes thirty seconds; kiss your wife goodbye, three seconds; put on shoes, fifteen seconds. In the garage, I know his car has already begun to purr with its silent electric engine. Everything here is electric, sustainable, green.

I tap the screen of my own tablet as soon as he's out of sight. There's an alert reminding me that Taryn has been up for twenty-two minutes now, and in three minutes and thirty seconds, she will be officially late for day care but I sweep it impatiently aside.

I tap the icons and swipe until the security camera footage fills the tablet screen. On it, I watch the electric car pull out of the garage, into yet another bright, perfect day in bright, perfect Venture, IL, the place where dreams come true. That's what the brochure said.

You don't know the half of it.

THREE MONTHS EARLIER

"So what do *you* do, Cecelia?"

I hadn't expected the question, seemingly innocuous. Although I probably should have. I blink.

"I'm looking for work, actually," I say. "I used to work freelance but then I went on maternity leave, and with a toddler at home—"

"Understandable." The woman who insisted we call her Clarisse gives a small nod and smiles. The smile is like a rictus because of the vast amount of plastic surgery I'm sure helped sculpt her face. I give up guessing how old she actually is. Fifty-five? Sixty? More? Clarisse seems like one of those women who find me pitiful. To give up a career and independence, all for a *child*, how pedestrian, tut-tut. Well, we can't all have high-ranking positions in major corporations. Billions of dollars in contracts with Chicago, Minneapolis, Cleveland, Toronto, wasn't that what she said? Everyone wants a piece of IntelTech and its products, Smart-Block and SmartHome, trademark registered, all rights reserved.

"Well, I'm happy to say you're exactly what we're looking for. A young, modern family. Modern values. Focused above all on self-fulfillment and deriving satisfaction from your life, experiences over possessions. This is exactly what SmartHomes are about. Experiences."

It sounds to me like it's the opposite. The cost of a SmartHome starts at nine hundred ninety-nine thousand nine hundred and ninety-nine dollars, for the most basic two-bedroom model.

"The concept behind the design is to reduce the amount of time you waste on trivial things every day," Clarisse says. Her gaze travels from me to Scott and back. "Have you ever wondered how many seconds, minutes, hours you spend every day on boring, useless things? Like waiting in line, setting alarm clocks, waiting for the bus. Time that adds up. Hours, days, whole years. Wouldn't you rather spend that time enjoying life?"

She doesn't wait for an answer. "Of course you would. So would anyone. That's where SmartBlock comes in. You may not have noticed but you—along with most people in most major cities, actually—have already used our technologies. Improved bus and subway services, for instance. Reduced waiting times, not to mention reduced traffic and nonexistent emissions, all thanks to an automated system that evaluates the volume of passengers and responds in real time by increasing or reducing the number of available transport units. I could go on but I'm not here to bore you . . ."

Did I look bored? I must have. I did zone out for a few seconds. Her voice has that quality, polite and pleasant but also bland.

"And now we're experimenting with entire neighborhoods that are custom-built and adjusted to the needs of the residents. The logical extension of that is the Smart-Home technology, which you will be testing. If you're interested, of course."

I chance a sideways glance at my husband, who is listening raptly, and I just know it. My heart sinks, and my stomach knots. He's already decided. There won't be any talking him out of it from this point on.

But I'll be damned if I'm not going to try.

CHAPTER TWO

The tablet beeps with another reminder. The episode of Taryn's favorite interactive cartoon has ended. Would I like to play another? In other words, technology is reminding me, in its usual passive-aggressive way, what a terrible and neglectful parent I am. I tap No, and as I set the tablet down on the counter, I find myself wincing, already bracing myself for what I know is coming. And she doesn't make me wait. I hear the high-pitched whine from upstairs with to-the-second precision. Right now my daughter is stabbing her chubby fingers into the screen, frustrated when it doesn't yield to her demand. Until finally I hear the usual war cry of "*Mommy!*"

"Coming," I say, too softly for her to hear. I guess it's meant for me, not her. As I start up the stairs, I throw a longing glance over my shoulder at the tablet, sitting peacefully on the kitchen counter where I left it, its screen dark. I could buy myself another twenty-two minutes of peace right now, play another episode. What happened to my best intentions? I won't have a child raised by screens. I did not go through all the anguish and trouble, the crushing depression, empty hopes, to plunk my precious baby in front of an iPad so I can have an extra quarter of an hour of me time.

Taryn is sitting in her crib, glaring at me, frustration written plain on her round face. "Another," she says petulantly before I'm even in the door. "Now."

"Good morning, sweetheart," I say on autopilot. She looks from me to the screen that's holding her favorite characters captive, frozen in midmotion at my mercy.

"Another," she repeats. Changing her strategy in that endearingly unsubtle way only a three-year-old can manage, she gives me a beseeching smile. "Please, Mommy. Just one more?"

"It's time to eat breakfast," I say, and reach to pick her up. She wiggles away. "And then it's time to go to day care. Don't you want to play with all your friends?"

She responds with a pout. When I reach into the crib and pick her up, she lets out a high-pitched scream right into my ear.

"Taryn," I mutter, wondering once again if I'm talking to me or to her. "Calm down. You love day care, remember? And besides, you *have* to go."

"Why?" She wiggles and kicks and flails her arms. I barely flinch away as her open palm hits me in the eye.

"Because," I snap. Ignoring her protests, I carry her downstairs, all the while dodging furious kicks and tiny fists, wondering if we're both going to go tumbling down the stairs. For someone so small, she's surprisingly heavy, like that little chubby body has bones made of lead. Finally, I manage to install her in her high chair. The microwave beeps, alerting me that her oatmeal is ready. Just as I turn to get it, she stops screeching and lets out a long, angry huff.

"You're home," she says, suddenly calm. "I stay home too."

I freeze, the bowl of oatmeal burning my hand. It's not what she just said; it's how she said it. With a meanness that's almost shocking, coming from someone so small and adorable. She is cute as a button, and even at this early age, it already makes a difference. She's a natural leader, her teacher at day care tells me. The other children just want to follow her in everything she does.

And frankly, why *can't* she stay at home? What do I tell her? The same thing I told Scott and the teachers? That it's time she learns to socialize? That I need time to focus on housework and my own projects? That's a crock of shit. The truth is that I just need a break from my own child. Every self-help book would say it's perfectly normal, that I'm a modern woman who deserves time for myself, et cetera. But it never occurred to me that Taryn might ever pick up on that. To be honest, I didn't think she was smart enough. Yet.

"Eat your breakfast," I say sharply, and set the plastic bowl in front of her with a clack. My fingertips are burning. Steam rises from the bowl in thick billows. The oatmeal is not the temperature I preset the microwave to. It's piping hot.

With alarm, I reach out to take the bowl but she's already grabbed her spoon and scooped an oversize glob of oatmeal. *Taryn*, I start to say. Too late. She raises it to her mouth, her gaze on my face, and I have time to see the hint of a malicious glimmer in her eyes as she stuffs the boiling-hot oatmeal into her mouth.

The oatmeal goes flying all over the counter, her chin, and her shirt, followed by a wail I'm sure they can hear down the street. As I pick her up, making soothing sounds, my thoughts are in a jumble. *Now she's going to think I did it on purpose* gives way to *Now everyone is going to think I did it on purpose* to *They're going to think I'm a bad mother*. I'm not sure what bothers me most.

Once Taryn has been soothed and cleaned up, she becomes placid and docile, as if she'd already spent all her angry energy. There's still a reddish spot on her upper lip that I can't look at without my heart clenching. But she lets me dress her, pack up her things, and take her to day care, all without a word of objection. I'm in a fog the whole time, and by the time I park my car in the garage and go into the house, I'm so exhausted it's hard to believe I still have the whole day ahead of me. So many blissful hours of quiet. I should be happy but I'm just listless.

"Run a bath," I say to the tablet. *With pleasure, Cecelia*, chimes the alert. Upstairs, I can hear the hum of water. Relieved, I kick off my shoes and set off in search of my book. I read paperback books, which Scott doesn't cease to make fun of. Once upon a time—before everything

went wrong—I was a freelance graphic designer who
settled into a career of making covers for ebooks. I
made quite a good living off it too. I was good at it,
and it was easy and reasonably lucrative—even considering Scott made more than enough money for the both
of us. But I liked the work, I liked keeping busy. I
liked making beautiful things. I was just branching out
into branding and websites when the renovations of our
old house began, and I abandoned the idea. And then,
after the whole nightmare happened, the ebook covers
fell by the wayside too. Now my own website, which
used to have hundreds of hits a day, has been reduced
to one static page with the brief message that says it
all: coversbycece.com is undergoing reconstruction—check
back here for more news.

But even when ebooks were my bread and butter, I
never could quite get in on the trend. I gave it a try but I
missed the weight and texture of paper and the distraction-
free experience a good old-fashioned paperback provides.
You can't click over to Facebook or Twitter like you do
when you're reading on a tablet or phone. And you don't
have hundreds of other books at your disposal, available
at the tap of a fingertip. I always thought that somehow
cheapens the experience.

At the moment, I'm finishing up one of those
Scandinavian mystery-thrillers that delight in their own
gruesomeness. You'd think I wouldn't be able to so much
as touch them, after what happened just over a year ago,
but on the contrary, I find them oddly comforting.

Right now, though, my copy is nowhere to be found.

Which is annoying because I was pages away from finding out who the culprit was and how the damaged female detective's love triangle finally worked out.

"Your bath is ready, Cecelia," announces a pleasant voice, accompanied by a faraway chime from the tablet. The house knows what room I'm in at all times, of course, due to advanced motion-detecting technology combined with the input from the identity chip. It would be great if it could also locate my paperback. With a groan, I grab a decoration magazine from a side table in the hall and head to the bathroom.

The house is true to its word, as always. The bathtub is full, topped with a shimmering heap of foam. The scent of lavender and eucalyptus pleasantly tickles my nostrils as I throw off my clothes. Magazine in hand—it's an old issue that I know by heart but it'll do—I swing my leg over the edge of the tub and lower it into the water.

The shock races up my nerves, from my toes to my spine. It's so sharp and sudden that I give a start, instinctively yank my foot out of the water, and lose my balance. My behind hits the ceramic, and my teeth clack. The whole thing takes less than a blink. I sit on the floor, numb with shock, trying to comprehend what just happened.

"Saya?" I yell out.

Recognizing the voice command of its name, the house's system beeps on. The pleasant electronic voice sounds from the speakers in the ceiling. "Yes?"

But my words have deserted me. "The—the water," I stammer. I stare at my foot, my toes a painful crimson, still throbbing.

"I'm sorry, Lydia," says the voice. "Would you like to change your temperature settings?"

"Yes," I snarl, relieved that finally, someone—something—decided to work with me. "Change them to—"

I stop midsentence. "What did you just call me?"

THREE MONTHS EARLIER

"What is your problem, Cece?" Scott struggles to keep his voice to a loud whisper. He doesn't want to make a scene here, in the waiting room. We were supposed to have "a few minutes of privacy to talk it over," as Clarisse put it, but this place hardly feels private. I think of all the hidden cameras and microphones that could be spying on us right this second. "Isn't this what you wanted?"

"What? To live in Big Brother's guest room?"

He groans and rolls his eyes. Just like I thought, he doesn't understand.

"This is what you wanted. This is what we need. Think of how secure it's going to be. No one can come within a mile of the place without being seen and recorded. And should anything happen, it'll call an ambulance . . . think of that! Think of Taryn!"

"They want to microchip us like purebred cats," I snap back.

"All that information will be private. You heard her—they have the country's top cybersecurity experts on payroll. The only way the information will ever be used is for our benefit."

"Do you even hear yourself?"

He gives a laugh, shifting his strategy—putting on the charming, boyish smile, just like in the early days when we used to affectionately tease each other, not snipe at each other at the first opportunity. "For God's sake, Cece," he says. "You think we're not spied on now? Your phone knows more about you than I do."

I sulk because it's hard to disagree with that.

"Face it, the time of privacy is over whether we like it or not," he says. "Unless you want to just leave it all behind and go live off the land deep in the Appalachians somewhere."

I can't help but shrug.

"That's what I thought. And you say you hate being spied on but I don't see you deleting your Facebook and Instagram. Or throwing your GPS out the car window. Only instead of selling our information to corporations for money, this place will use it to better our lives. Sounds like an improvement to me."

I can only shake my head. I know he's winning the argument, and I have nothing to say. Nothing I can put into words.

"And anyway, this is a trial. We can't afford to be early adopters. At least not yet, not until I get the promotion. Because yes, people like us pay millions of dollars to live there. Are they all idiots too?"

"I never thought you were an idiot," I point out. *Just gullible.*

"Worst that can happen, we live there for a couple of years—we're not going to sell the house yet—and then we can leave! At the very least, it's a break from the same old. A change of scenery. Isn't that what you wanted?"

Here we are again, with whatever it was I said I wanted.

For God's sake, what I wanted . . . what I really wanted was to simply be out of the house where a man tried to kill me.

CHAPTER THREE

I run my fingertip over the thin skin on my outer wrist, right below the wrist bone. You can't tell—there's no scar and not even a mark—but this is where the microchip is embedded. A microchip that, according to the brochure, "thousands of sensors all over the house will detect and react to your unique DNA signature."

I don't see why they couldn't have gone with facial recognition or any similar technology instead but, according to Clarisse, the DNA signature offers superior possibilities. The chip is powered by my own body heat, and, apart from identifying me flawlessly to every feature of the SmartHome and SmartBlock, it also takes my vital signs and will activate a call for help if it picks up on any distress. For instance, if I have a heart attack in the middle of the day with no one to see me and I can't get to the phone, the chip will transmit a distress signal to the central command system, which will call an ambulance, sending the data along for good measure. *Not wasting a single second to get you the help you need*, the brochure read.

Think of what it'll mean for Taryn, Scott said. No more panic in the middle of the night because of a rash or a fever—the chip knows best when the situation is urgent and makes the decision for us. He presented it as a good thing.

But I balked at the idea of microchipping my child, sticking that needle into the perfect, creamy skin on her chubby arm. It feels wrong, I told Scott. It feels like despoiling her. Taking away her integrity somehow.

He rolled his eyes and said I get it from my mom. Which made my face flush with embarrassment and put a definitive end to the argument, like he knew it would.

Whenever he thinks I'm acting "crazy"—his term—all he has to do is insinuate that I'm turning into Therese. It never fails. Whether it's me suggesting—just suggesting, in passing—that we have Taryn baptized, to expressing concern that having five mobile devices for three people, two phones, and three tablets, might be less than healthy—it always means I'm turning into my mother and will inevitably go off the deep end. And this was before the SmartHome project was even on our radar.

So Scott won the argument. On the same afternoon we were handed the keys to the house, we were officially given our chips. The needle has a built-in anesthetic that kicks in with surprising speed, and I barely felt a pinch. I was so worried that Taryn would throw a tantrum when she saw the needle, with tears and wailing, and I wouldn't be able to go through with it. But Taryn was too busy looking around the office, twisting her neck this way and that, her brown eyes the size of saucers, and she didn't even see the technician approaching her with the needle, cooing soothingly. When she pressed the device against Taryn's arm, there was just a soft hiss that lasted for half a second, and then it was done. Taryn blinked, bewildered, wondering whether she should cry but there was already nothing to cry about. She got a little plush teddy bear for her good behavior, a logo of IntelTech on its belly, and that was the end of that.

Now, she would be safe at all times, Clarisse said—the house's sensors would know if she got out of her playpen, if she toddled too close to any stairs or kitchen appliances, if she took a fall. Both Scott and I would get instant alerts on all our devices.

Clarisse shook our hands. We were in.

At my request, the house obediently changes the temperature settings for the bath but I'm no longer in the mood. I drain the tub, go downstairs, and get on my laptop.

There's an app we installed on all our computers and devices that lets us access the SmartHome portal to report any bugs and malfunctions, among other things. I think that trying to boil me alive counts as a bug. Plus, this is part of the reason for the trial—to help them improve the system. At the price of some occasional boiled toes and burnt palates, I guess. I click on the app impatiently, and it loads in the blink of an eye. I click Report a problem.

The house's operating system is named Saya. Each house on the street has its own: The one to the right has

Sandy and the one on the left has Sophia. Always women's names, and the default voices are soft and pleasant.

Any malfunctions with Saya? Let us know! prompts the page.

I enter the date and time. Microwave oven setting malfunction, I type in. Bath temperature malfunction. The system registers both.

Used the wrong name, I type, then backspace. Did it actually use the wrong name? I can't be sure. Maybe I misheard. My ears were ringing from the impact. While temperature screwups merely caused annoyance, this one makes me nervous. So much for the unique DNA signature. Who on earth would Lydia be, anyway? We were the first to live in this particular model, Clarisse said. And if "Lydia"—if that's what I actually heard—is real, why would she take her bath at eighty degrees Celsius?

I decide to forget about it for the time being. The important thing was the temperature, and that's taken care of. I'm so sorry you experienced this inconvenience, the page informs me. Please accept our sincere apologies on behalf of SmartHome.

This does little to mellow me out. "Saya," I say out loud.

"Yes, Cecelia?"

"Can you find me some vegan recipes, please?"

Number one item on my to-do list is to prepare for the party tonight. *Party* is a bit of a strong word for what's going to be more of a pretentious dinner.

"Of course, Cecelia. Today's most popular vegan recipes are uploading to your tablet."

Scott's colleague's wife is a militant organic-vegan who

I suspect actually has some form of an eating disorder. So although she'll be the only vegan at the table of six, no dead animal flesh must come within a mile of the kitchen.

"Never mind," I say after a moment's thought. "Find me some vegan caterers who are available for tonight."

"Of course, Cecelia."

Of course.

*   *   *

As usual, Saya—and the last-minute caterer found by Saya—doesn't let me down. All the food is in place, waiting for its time in the vast downstairs refrigerator. Only a couple of items need to be heated up beforehand. The menu is basically different combinations of various rabbit foods, profoundly unappetizing.

Not that I'm all that hungry to begin with. Little work to do means little energy expenditure. Taryn has been picked up and is safely absorbed in her tablet, in one of the many educational games I downloaded on it. It makes me feel less bad that the games are educational. She's not just out of my hair for an evening—she's also learning about the fauna of African veldts or something like that.

Scott shows up pretty much at the same time as the guests. Which is not a surprise—since another handy app on my phone sends me a notification when he leaves work and when he's approaching the house. But still, it's a small annoyance.

Scott's coworker is Kyle, and his wife, the rail-thin,

red-lipsticked vegan, is Emma. The other couple was invited, I'm guessing, for my benefit: one of Scott's old friends from his previous job and his wife, Mia, who I used to get along with quite well. I alienated most of my real friends over the last few years, the dark years of the fertility struggle. And the few who remained dropped off after all the drama went down.

I can't blame them. No, that's not true. I totally blame them, even though it's hardly their fault. They just never were the type of friends to stick around in dark times. More the fair-weather kind, far more common these days, more suited for wine-soaked girls' nights and shopping sprees. That's who I surrounded myself with because that's who was available. In the age of smartphones and apps, there's no need to stick around for someone's moping. Why bother when a brand-new partner in crime to sip wine with is just a tap of a fingertip away?

Lounging in the living room while Scott goes to make drinks and uncork bottles of wine, Emma the vegan and Mia politely admire the house, like they're supposed to. I say I wish I could take the credit but everything was here when we moved in. Emma runs her hand appreciatively along the lacquered surface of the hardwood coffee table, tracing the whorls in the exotic wood frozen forever beneath the thick layer of gloss.

"Good materials," she says. "Hard to find these days. Everyone cuts corners where they can."

I think of the tree that had once been, a magnificent exotic species from South America or maybe Africa, sawed into neat slices meant to adorn rich people's houses. That doesn't seem to bother her, for all the posturing about ecological footprints and animal rights. Then again, if her five-hundred-dollar pumps aren't genuine leather, I'm willing to eat them.

But you don't point these things out. Not in this crowd.

"Yes," Mia chimes in. "My sister had a house built to measure last year. Cost a ton of money. Imagine her surprise when she dropped in on the contractors to find them painting her walls with six-dollar-a-gallon paint."

Emma commiserates, while I wonder what I could possibly talk to them about. Scott tops off Emma's wineglass and gives me a meaningful look. Or maybe it just seems meaningful, because the conversation is now about swapping renovation horror stories. Not a direction I like at all. My face grows warmer. I fidget on my chair.

He gets it and comes to my aid. "Food, anyone?"

The women are annoyed at the interruption but the husbands eagerly agree so we move to the dining room.

As we sit down to the rabbit-food feast I set out on the dining room table, I can tell the drinks are starting to kick in. Everyone visibly relaxes, and the slight air of formality slides off them as they tuck unselfconsciously into their appetizers. I excuse myself before picking up my tablet and remotely starting the preheat of the main course, some kind of tofu curry.

"Lucky, lucky you," Mia says to me. "You must get everything done in the blink of an eye with all this tech around."

"I won't lie," I say with a chuckle. "There are advantages."

"She's being coy," Scott says. His face is a bit flushed,

and I wonder how many times he's refilled his wineglass. "She loves it here. Who wouldn't?"

Later, once the main course has been eaten (or, in Emma's case, picked at and left mostly intact) and the third or fourth bottle of wine has been opened, I realize I'm actually having a good time. I'm relaxed in my comfortable chair. The lights appear to have dimmed—I don't remember presetting that but it's nice. It smooths the edges of everything.

Emma, who's not nearly as discriminating with alcohol as she is with food—I suspect two of the three or four bottles of wine ended up in her glass—has finally let loose and is telling a story about one of her friends' Botox disaster. Scott is talking to Emma's husband about work. I'm getting lulled into it all when a discreet notification chimes on the screen of my phone.

"Sorry," I say, and I really am sorry to have to get up. "I have to put Taryn to bed."

"Wow," says Emma, interrupting her story, "I hardly even noticed you *had* a kid!" Her face is flushed from the wine, and nobody, least of all her, seems to notice the tactlessness of her little slip. "It's the robot nanny?"

"Entertainment center," Scott corrects.

"One hell of an entertainment center. We should get one for Jason," Mia chimes in, howling with laughter. "Oh, he's just hell on wheels. Taryn is cute now—wait till she's five!"

I excuse myself, letting them continue that train of thought. Upstairs, the credits of the latest educational cartoon episode are rolling on the tablet screen as my daughter blinks sleepily at it.

At once, I'm overcome with tenderness. Maybe it's the wine amplifying my emotions but I just want to pick her up and cuddle with her on top of her tiny bed. All this, I think to myself as I reach out and switch the screen off with a tap, all this is for her. So she'll grow up with every possible comfort and every possible opportunity. So that she's safe at all times, sheltered from the scary parts of life—at least for now. I'm not dumb. I know it can't go on like this forever, with her hidden inside this cozy digital cocoon. Kids grow up and venture out into the world, and she will too. In time.

For now, I'll do everything I can do.

As soon as the screen goes dark, Taryn lets out a high-pitched squeal of protest that splits the silence and makes me wince in spite of myself. Shredding my peaceful little mind-image.

"It's sleepy time, Taryn," I coo automatically as I reach to pick her up. She swats violently at my hands, trying to bat them away. Her face is quickly turning red—a sign that a tantrum is coming.

"Taryn," I say, with a soft but present note of warning.

"No!" she shrieks. "No sleep!"

Her eyes are red and shiny, and her upper lip is already glistening with snot. She wiggles with all her might when I finally pick her up. Her small but pointy little foot connects with just the right spot under my ribs, making me hiss and stifle a bad word.

A headache throbs in the back of my head. Maybe I had enough wine after all. When did she become this bad? She was such a sweet baby. She slept through the night at a mere three or four months and was always smiling, eager to be picked up.

Shame floods my face with heat, followed quickly by anger. Anger I have no outlet for because there's no one left to be angry at, except myself. That's what the child psychologist said. I thought Taryn was too young to understand but he said she could still pick up on subconscious cues. Detect my distress and fear, sense my lingering trauma for weeks and months afterward. Is that why she's acting out? Because I, her mother, the person responsible for taking care of her and making her happy and safe, had failed?

At least her screen is consistently there, present, unrelentingly cheerful and entertaining, not sneaking away into corners to cry ten times a day. And Scott was absent then and he's absent now—his solution was to throw money at the problem, and this house is just the culmination of it. No wonder she prefers the screen.

By the time I get Taryn to sleep—it feels like it's been hours, although it can't have been more than thirty minutes or so—the headache has evolved into a migraine, and all I want to do is follow her example and hit the hay. The room is dimly lit by Taryn's moon-shaped night-light, and the only sound is her soft, little snore, which I used to find so adorable. Of course, once she was in bed and tucked under the ethereally soft blankets, she passed out almost instantly without further argument.

I come to the window and lean my forehead on the cool glass pane, closing my eyes. When I open them, I see what I first think is a reflection in the glass, a glimmer of light.

I blink but it's still there, and I realize it's not reflected in the window but outside of it.

I take a tiny step back and look across the dark expanse of our backyard. Right now it's an empty space. We had big plans, if we decided to stay on board and buy the place, to build a gazebo or a swing set for Taryn or plant a lush garden. For the time being, I planned to at least bring in some flower boxes, to plant lilies and other low-maintenance plants to dress up the acid-green expanse of empty lawn. But I've put it off and put it off, and now it's nearing fall and it's too late.

The lawn eventually ends with a fence, and behind it looms the neighboring house. It's not like ours—the designers have no doubt decided to avoid the trap of having rows of identical buildings, which the target clientele would consider tacky and suburban. So instead, each street is an assorted set of houses that nonetheless complement each other, with variety to suit tastes and price ranges.

The house out back is bigger and starkly square and modern in contrast to our more traditional-looking abode with its slanted roof. The wall facing us is made up of floor-to-ceiling windows, all of them one-way glass, of course. But in that moment, it had let something through. Just the glimmer of our terrace light when it caught on the round shape of a lens.

CHAPTER FOUR

I come back downstairs, unnerved and stone-cold sober. Even my headache has somewhat faded into the background. I linger in the door, observing the scene. My husband is topping off Mia's glass, while Mia's husband, Eric, is telling something to Emma in a hushed voice, which makes her giggle drunkenly. They don't notice me at first.

Scott is the first one to look up. "Taryn is sleeping?"

"Yeah," I say.

He nods at my glass, which he—or someone else—has refilled, pretty much to the brim. Since those giant glasses fit half a bottle each, you're only supposed to splash wine into the bottom, to let it breathe. But right now it's welcome.

"Thanks," I say, and take a generous sip. He looks at me expectantly, and I sit down, hovering on the edge of the chair. I look over the faces around the table—wine-warmed, content faces—and realize there's no good way to blurt, *By the way, honey, someone is taking pictures of our daughter's bedroom window from the house next door.*

"We have to go home," Eric is saying, slurring his words. Mia groans theatrically, stretching her arms over her head.

"No," she pouts.

"You know I have to get up tomorrow. We all do."

"Except Cecelia," Emma chimes in.

"Yeah," Mia picks up with a giggle. "Except Cecelia."

Scott and I exchange a glance.

"You're tipsy," Scott says to Mia's husband, to break up the tension and shift the subject. "You're not going to drive like that, are you?"

"Well, I'm not going to *walk* like that, am I?" the man says, which elicits another burst of laughter from Emma. "Weren't you supposed to be the designated driver, honey?"

Mia looks embarrassed. "Oops."

Oh no. We're going to have to offer to let them stay over. We have no excuse not to. We have three unoccupied rooms in the house and a fold-out couch in the basement. The thought of having to make Emma organic-vegan-fair-trade breakfast tomorrow while attempting to make small talk with the husbands through my hangover at six a.m. doesn't appeal to me in the slightest.

Scott saves the situation. "I'll call you guys taxis," he says. "Hey, Saya!"

Everyone goes quiet with a sort of reverence as the electronic voice springs awake. "Yes, Scott?"

"Can you call two taxis for my friends, please?"

"Of course, Scott." She proceeds to list the plate numbers and inform us all that the information has been sent to Kyle's and Mia's phones.

Mia shakes her head in disbelief, checking the screen. "Wow, Cece. I'm so freaking jealous, you have no idea."

I'm not sure how I'm supposed to react or what she expects from me. So I decide to laugh it off. "Well, if you don't care about your privacy at all, I guess you could say I'm lucky."

Instead of laughing, she gives me a blank look. The tension grows, visible only to me.

Her husband saves the day. "Well, I'll bet the crime rate in this part of town is really low, though, huh?"

Everyone dutifully laughs at that.

"Won't people just come up with new ways to get away with it?" Emma asks. "Don't they always?"

The laughter dies down, giving way to an awkward silence. "I suppose," I say.

"Oh, you girls have no idea," Kyle exclaims. "The lengths people will go to, it's nuts. Just last week I was dealing with a client's wife who tried to squirrel away assets before the divorce. Her scheme would put Bernie Madoff to shame, I tell you."

But we never find out what the scheme was because, in that moment, the phones ping, and Saya's voice informs us the taxis are here.

The door barely had time to close behind our guests,

leaving Scott and me alone at last, in the silence that felt heavy somehow, filled with the barely perceptible buzzing of the electronics in the background. The headache that had been scratching behind my eyes takes over, filling my entire skull. Too much wine.

"Thank God," I mutter, pressing the heels of my hands over my eyes.

"Thank God?" Scott echoes. "You've been looking forward to it all week. You always say we never see anyone anymore."

"I'm just tired," I snap back.

"You couldn't get them out of the house quickly enough," my husband points out.

"All the noise made it impossible to put Taryn to sleep," I say. I don't know why I feel the need to justify myself. What I really want to add is, *And it's not like* you *ever have to deal with Taryn's temper tantrums*.

"Nonsense. The rooms are all soundproofed. It's what you wanted," he says pointedly. This is becoming a regular refrain in our household: *This is what you wanted, Cecelia. It's all for you*. As if it's my fault that I couldn't sleep anymore in the old place, that I never ever felt truly safe.

But I can't just blurt this all out, throwing it in his face. I want to sleep, not start another argument. My bones ache with fatigue. Maybe I won't even need the sleeping pills tonight.

I still take them, just in case. It's happened in the past: I assumed I was exhausted enough to pass out naturally only to end up staring into the dark ceiling at three in the morning, my bones humming with fatigue but my mind restless, racing around and around in circles, unable to relax against all logic.

Downstairs, Scott finishes piling the dishes into the dishwasher. Through the open door, I hear the soft beep of commands and then the gentle whir of the machine springing to life. I listen to his steps as he climbs the stairs, the rush of the faucet in the adjacent bathroom as he brushes his teeth. And finally, I can feel his presence next to me as he climbs into bed. The mattress barely moves, not even a vibration to disturb my sleep. But I haven't drifted off yet. The sleeping pills are only starting to act.

"Scott," I find myself murmuring. As if I need to reassure myself that it's really him and not some stranger who took his place.

"Yeah?"

"What do you know about the neighbors?"

"The neighbors?"

"The house behind ours. Do you know who lives there?"

"How would I know that?" he says and gives a soft snort, as if it were a truly ridiculous thing to ask.

People used to know their neighbors, didn't they? They used to have neighborhood associations and block parties and things like that. Welcome baskets full of homemade muffins and what have you. In this sleek bedroom with its windows that black out at a set time like screens switching off, with its lights that gradually fade to sepia before dimming out to help with relaxation, with the hidden speakers gently humming with white noise, such things seem not even retro but antiquated. What would anyone need homemade muffins for, anyway, when you can order them from a bakery and have them at your door in minutes?

"I was just wondering," I murmur. The urge to sleep is stronger than me, pulling me under fast. "Maybe I should go introduce myself, or something."

"Why would you do that?"

"I don't know, Scott." The amusement in his tone that he doesn't try to hide annoys me, momentarily tugging me back out of dreamland. "Because it's civil?"

"There's no point," he says, again with that little derisive snort.

"Why not?"

"They're either early adopters or testers, like us, which means they've been selected by IntelTech. And that place does background checks like it's hiring for the FBI."

He is right, of course. *Everyone on the block has been preselected and carefully vetted,* says Clarisse's voice in my head, clearly like she's standing right there over my bed. I took it to mean everyone was thoroughly background-checked but of course, that's not what it really means. Kind of classist, some of my old friends would say. Did it really not cross my mind until now? Of course it did. I just didn't care and decided not to think about it too much. Because in my mind, it would mean that it's safe.

I am safe.

I close my eyes, and in that moment, the image in my head becomes softer, less real. Did I see a lens? Or did I mistake something for a lens, some techy gizmo? There's no reason for it after all. Why would someone be spying on my daughter? On me. On us.

"Anyway," Scott says. He puts his arm around me, which takes me by surprise. It takes me a heartbeat or two to relax into it. "Why don't you look them up? There's probably some kind of app for that too."

I pick up my phone blindly from the nightstand—how long has it been since it was farther than arm's reach at any moment?—and check the screen. As if by serendipity, that's when it gives a short buzz.

"Will you put that away?" Scott groans into his pillow. "You can check tomorrow. Anything interesting?"

"Just an email."

I swipe left and delete the message without reading.

CHAPTER FIVE

TRANSCRIPT: Session 8, Lydia Bishop.
Dr. Alice Stockman, PhD.
May 29th, 2018

LB: Is this being recorded?

AS: Yes. It's something I'm trying. That way I can focus more on you and less on taking notes.
[pause]

AS: It's solely for my personal use. It will never leave my office. But I'll understand if it's making you uncomfortable, and I can stop.

LB: No . . . no. Not at all. It's fine. [nervous giggle] I mean, yesterday I went and signed release forms to live in a high-tech aquarium so I can hardly object to a little tape recorder, right?

AS: Is that a question you're asking me or yourself?

LB: I'm just . . . I still can't believe I did that, you
know? And a tape recorder. That's so quaint somehow. With a cassette inside and everything. I didn't
know they still made blank cassettes.

AS: Sometimes I think it's best to go low-tech.

LB: I couldn't agree more! Well, I know I'm a total
hypocrite for saying that.

AS: What was it like, signing those papers? Let's
unpack this.

LB: Oh. They wooed us. I really can't come up with
another word. They sat us down in this gorgeous
room, one table and three chairs, two for us and
one for that woman, Clarisse. I guess they were
going for intimate—the irony. And an assistant
brought us espressos and a plate of biscotti. But if
we'd wanted to, we could have had champagne.
She offered. I thought it was weird, kind of in-
appropriate. To be under the influence while
taking a step like this? But they were just trying to
put us at our ease. They gave us a week with the
papers so there was nothing new in them. They
actually encouraged my husband to have his lawyer
look at them. But he ended up asking Faye. I
wasn't so sure about it.

AS: Why?

LB: I don't know . . . I would have paid someone.
Someone qualified. Someone impartial.

AS: And your sister wasn't qualified enough? Or impartial enough? You mentioned that she just got
promoted at her law firm—

LB: [laughs] Oh no, she's plenty qualified. Of
the two of us, she's the one who went to an
Ivy League school, you know, and I swear, she
has worked that fact into every conversation for
the last ten years. And yes, they love her at the
law firm. She went over the contract and said it
was all pretty standard stuff. There's worse on
your iPhone user agreement—that's how she
phrased it. And that never stopped anyone,
did it?

AS: The real question—and the reason we're here—
is, does it bother *you*?

LB: Oh, I don't know. I guess it doesn't. She knows
her stuff. It's just that this seems like a family
matter, and by family I mean my husband and me,
not my sister. Besides, she's going to go and discuss it all with our parents, and I like that idea
even less.

AS: That's not what I meant, Lydia.
[brief pause]

LB: If you're talking about the house...

AS: I am.

LB: I can't explain it. I thought it wouldn't bother
me. I mean...I should be glad, right? After everything that happened. After Walter.

AS: I hear a lot of uncertainty. A lot of *should* and
would and *might*.

LB: One thing I'm unequivocally happy about is the
safety. That's for sure. I don't doubt that part for a
second. I'm much safer there than I ever was in my

old house. Most people take it for granted but I don't.

AS: Would you like to talk about what happened at your old place?

LB: I thought we talked about this. Not yet. I'm not ready.

CHAPTER SIX

The truth is I liked my old life. I liked our old house. It was old in more ways than one. It dated back from the 1910s, a quaint art nouveau beauty that was a bargain, comparatively speaking, because it hadn't gotten as much care as it should have over the years. The former owner, an elderly lady, was happy to sell it to a young couple who planned to raise their family there.

Even considering all this, we offered twenty thousand dollars more than the listing asked. That, our real estate agent explained to us, was the market. The neighborhood was up-and-coming, trendy. On a nearby commercial artery, an organic grocery had just opened, and little high-end cafés and shops were popping up like mushrooms. Hip young families were buying up the duplexes left over from the neighborhood's working-class origins and turning them into airy condos or single-family homes, keeping only the picturesque façades with their brick patterns as an embodiment of living history.

It was the exact opposite of the place we live in now. I loved being able to walk for five minutes and have a cup of fair-trade French roast in a cozy coffee shop while reading a book. It added something to the monotony of my days as I worked from home, gave me a break from staring at the computer. Most important, it fit the image I had of myself, of us, the kind of family we would be. McMansion in the suburbs—not for us, not for the Holmeses.

Our old house was one of the nicer ones. Fully detached, on a street corner so we only had neighbors on one side. Back then it was an asset, not something I ever thought would turn against me. It had a vast, albeit overgrown, yard out back, and a beautiful maple out front that provided a little shade in the summer, without its bare branches blocking too much light in the winter. It hadn't been remodeled in decades and was full of those old-house quirks: rooms a touch too big or too small, closets in odd places, a little nook in the hall that had probably been designed to house a little console for the phone and the chair next to it, back when such things were practical. The door had a stained-glass insert at the top, as did the windows. Multicolored light fell on the parquet floor on sunny days.

It had a habit of creaking and groaning in windy weather and in winter when you just turned on the heat for the first time and the house seemed to stretch its old articulations and bones as the boards adjusted to the temperature. For no reason at all. It was cozy instead of creepy. If there were ghosts, they had to be friendly ones.

I liked living in it. I liked cooking in the too-small kitchen. I'd weeded the overgrown garden, mowed the grass, and put up boxes of flowers. Scott started to complain almost immediately. Small things got on his nerves. He'd bump into walls and trip over floorboards. The bathroom, he said, was too small to put in a bigger tub, the kitchen needed a remodel, and the wall between the living room and the adjacent bedroom could stand to be torn down *to get some light and air into this place*. The floors had to be sanded and the tiles replaced. We have the money, he'd say. Why not just hire a company and have it all done within a couple of weeks?

I'd say something about the noise, the dust, how annoying it would be to have all that banging in the background while I tried to work. But the truth was that I could have gone to a café or outside into the yard or taken a break from work altogether, two weeks wasn't that long. But I was reluctant. I didn't want the house to change. I was afraid, against all logic—Scott's logic, in any event—that I would love it less.

But then the other problem became evident, harder and harder to ignore every day. And that one had nothing to do with the house, with the supposed decrepitude of its fixtures or the outdated bathroom cabinets. It was a problem with me. With us. I put off the doctor's appointment as long as I could but knew I couldn't put it off much longer.

That's the real reason I caved on the renovations. I was

conceding something to distract from my failures else-where. Giving my husband what he wanted—one of the things he wanted, anyway. Maybe I hoped it would change something in me too. New surroundings, a new start.

Maybe that's when everything went wrong. We angered the house, and it turned against us. Instead of my home, it became the place of my torment.

* * *

My mission for today: get to know the neighbors.

To be honest, it's also the last thing I want to do. Especially when it comes to the house behind ours. That forbidding structure alone is enough to give me the heebie-jeebies. And now I have to knock on the front door and find a way to ask, *Excuse me, are you the creep who took pictures of my toddler's room last night?*

I suppose it's not a bad thing to know the people you live next door to, even though when it comes to Rosemary Road, I'm clearly the minority in thinking that. Scott was right. There's an app but when I sign up, I notice that I'm the only one on the street to use it. Feeling awkward, I sign out and then delete the app from my phone.

Next, I search for our contract. It must be on my device somewhere but I can't find it. I remember clearly that Scott printed a copy because we made a joke about it. So I head to his office.

It's pristine in there. He hardly ever uses it anymore, since he's stuck at work so late every day. He hasn't had time to put up the pictures that used to be on the walls at the old place, or he simply hasn't bothered. Our old attempts to decorate look kind of sad in this new environment, replete with details chosen with a keen eye for style but lacking that something that makes a house a home—soul, perhaps. Why hang up that little seascape we bought on vacation that one time, or that framed photo collage of us I made for him a few years ago, when there's already artwork on the walls?

His laptop sits in the middle of the desk, a shiny, un-scuffed MacBook Pro. When I run my fingertip along the lid, it comes away gray with dust.

Next, I try the drawers of his desk, which have locks but open without resistance. In the bottom one, I find the little seascape and, wrapped in an old terrycloth towel, the framed photos. It reassures me deep down that he hasn't gotten rid of it all.

I unwrap the frame and hold it up. We look so happy in those photos. The oldest one dates back to college where we first met. Even though we're only in our very early twenties, the low resolution and bad light makes us look worse than we do now. Unfortunate makeup and clothing choices don't help—my eyebrows are way too skinny, and, in contrast, Scott still has some puppy fat around the chin.

I remember making the collage but as I look at our care-free faces I can't remember the exact date it was taken. Maybe there's a date or a time stamp on the back. I turn over the frame and something small clatters to the floor.

I set the frame down and pick up the small object. It's a key. Which is odd, because nothing in this house needs anything like an old-fashioned key—everything responds to our personal chips or fingerprints. It's a smaller key, like something from a suitcase lock. There's a tag attached but it's no help: It's just a red-and-white plastic tab with nothing written on it. I inspect it and then put it back in the bottom of the drawer, the picture frame on top. I slide the drawer closed, realizing I had forgotten why I had come here in the first place. Right. The contract. The neighbors.

For the time being, we have two. One of the houses next door is as yet unoccupied—it looks brand-new, like they just finished building it. The grass on the front lawn hasn't even fully grown in yet. I can see through the curtainless windows during the day. I assume they have dimmers like ours do but there's no one there to use them so I can glimpse the big, empty rooms waiting to receive their inhabitants.

In the other house lives a couple with no children, as far as I can tell. I've only seen them once or twice since we moved in, as they planted flowers in a flowerbed out front. Otherwise I just see their cars as they leave in the morning, his big gray SUV, which exits the garage at seven, and her blue sedan that comes and goes occasionally. Which must mean she's a housewife. Like me, I remind myself reluctantly.

And of course, there's the house behind ours. I hadn't given it much thought, to be honest. Not until I saw that camera lens in the window anyway. I'd never seen a person or a car leave it but I assumed it was inhabited because, unlike the vacant house, the windows were always dark, and the decorative lights that lit up the façade went on every evening.

Now I find myself at a loss. Do I just go and introduce myself, bearing a basket of muffins, like something out of an '80s movie? Do people still do that? Do people *my age* still do that? Will they think I'm a weirdo?

Finally, I decide to forgo the muffins and instead buy two bottles of midrange chardonnay. No one ever turns down free wine, right? At this time of day, our friendly neighborhood grocery store is almost empty, and there's no wait to pay. There's never a wait because there are no cash registers to speak of. At the entrance and exit, our chip is scanned, and the amount for every item we take out the door with us automatically charged. Those from out of the neighborhood have to make do with three self-checkout stations that I've never seen anyone use. Living in the future has its benefits.

Not that we *have* to do our shopping here, or at the luxurious shopping mall that takes up the less desirable terrain by the highway. And at first, I resisted, hesitant at the idea that something—someone—is always keeping track. What did we look at but put back on the shelf? What did we load our cart with? Recording our habits and preferences, adding up the data, sorting it into complex algorithms. Judging your less than healthy habits, the ramen noodles, the potato chips, and soda.

In exchange, you never drop in to get a new bottle of organic sriracha only to find yourself facing an empty shelf or wondering if the prepackaged chicken thighs are about to go bad. Everything is stocked in just the precise quantity, always fresh, never gathering dust on the shelf for God knows how long. And if something we want or need is missing, all we have to do is request it from our Saya, and the next time we go shopping, it'll be there.

As I exit with my wine bottles, I wonder how many other bottles of wine and booze we've logged in the last month. I can't remember but I'm sure the computer didn't miss a single one. Lately, I don't even bother to review the monthly bill.

Perhaps I should start.

I decide to begin with the house next door because the blue sedan is sitting in the driveway. She's home. I make my way up the neatly paved path to the door. There's a doorbell, although I don't see why it's necessary. The second I set foot on the paved path, the house's inhabitant gets an alert, and the video feed on her tablet shows me from three different angles, in high definition. At least that's how it works in our house.

But I perform the motions even though they've become obsolete. Still, she takes a while to come to the door, and for a moment there, I wonder if she won't come at all. Just as I contemplate leaving, feeling like a fool with one of the bottles of wine sweating in my hands, the door opens.

"Can I help you?"

She doesn't look unfriendly—only surprised. What could I possibly need from her after all? To borrow a cup of sugar for a recipe?

"Hi," I say. "I live next door. We just moved in a short while ago."

"I know," she says, a little flatly.

"You do?"

I'm unprepared for this conversation. She must see the surprise on my face because she gives an awkward chuckle.

"So sorry. We were alerted that another family was moving in," she says cryptically. Alerted, huh. "And that you were pre-vetted. It was one of our conditions."

"I just thought I'd introduce myself," I say. "Maybe they don't do that around here—"

"Oh, on the contrary. I'm Dorothea."

"And I'm—"

"Cecelia Holmes," she says, nodding. "I know. Why don't you come in?"

Minutes later, we're sitting in Dorothea's living room, drinking the wine out of those giant glasses. Observing her house, I can only marvel at SmartBlock's dedication. It has nothing in common with our own. The style is completely different, all its own. While ours favors clean, contemporary lines and a cool palette of colors, this one perfectly reproduces the look of a distinguished century-old Victorian. It reminds me a little of our old house, before we butchered it, and our life with it. Reminds me enough to give me a pang. There are even stained-glass inserts in the windows. The light is warm. There's wainscoting and art nouveau moldings on the walls and ceiling and an antique-looking chandelier.

I wonder if each house is like that, a unique creation. And if yes, it means someone designed it, put it all together, chose the materials and the furniture, the shades of the paint on the walls. Who? Not us, the testers. We only filled out a most rudimentary questionnaire. Yet somehow, they seemed to know our favorite styles and colors, grays, blues, and olive greens, right down to the matte finish of the appliances.

Dorothea chatters away, seemingly oblivious of my sharp gaze on her. Or maybe she is aware. We talk about our husbands' jobs, our own jobs—she's not a housewife, it turns out, but a freelance journalist, currently between gigs. Yet something about her feels off to me. Just like this house posing as a turn-of-the-century mansion, a beautiful replica, down to the smallest details, but a replica nonetheless. Like she's telling me a story. And when it's my turn, she nods along with a little too much ease, like I'm telling her things she already knows. Even when I talk about my career designing ebooks, she expresses polite interest but hardly any surprise.

"Your daughter is adorable, by the way," she says. This makes me refocus. When has she ever seen Taryn?

"I see you guys going out for a walk every once in a while," she adds, apparently seeing my frown. "It's such a perfect place for children. You really couldn't do better."

Finally, something we agree on. "All these safety features have been a godsend," I say.

"And all the neighbors are pre-vetted," she adds, and takes a generous sip of wine.

"By IntelTech."

"And by the board. Wait." Her eyes glint as she leans forward. "You didn't know?"

"Know what?"

"Before they move in someone new, IntelTech submits

the candidates to the board of residents. What? It's not that strange. They do it in fancy condo buildings—"

"We're not a condo building. Is that even legal?"

"Not only is it legal, it's great. You'll see the benefits soon enough. If you decide to stay. Then you'll be on the board too, and you'll always have a say about who moves in down the street from you and your *young children*. Better than nothing."

So that's how she knows my name. And my husband's, and probably Taryn's.

What else does she know?

But another thought occurs to me, eclipsing this troubling one. "Definitely," I say. "Do you, by any chance, happen to know who lived in our house before us?"

I drop it into the conversation casually. Or I think I do. Because she stiffens, her spine straight and gaze alert. A moment later, an uncertain smile floats to her lips. "What do you mean?"

"Someone lived in our house before, right? Other testers. I guess they didn't choose to stay. Do you know why?"

"Cecelia," she says, "I don't know anything about that."

"But you're on that . . . committee."

"Board."

"Right. Board. So didn't you guys vet them too?"

"Cecelia, if I'm not mistaken, you're the first ones to live in that house. If there was someone else, I had no idea."

"There was someone. I think they mentioned it in passing. At IntelTech," I lie. "Someone named Lydia?"

Dorothea blinks. It's hard to make the act of blinking aggressive but somehow she pulls it off. "I don't know who would tell you such a thing. Even if there had been, it would be confidential information."

But the confidentiality is one-way, I think. I get up and make a quick exit—she's not exactly begging me to stay.

Outside, the sunlight is blinding, and the perfection of the clean lines of sidewalks and lawns is a sharp contrast to the jumbled chaos of my thoughts. I now realize I must have had too much wine. And a second bottle is still in my bag, tugging on my shoulder.

Right. There's still the house behind ours. Can I take on another Dorothea? Maybe it's the chardonnay talking but I'm filled with determination. I'm going to march right up to that house and ask whoever it is why she was taking pictures of my daughter's bedroom window. Yes. And I won't leave until she answers. That's what I'm going to do.

I storm down the sidewalk, around the bend, and up to the front door. The house looms, a giant rectangle of dark stone and darker one-way glass, practically sucking up the sunlight. This one isn't shy about it: I can see the surveillance cameras, which means the house's inhabitant wanted them to be seen. I march up the short ramp to the porch of flat, square granite, also shiny and black, and when I look up, there are the cameras, not one but two of them above the door. There's also no doorbell I can see. I know she knows I'm here.

"Hello?" I call out. My voice is cowed and insignificant all of a sudden, pitiful even to myself. As if the house absorbs not just light but sound as well.

"Hello," I repeat, trying to be more assertive. I look up,

defiant, straight into the cameras. "I'm your neighbor. I have a gift."

But I feel stupid, standing there with my bottle of wine. Suddenly, in the middle of the searing-hot day, I feel a chill. The house casts a deep, icy shadow.

"I'd like to speak with you," I say, louder. "Please open the door."

There's no answer. Yet somehow, I know that I'm not talking to an empty house. I don't know how to describe it. Just a feeling. Intuition.

"This is important," I say. My fists are clenching. I feel intense anger at this house, at the cameras, at the indifferent stranger within. "Open the door."

It occurs to me that I'm acting crazy. That for all I know, I'm scaring her to death, and she's about to call the police. "I saw something from the window last night," I add, trying to keep my tone normal, if not friendly. "I just wanted to speak with you. It'll only take a minute. Please."

The sound startles me because it seems to come out of nowhere. I didn't hear a crackle of speakers humming to life, nothing, just, all of a sudden, a voice. A deep, raspy, male voice.

"Go away."

"Sir," I stammer. "Wait. I just wanted to—"

"I said go away. And don't come back."

I start to say something else but stop myself. What if he does call the police? He could accuse me of harassment. Which could get us in trouble with IntelTech. Scott will be pissed if that happens.

Reluctant, I start to back away, nearly tripping on my

low heel and stumbling off the porch. Then I finally turn around and walk slowly back down the arrow-straight path.

Only once I'm at the sidewalk do I chance to turn around. And maybe it's my imagination or the wine and the heat. But in the shiny, pitch-black glass panel of the front door, for just a fraction of a second, I think I see a hideously distorted human face.

CHAPTER SEVEN

"So how did it go today?"

It's nearing nine, Taryn has long ago been put to bed, and we're on the living room couch. The couch is easily twelve feet long, and we're on the opposite sides of it. Something is playing on Netflix, some show we've been half watching.

"How did what go?"

"The welcome wagon."

Oh. "Well, the one next door is a Stepford wife, and the other is Boo Radley," I say. "Totally normal people and not creepy at all."

Scott gives a soft chuckle. "You do know Boo Radley wasn't the bad guy, right?"

"I'm surprised you remember what book he's from."

"You seem tense. I take it, it didn't go well?"

"Oh, it went fine. As well as can be expected. Right up until I asked her who used to live in the house before us. Then she couldn't get rid of me fast enough."

Scott frowns. "What do you mean?"

"It's a simple enough question. Who used to live here before us? You'd think—"

"No one," he says. "We're the first."

"You seem awfully sure."

"That's what they said, didn't they? Why would they lie about it?"

"And apparently, there's some sort of committee. No, board. That vetted us before we moved in. No one mentioned that."

"It's standard. They already do it in condo buildings."

Clearly, I'm not getting through. "Scott," I say, "the house is weirding me out."

"Oh, the glitches?" He has had time to turn his attention back to the Netflix show, and now he's reluctant to turn back to me. Light from the screen flickers on his face. "You should just report those."

"I did. And it's not just the glitches. It called me the wrong name."

Even that, it turns out, isn't enough to make him look me straight in the eye. "And that's why you think someone else used to live here? That's ridiculous."

"Ridiculous," I echo. "Yeah, sure. Like so many other things. If I remember correctly, you thought changing the locks was ridiculous too."

In spite of the TV, droning at low volume, I feel the awkward tension in the room. At least now my husband turns to me. "You don't have to go there. I was wrong. I admit it."

"How generous." My voice drips with sarcasm. He ignores it.

"And I like to think I righted the wrong. I found this place, I got us in, and now we're living in a million-dollar home with security features straight out of a sci-fi movie. What more do you want?"

"You know what?" I say. "I'm tired. I'm going to bed."

With that, I get up from the couch. At once, little lights flicker on, guiding me to the door so I can avoid any lurking furniture corners.

"Cece," I hear Scott say behind me as I leave, "why don't you do what I ask and—" but whatever he says next is cut off by the soundproof door sealing off the hum of the TV.

"Saya," I say, "please warm the sheets. And set the alarm a half hour later than usual."

The electronic voice doesn't make me wait. "Of course, Cecelia."

*   *   *

I know what he was going to say. Why don't you do what I ask and go get help? We discussed it several times but it never went beyond the five appointments of PTSD-preventive psychological counseling. And now I'm wondering if I made a mistake stopping. Scott certainly seems to think so. And I'm not blind, I can see that it's damaging my marriage, and soon enough it'll bleed into my interactions with Taryn, if it hasn't already.

This morning, my little ruse worked. Scott was pissed at me for oversleeping. I'm not proud of myself. What I did was childish. And now I'm driving Taryn to day care and wondering if I should give therapy another go.

Here, they probably have a nice, white-walled clinic with smiling, white-clad staff for all my needs. And all of it logged into my file, wherever it might be on some cloud up on a satellite, from which I'll never be able to erase it.

"Mommy?"

"Yes, sweetie?" The descent back to reality takes me by surprise. I hurriedly glance in the mirror above the windshield to see Taryn in her seat, looking anxious.

"We passed the day care."

Wait, what? Disoriented, I glance sideways, only to see that she's right—the bright-colored building is receding in the rearview mirror. The GPS, that traitor, stayed silent.

"We're not going?" Taryn asks. I can't tell if she's happy or not at the prospect. "We're not going!"

I give it some thought. It's not like it's high school or they have homework. Maybe we can skip a day. Have some mother-daughter time, maybe hit a museum. But as I wonder which street to turn onto, Taryn gets more and more agitated in her seat.

The first street I pass is one-way. So is the second. Feeling powerless, I glance at the GPS for help but the red dot that's supposed to be my car doesn't even show up at the right place. Bad connection?

Here, in this place, where the air itself is made of Wi-Fi? Yeah, right. Annoyed, I tap the screen. "Saya?"

No answer. What the hell?

"Taryn, honey," I say, glancing in the mirror at my daughter. Her face is red and scrunched up, a sure sign of upcoming tears. "How about we don't go?"

"Go!" she shrieks.

"We can go somewhere else. Just the two of us. We could go for ice cream."

"Day care!" Taryn yells, her voice rising in pitch.

"We could go to the park, to ride the carousels. And pizza for lunch!"

Her face becomes redder, until it's almost purple. What kind of kid doesn't want to skip day care and go ride the carousel instead? "No!"

"Taryn," I say, "please behave yourself, or . . ."

Or what? Mommy will leave you at day care forever, which seems to be what she wants anyway?

"No!" Taryn shrieks. "Day care! Day care! Saya, take us to day care!"

Excuse me? "Saya doesn't decide where we go, Taryn," I say. I'm starting to sweat. Finally, a street that goes the right way. I turn onto it, a little too abruptly. I'm sure a million sensors and cameras and detectors record it all and send it to my file somewhere. Bad driver, minus ten points.

Taryn rages in the back seat but I manage to tune her out, circling around until I'm back on the main street and the colorful building looms ahead. Taryn has never talked to Saya before, although of course she's seen us do it a million times. Saya isn't programmed to answer to her. Even when choosing her cartoons or games on her personal tablet, Taryn only has an illusion of choice—everything is pre-vetted not just by me but by the software that selects things that might suit her based on a bunch of different factors.

Just who does she think Saya is? Someone who can override her mother's authority, apparently.

As soon as we pull into the parking lot of the day care, Taryn calms down as if by magic. By the time I go around to get her out of her seat and help her down, her face has magically returned to its normal color, and the only indication that she was having a tantrum just moments earlier is her light sniffing and two damp trails down her cheeks. She's adorable in her blue dress with a bow at the collar, her light brown curls escaping from her ponytail. A little angel where the little demon was just a second ago.

She skips ahead to join her friends in the day care's yard as I awkwardly nod hello to the teacher in charge today. It's the same one who told me, at the last parents' meeting, how great Taryn was, a quick learner ahead of the entire class, not to mention a natural leader. Taryn has a great future ahead of her, she'd told me, beaming.

But now she barely acknowledges me, quickly turning her attention to one of the other children. After I make sure the gate closes after Taryn, I head back to the car.

Once the door has closed and the AC kicks in, my shirt sticks to my sweaty back, and I start to shiver so I adjust the temperature settings. Yet it seems to have no effect: The vents keep pumping out arctic-cold air. I poke and prod at the frozen GPS. "Saya?" I ask. No answer.

I roll my eyes. Another report to make when I get home. I start the car and pull out of the parking lot. Home is ten minutes away, and I don't need a map.

The hum of the vents is the only sound. This car, like all vehicles residents are allowed to have, is fully electric. It feels eerie. Some music would be nice. "Saya, play the driving playlist," I say before I remember Saya's playing hooky. But just as I reach for the control panel to start the music by hand, sound blasts from the speakers at full volume, exploding into my eardrums.

My hands jump on the steering wheel, and the car swerves right into the wrong lane.

CHAPTER EIGHT

It all happens so fast that I don't have time to get scared. Instead of pulling gently into my lane like I intended, the car turns too far, and the bumper collides with that of another car that has just been pulling up to the day care.

Mechanisms activate in the car's computer core, faster than any human reflex. My seat belt pulls in sharply, cutting into my shoulder, and pins me to my seat, which instantly pulls back. I'm frozen in shock, my heart hammering as the music continues to blare.

The driver's side door of the other car opens, and a woman climbs out, a tall, thin redhead, dressed in a sharp and expensive suit. She slams her palms on my car's hood. I can't hear a thing through the music but I can see her lips move as her face distorts with rage. I can read what she's yelling clear as day: *What the hell is wrong with you, you crazy bitch?*

With shaking hands, I feel around the control panel but everything seems to have frozen. I don't know how to turn off the music, or open the windows, or do anything for that matter.

And then silence falls like a rock. In it, Saya's calm, pleasant voice: "Collision detected. Calling for assistance. Sending report."

"Let me out!" I bellow. The window slides down, and, with a click, the doors unlock. The redhead descends on me like a bird of prey.

"My child is in the car! Watch where the hell you're going! Are you drunk?"

Her face creases in spite of what must be abundant Botox and turns the same shade of raspberry-red as Taryn's before a tantrum. In the face of all that fury, my own fades, and I find myself trembling and helpless, raking my brain for words.

"I'm so sorry—"

"They'll be hearing about this at IntelTech. This is exactly why I moved here—so I wouldn't have to deal with this shit."

"You know I'm not drunk," I say. Otherwise, my chip would have detected it and wouldn't have let me behind the wheel in the first place.

But I don't think she hears me. In any event, my protestation does nothing to stop the verbal onslaught.

"Do you realize I don't have time for this? I have to be at work! The stupidity of some people. It's baffling."

I start mumbling something about calling assistance but cut myself off. She keeps cursing, calling me all kinds of names, but it all recedes into the background. Behind her, I see the fence of the day care's front yard, like multicolored Popsicle sticks, and all the children are now clinging to it, desperate to see what all this racket is. Curious little faces, their eyes shiny like marbles.

And among them, I see Taryn, standing at the front, peering intently between fence posts. On her face is a look that I can only describe as utter fascination, her adorable face full of evil glee.

*   *   *

The redheaded woman is Anna Finch, this or that executive at some big company or other. Her husband is a lawyer—not just any lawyer but the kind of lawyer the firm is named after. I couldn't have chosen a worse car to lightly dent. And that's really all it is, a somewhat dented bumper, a bit of chipped paint. And, of course, "emotional distress." Anna Finch must have said this phrase at least eleven times in the last five minutes.

It turns out that Venture has its own clinic, five grocery stores, a number of pharmacies, gyms, and recreation centers but no police station. Sure, we have our very own SmartBlock Assistance but technically we're still in the jurisdiction of the station that also serves the adjoining neighborhood, situated in the semi-industrial area on the outskirts of the big city and consisting of crumbling working-class homes and housing projects.

The police officers probably see all kinds of devastating things day in and day out but they somehow manage to keep their cool in the face of two rich ladies and two lightly damaged $100,000 cars. I can't help but feel uneasy around them. Guilty for existing.

One of them tries to calm down the raging redhead while the other patiently questions me about the event. He's old and grizzled looking, and he reminds me of the officers who came to our home—our old house—after the invasion. They were nothing but kind to me, just like these are. They have no reason to be unkind. I'm the very profile of the good victim, a woman, a white woman, well-to-do, a mother to boot. Even if we weren't in the heart of the costly new development for the (mostly) rich, there's no reason for them to tackle me to the ground and handcuff me. Which I should be grateful for, I guess. The redhead obviously takes it for granted.

I try to answer the officer's questions but I'm stammering, forgetting my words. My mouth is dry and my hands clammy. Posttraumatic shock? If one can call this minor inconvenience trauma, that is.

Anna Finch sure thinks she can. Her offspring, tucked into a state-of-the-art security seat in the back of her car, barely felt any impact at all but started to wail its head off pretty much immediately. And for all her shrieking about her child in the car, she doesn't seem to give a shit. Which only makes the little demon scream louder and louder.

I never much cared for other people's children. Having one of my own, finally, didn't change anything. I still don't. Whereas Taryn's crying makes my heart clench with pain, the only thing I feel at the sound of a bawling baby at a restaurant is annoyance.

"Ma'am," the officer repeats, and I blink, confused.

"Yes?"

"Is this an autonomous vehicle?"

"What? No, no. It's just—connected."

"Connected?"

"You see, there's this—" I only begin to wonder how to explain, in my current state, about the SmartHome and Saya, the personal assistant uploaded into my car. But thankfully, a sleek electric car pulls up, smooth and white as a pebble polished by the ocean and bearing the unmistakable logo: a tree inside a circular green arrow with the caption underneath: *live smarter. live better. live IntelTech.* Speak of the devil—SmartBlock Assistance has come to the rescue.

Within minutes, three pleasant-looking personnel in civilian clothes dispatch the police officers back to the station and arrange for the cars to be towed. Presumably, to be taken care of somewhere out of sight of the neighborhood's population. To be restored and returned shiny and new.

"This is unacceptable," shrills Anna Finch. "I demand that there be consequences. You can't just drive around like a crazy person here."

They assure her that they'll get to the bottom of it.

"My car," I say, finally finding my voice. "Saya malfunctioned. It blasted random music at top volume. I was startled."

"If Saya had been malfunctioning," says the pleasant-looking woman from IntelTech, "it isn't recommended to use the vehicle at all."

"The vehicle was fine," I snap.

"It's all in the terms of service," she says, still pleasantly. I remember her. She was there with Clarisse and us when we signed the papers. She wears her ash-blond hair in a low bun, a style that looks too conservative on someone so young, and the tag on her uniform reads JESSICA.

"There you have it!" exclaims Anna Finch. "She ignored the TOS. Shouldn't there be consequences?"

"It's a complex issue," says the mediator.

"I don't see what's so complex about it. I thought you have everyone here prescreened. Clearly it didn't help much. You should have a zero-tolerance policy—"

"Saya's been malfunctioning for a week," I snarl. "I've been reporting and reporting. Nobody does anything."

"Please be assured that all your reports reach those who are concerned," says the woman, "and are analyzed and acted upon as the situation demands."

I want to grab her and shake her. This seems to be the thing Anna Finch and I have in common. The mediator is one of those flawless IntelTech employees. Neither her clothes nor her face has a single crease. You can't quite tell her age, and her hair in its bun looks like it's been molded from plastic. Is she an actual robot? Like Saya but also in a silicone body.

"Ms. Finch, Ms. Holmes. Let's regard this as what it is: a minor accident. Ms. Finch, your vehicle will be restored to its original condition and returned to you in the briefest delays. In the meantime, an identical one will be provided for your daily needs. Ms. Holmes, your concerns will be addressed—"

"I want to speak to Clarisse," I say.

"Good idea," sneers Anna Finch.

"There's no reason to bother Clarisse. She's very busy, as you can imagine."

"First, my house nearly boiled me alive in the tub. Now, it's calling me Lydia." My breath catches, and the next phrase comes out not menacing, as I intended, but whisper-quiet. "I need to speak to Clarisse."

Sensing that the mediation efforts aren't being as effective as she'd like, the woman switches gears. She addresses me with an apologetic smile.

"Clarisse will contact you herself. Within the briefest delays."

"What does that even mean?"

"Now, I'll call two cars to deliver you to wherever you need to be. Will that be your office?"

"My home."

"Of course. It won't take a minute."

CHAPTER NINE

I would have avoided telling Scott at all but the replacement car in the garage was a dead giveaway. Even when I do tell him, I don't get much of a reaction.

"You got into a fender bender," he says. "Happens to everyone."

"Not like that it doesn't."

"I know it's stressful but I don't think IntelTech is making a big deal of it. And neither should you."

"You should have been there. That shrew from the other car looked ready to murder me. I was humiliated. Everyone was staring..." I remember Taryn, watching so calmly through the fence, and trail off.

"The important thing is that nobody got hurt," he says, clearly eager to move on. "They'll fix up the car—you said so yourself."

"Scott," I say, "do you think this place is having a bad influence on Taryn?"

Now he's paying attention to me. He looks up with some interest. "How do you mean?"

"I wanted to take the day off day care today. But she wanted to go."

He shrugs. "She has friends there. She wanted to hang out with them rather than with her mom. Isn't that kind of normal?"

"For God's sake, she's three."

"And they grow up faster and faster."

"Maybe we should do something about all that screen time."

He chuckles again and shakes his head. "Now there's a change of pace. Didn't we want this place *for* Taryn? We knew there would be screens."

"Understatement of the century."

"Look, I know you want the best for her. And I guess it's your decision, you're her mom after all—"

"And you're her dad," I interject. "And you should be concerned too."

"—but I think you should reconsider," he says, ignoring my remark. "Remember how our parents forbade us to play video games or listen to music? Remember how annoying it was? And most of all, how freaking pointless? It was a losing battle.

"Well, you're being the same way right now. Screens are the future. Social media is the future. By the time she's a teenager, they'll probably be wiring our phones right into our eyeballs." This last bit was intended as a joke but it doesn't exactly lighten the mood. The pause hangs awkwardly in the air until he breaks it. "So, you're not giving her a childhood by forbidding screens. You're depriving her of a childhood. *Her* childhood."

"I never said anything about forbidding," I argue feebly.

"Limiting. Same thing. You're being Therese right now. Is that what you want for Taryn?"

I grit my teeth. Therese. My mother. My mother went beyond unplugging the PlayStation and monitoring my CD collection. Far beyond. And in the end, did it change anything?

Maybe he's right. I don't want to be that to Taryn.

"Maybe we can just spend more time doing family things," I say uncertainly. "Out in nature. Or something."

"Yeah, we should go to the park," Scott picks up with enthusiasm. "I drive past it every day. It's beautiful."

I didn't mean the local park. At all. I meant camping in the wilderness, or a trip to Yosemite, maybe, for a week or two. But not the SmartPark, with its perfectly shaped trees and acid-green lawns and ergonomic playground equipment and sensors, sensors, sensors. Logging the time Taryn spends on the swing versus the merry-go-round. The one time I was there, I looked at the park and wondered whether it was real—the trees, the grass, the flowers that never seemed to wilt.

Lately, I often wonder whether any of this is real.

* * *

The old house is still real to me in a way this place never manages to be. A place where I was once so happy can't just fade from memory, not even after all the evil things that happened within its walls. By the time police-car lights were flashing through the windows and the dreaded crime-scene tape was stretched out across the porch like a bad Halloween decoration, it was no longer the same house in my mind. It was a different, soulless house, wearing the old one's façade like a mask.

When the police got to the house that day, they found me sitting on the porch with Taryn in my arms. I was hugging her, squeezing her close to me way too hard, and she wailed and screamed her head off, tears and snot running down that little red face. If I'd looked up, I would have probably seen the neighbors peeking from behind curtains, morbidly curious but not daring—or just not wanting—to go outside and get involved.

I learned later that not one of them called the police, even though they must have heard the gunshot. They can't not have heard it. Our old street, so unlike Rosemary Road, was in the heart of the city, buildings sitting as close together as the builders a hundred years ago could manage. I heard other people's wailing babies and barking dogs and the occasional explosive argument. But there, just like here, everyone prioritized their own peace of mind.

So I sat there until the police cars pulled up, flashing lights and sirens and all. And then someone tried to pry Taryn from my arms, and I screamed so loud I startled myself. It was hardly a normal human scream, no words, more like an animalistic howl I never thought I was capable of. And it made Taryn cry even harder. And then the EMTs descended on me, and of course they took Taryn away, telling me all the while everything was going to be fine, she was in good hands and so was I.

Only then did the neighbors creep out of the safety of their homes and circle the scene. I remember their faces, colored red and blue and white by the police-car lights, and their big, shiny eyes trained on us. On me. Where were you? I wanted to shriek. Where the hell were you ten minutes ago?

That's when I knew I couldn't trust other people. No one has my best interests at heart but me. I have to watch out for myself, and for Taryn—I owe it to us. It's the only thing I owe anybody.

And this house, with all the cameras and sensors and detectors, was meant to protect us. That's all that matters. That's all I care about.

I won't let anyone mess with me, or with my daughter, ever again.

*　　*　　*

Jessica exits her boss's office in a measured step and heads straight to the bathroom. Once there, she washes her face with cold water. Only when she looks up into the mirror above the row of square, modern-style sinks does she remember she wore mascara that morning, and now it's all under her eyes. She gets a gob of toilet paper from one of the stalls and tries to wipe off the mess with little success.

They're not forbidden to wear makeup, exactly, but encouraged to keep a natural appearance, as her contract worded it. No garish colors of lipstick or smoky eyes. They're not flight attendants after all. Their uniforms resemble casual clothes as much as possible, or at least the big bosses' strange idea of casual clothes. Low heels and pencil skirts, and collared shirts under a sweater. Who on earth wears that of their own free will, let alone *casually*?

In a way, it's probably for the better. If by some unlikely hazard she were to run into someone from work when she's on her day off, they'd hardly recognize her. And lately she's been looking forward to those days off more than ever before. She gets home, changes, and then goes out all night and gets blind drunk. She'd get stoned too, if she could. But they do routine drug tests at work, and that stuff lingers in your body.

She can't afford to lose this job. She can't afford to tell them to go to hell and quit. For now. The look on Clarisse's face when she tells her to take that job and shove it—that'll have to wait.

Over the past two years, she's mediated an untold number of conflicts, which is a fancy way of saying that she's pacified entitled rich bastards throwing tantrums like babies. The things she's seen. The things she's heard them spew out casually like it was the most normal thing. And through it all, she's had to keep her pleasant smile and not punch anyone in the face when confronted with some executive who throws a shit-fit because an ambiguous-looking family moved in across the street when they were supposed to be living on an all-white block.

She has a degree from MIT, for crying out loud. She had a full scholarship. She was top of her class. And this is what it got her. Had anyone told her this when she was graduating with honors...

When she first got hired at IntelTech, she marveled at the ironclad NDA, a bloated stack of papers she had to sign. Now she knows why.

But the thing that stuck in her head the most—the thing that floated to the top of her consciousness every time she lay down and closed her eyes to try and sleep—that thing was Lydia. IntelTech's dirty secret. One Clarisse would kill to keep hidden... literally, Jessica is sure. The woman living in that house is now starting to act unhinged too.

Jessica would laugh about it if she could and if her job wasn't on the line. The irony of it. Can a brand-new house, a marvel of gleaming marble and chrome and glass, packed full of circuits and chips, be haunted like some old Victorian manor?

No. It's people who are haunted, not houses, and all the technology in the world can't set them free from themselves.

Jessica exits the bathroom and heads back to her office where she discreetly slips her headphones in her ears and presses Play on an old-school MP3 player that hasn't been on the market in a decade. Instantly, the tender voice flows from the device and into her ears, like honey.

There's a saying old, says that love is blind...

CHAPTER TEN

The morning I'm supposed to meet with Clarisse, the house messes up my morning coffee. A poor start. I come down-stairs to find an unknown beverage steaming under the coffee machine, a fluffy thing I'd never drink in a million years, sprinkled with something—is that ground cardamom?

"Saya," I say, annoyed.

"How can I help you, Cecelia?"

"Whose coffee is this?"

"This is your coffee, Cecelia. Would you like to change the default settings?"

"I would like the settings as before," I say testily. I pick up the unknown creation. The mound of whipped cream on top of it wobbles, and the cardamom trickles down onto my hand.

"I do not understand what you mean, as before."

I grit my teeth, take a teaspoon, and sweep the whipped

cream off the cup into the sink. I take a sip of the coffee and nearly gag—there's more syrup in there than actual coffee, some weird flavor. And why do we even have whipped cream? I never put it on the shopping list. I only drink my coffee black, and Scott is watching his weight so the only dairy he ever consumes is skim. Who in this house would ever drink a coffee like that?

Lydia, that's who, says a mean little voice in the back of my mind.

"Saya, please make me a long double espresso," I say.

"Coming right up, Cecelia."

"And make that the default from now on."

"Of course."

I drink my coffee and scroll through my phone. This morning I got another text message. I'll need to deal with this, and soon. I could just block, block, block. Technology to the rescue. And with this technology, I can literally block someone—they won't be allowed past the gates. I toy with the idea, promising myself that, as soon as it gets hairy, I'll do exactly that.

By the time Clarisse arrives, with that assistant of hers in tow, the one with the face like a doll molded from plastic, the house is on its best behavior. It alerts me two minutes before they arrive that I have visitors incoming and confirms their identities in a loud, clear voice before asking for my approval. I let them in.

"Cecelia, it's lovely to see you." Clarisse is beaming like we're long-lost friends. The doll-faced woman hovers by her side with that unshakable smile. But I'm not having any of it today.

"The house is malfunctioning," I say, skipping the hellos. "I keep sending reports but no one ever comes to fix anything."

"Rest assured, we're analyzing the situation," says Clarisse. "Jessica is the one in charge of Rosemary Road, and she's been working round the clock."

"What about what happened with the car?" I ask.

"We're working on that too. For now, there are no guilty parties. Just ill luck."

"Well, that ill luck could get someone killed," I mutter. Somehow, in the face of that compulsory friendliness, it's so tempting to be rude. Just how much could I get away with before the veneer cracks?

"We're working hard to resolve the issue."

"The map wasn't working. And when I tried to play music, I was blasted with some song I never uploaded."

"Sometimes, the AI makes suggestions based on things you've listened to in the past," the assistant speaks up. She introduced herself but I struggle to remember her name.

"Well, I—" I'm not a fan of the oldies, I'm about to say.

"As for the volume, is it possible you accidentally changed the settings yourself?"

"Oh, so now it's my fault?"

"Nobody is saying that," Clarisse cuts in. "We're just trying to get to the bottom of what happened. And there's no record in your car's system of anything at all going wrong right up until the collision."

"Oh. So I'm making things up."

"Not at all. You're saying you had your daughter in the car right before?"

"I dropped her off at the day care."

"Is it possible she could have changed the sound setting or picked the song?"

I give an incredulous chuckle. "She's a child. How could she do that?"

"Children have been known to figure out technology surprisingly well." Clarisse's smile is beatific. Sure, my three-year-old can figure out stuff I barely understand. But then I remember the look on her face as she watched through the fence posts...

Could Taryn have changed the settings? Saya doesn't answer to her, and the car has safety features. For instance, she can't open the doors by herself. But could she have found a way to raise the volume? To do what? To hurt me? But she couldn't have known the collision would happen. She's three. She can't make those logical connections yet.

"Can we not blame my toddler for your failings?" I snap, my voice shrill.

"It's a possibility. We'll review the settings in your car to make sure she can't access any features at all. And we can't blame her—she's just a small child. Right?"

"Exactly," I fume.

"So, as you can see, no bad guys," Clarisse says, smiling. She seems to have come to that conclusion awfully quickly. Reminds me of one of the police officers on the scene, who kept asking me the same things over and over, hoping I'd slip up and he could somehow make what happened my fault. *Are you sure you locked the door? Are you sure the windows were locked? Are you sure of this and are you sure of that.* As though, if I'd forgotten to turn a latch on some window somewhere, I deserved the home invasion.

"Cecelia, we want to create an atmosphere of safety and trust here at SmartBlock," Clarisse is saying. I guess she noticed my spaced-out look. "It's very important to us that everyone feels heard. We are constantly collecting feedback and improving."

"This house," I find myself saying, "it could kill someone."

The smiles don't waver.

"I'm not sure what you mean," says Clarisse at last, echoing Saya in a jarring way.

"Well, technically, it's a possibility," I stammer. Somehow their imperturbable faces make me feel like the crazy one, some tinfoil-hat conspiracy theorist. Like my mother. "The AI controls everything. What if I were in the bathtub, for example, and it just decided to crank the water temperature to boiling?"

Jessica gives a polite laugh. "That's not possible. Such a thing isn't even in the settings."

"I'm just making an example."

"And we've thought of everything," says Clarisse. "Our techs have. Pretty much everything is preprogrammed to prevent harm, accidental or intentional. This goes without saying."

"Intentional?" I ask.

Clarisse sighs. "These aren't fun things to talk about, of course," she says, "but, since you asked, it's all in the fine print. If . . . someone in the house were to try to harm you, the house will go out of its way to prevent it. And alert emergency services at once."

"Interesting."

"Indeed. And we're always working on improving these features. So we would like to thank you for your patience with the house's little snags. Please continue to report anything that's not to your liking. You can be sure your reports are being read and addressed."

They leave me with a bad taste in my mouth and a weird sense like I'd been cheated. They answered all my questions without answering anything at all. I wander the house aimlessly, taking a mental note of every single automatized feature, my mind concocting one crazy scenario after another. I'm living in an Asimov novel.

This is why, when the house announces that I have a visitor, I give a start.

When the house tells me who the visitor is, I nearly jump out of my skin.

CHAPTER ELEVEN

I never could have imagined my life would take this science-fiction twist. In fact, growing up, I didn't imagine much for myself in the best-case scenario.

I understood early on that my family was different from those of other children my age. If I had to pinpoint the exact moment, I doubt that I could but the definitive reckoning came the day the authorities told Therese she had to enroll me in school or have me taken away and placed in a foster home.

Until then, Therese was home-schooling me—or that's what she called it. Child Protection Services asked her a couple of questions about the curriculum and decided that such an education was insufficient, to put it mildly. The reason they didn't just take me away immediately remains obscure to me. Maybe because Therese was a white Catholic, and also not a drug addict or prostitute, which was already pretty good considering the averages in our neighborhood at the time. But CPS assigned us a social worker to check up on my progress and make sure I started second grade immediately.

Until then, my primary exposure to children my age was the church play group. Even there, it wasn't hard to realize that I lived in a completely different world. The rest of the children stayed an hour or two after Sunday school to tumble around the playground and then went home, to their otherwise secular lives of cartoons and video games and Twinkies for snacks. I'd spend the whole day there, waiting for Therese to be done with her volunteering, and in the evening, we'd go back to our crumbling rental apartment.

Much later, I'd be shocked to learn we weren't actually poor. *Shocked* is too kind a word. We lived in that one-bedroom for years, and in the meantime, she had close to six figures squirreled away in the bank. But at our apartment, we slept on secondhand cots. We didn't have a television, let alone a gaming console or a DVD player. She got our clothes at the Salvation Army and made me wear them until they literally fell apart.

I guess I shouldn't have been so surprised to find out we weren't broke—she never outright said we didn't have money. That lifestyle was Therese's all-consuming crusade against sin. Anything pleasant or pleasurable or aesthetic had to be mercilessly rooted out of her life, and mine by extension. Pizza or takeout was a sin, new sneakers were a sin. Cartoons were the Devil's work upon this earth, with subliminal messages to brainwash children and lure them away from the righteous path. Regular school would corrupt me, and so she decided to school me herself, teaching me how to read with a Bible.

Who knows where Therese got these ideas, more suited to some Bible Belt small town than to the middle of a large, multicultural city. She mellowed out with age, moving from the decrepit rental with mold on the walls to a small but comfortable condo, and the very fact that she now talks to me again speaks volumes. But she remains reluctant to answer questions about the past. Clearly, something must have happened, something pretty damn drastic, but all I know is that she got pregnant at a young age, had me, and then became a born-again Christian. The how and the why remain a mystery.

But back when I had to integrate into normal society— at least from eight until four p.m. five days a week— she was beside herself. The moment I'd step over the threshold she'd descend on me, bombarding me with questions, trying to suss out if I'd been seduced by the Devil's works. What did I learn, what did the teachers say and do, but, especially, who did I talk to, hang out with, play with?

She had nothing to worry about. The moment I first set foot inside the school gates in my secondhand, ill-fitting clothes and shoes with holes, I became a target. Hardly surprising, when even the Sunday School kids kept their distance from me, somehow figuring out that I wasn't like them. That whiff of crazy from Therese rubbed off on me, and children are great at picking up on these things. If ever a new child joined the group on the playground, someone would elbow her in the ribs soon enough, whispering in her ear, *Don't play with her, she's weeeeeird.*

Regular school was no exception. I couldn't keep up with their conversations about Barbies and Pokémon cards. I became the butt of jokes. Kids avoided going near my desk like it was contaminated.

I should have hated it and longed to run back under Therese's skirts. But instead, I was fascinated. I was too consumed with wanting to *be* my tormentors to loathe them. Even as my classmates spat on me and tripped me up in hallways, my envy was stronger than anything, even my hatred.

And pretty soon, I had a chance to join the world I longed for.

By that time, second grade, I had a pretty good idea that my relationship with my mother—or rather Therese's relationship with me—wasn't the same as what most kids my age had with their parents. Therese rarely showed love or even the most basic affection. Only after starting second grade did I understand this had something to do with that dad I was never allowed to mention. My one innocent question about my dad cost me a whole evening in the corner. Some girl in my class had heard from her mom, who knew some school worker, that when she enrolled me, Therese requested that the field for my father's name be left blank. And I remembered enough from the Bible reading lessons to put two and two together. Therese hated me because of that. Because I, myself, was proof of some kind of deadly sin.

The children in my class caught on with remarkable speed. They called my mom a Jesus freak—the first time I'd ever heard that term—and me, devil-spawn. My desk went from contaminated to cursed. One girl in particular—the very same one who started the rumors—victimized me the most. The pleasure she took from it was evident, from her wicked grin to the evil gleam in her eyes any time she glimpsed me, and whenever I saw those I knew I was about to be subjected to some new ordeal.

And so, one day, I took advantage of a moment of inattention and stole her prized possession, some sort of pencil box made of bright plastic, with buttons that played music and a little built-in calculator. She turned away just as I was passing by, as always, discreet, shrinking into myself, and for once, she didn't notice me. I slipped the pencil box right off her desk and stuffed it in my pocket.

Long story short, she had an absolute fit when she realized her thingamajig was missing. No matter that she would have forgotten about it by next week, and it would be gathering dust at the bottom of her school bag, replaced in her favor by some new toy. But right now, it was gone, and something had to be done quickly. They searched everyone in class and found the pencil box.

Later, at home, was the first and only time Therese ever hit me.

Honestly, it's surprising it didn't happen sooner. And it

definitely wasn't out of love for me that Therese had kept her hands off me thus far. But she hit me that evening. Or, rather, slapped me—slapped me hard enough that my head snapped sideways.

My ears were ringing, and, shocked by the suddenness of it as much as the pain, I spun around and ran from the room. Maybe I ran too fast, in the apartment that was too small and cluttered. But I tripped and fell and hit my head on the side of a table. The next day, I had to go to school with a bruise.

And that's when I did something I'd never thought possible before. When a teacher asked me about the bruise, I flat-out told her it was my mom who hit me.

I still don't know what possessed me. It wasn't an outright lie—she did hit me; it just didn't cause the bruise. And it was the perfect way to draw attention away from what I had done, for which I had already been given detention for the whole week. I didn't exactly think my little lie of omission would get me out of detention. But I needed something. The bruise was something.

Little did I know the far-reaching consequences my fib would have. I only had the vaguest idea why I ended up in regular school after all. I remembered the conversation with the social worker, who had been nice and friendly and smiling, so I didn't suspect any underlying motivations.

For once, the machine whirred into action with frightening efficiency, and by the end of the week, I was whisked away from Therese's care and placed with a foster family.

I would spend several months with them, a time that is mostly lost in a fog of sheer wonderment. I got a set of cheap but clean clothes from the local department store, I ate boxed macaroni and cheese three nights a week and breaded chicken fillets the rest of the time, and watched cartoons with four other children. It was utterly incredible, and I couldn't believe my luck.

Although I didn't know this at the time, Therese went into a frenzy to prove to social services that she was a fit mother. She attended those classes they signed her up for, she rented a new apartment, and got rid of the hoarded clutter. I don't know how sincere it all was, whether she really decided to change or it was all an act. But if so, why go to such lengths to get me back when she didn't much care for me in the first place? When I certainly didn't need or want her to?

But get me back she did, and one fine day, I returned to her with my possessions folded neatly in an old suitcase provided by a special charity organization. The first days were strange, the Therese I knew and the new, social-services-approved Therese warring within the small space of the new apartment. There was a TV now, which stayed off most of the time. There was nutritious food beyond plain oatmeal and peanut butter on toast—to this day I still can't stand the sight of peanut butter, and for the longest time, I pretended to be allergic to it. I had clothes that fit. Therese was polite to me, the way one is to an exchange student. At first, every day I expected her to ask me why I lied, whether I remembered what a grave sin lying was, and whether I had repented.

But she never asked. I guess she knew she wouldn't like the answer.

With the new apartment came a new school district and a new school, which meant the end of the bullying. Not just because my clothes were better and my lunches didn't call attention to them with their shabbiness. This time, I was smarter. I learned to hide from people the things I didn't want them to see. Things were so much better now, and all I did was tell a little white lie.

CHAPTER TWELVE

"Anna Finch is here to see you, Cecelia. Should I let her in?"

My initial reflex is to say no. To send a message to Anna-fucking-Finch that I'm out, that I'm away on vacation to Honduras for the rest of the year, that I died, whatever. Or better yet, to tell Anna Finch to please go to hell.

But then I think about it. "Sure," I say.

"Very well, Cecelia. Anna Finch has been notified. She's at the door."

I go and let her in. She's wearing a suit again but a different one. Still in a similar style, and, by the looks of it, just as expensive. Only now her hair is down, and she's wearing less makeup. I can see her freckles.

"Hello," she says. When she's not screeching or spewing insults, her voice is poised, pleasant. Something is very corporate about it. It's the voice of a person who gets promotions. "Cecelia? I apologize for dropping in on you like this. So kind of you to let me in."

She holds out a wine bottle. What is she playing at now? I'm in my own house. She can't have another fit. I remember Clarisse's words: The house will protect its inhabitants from any threat, internal or external. So if she plans to break that wine bottle over my head—

"A little offering. I wasn't sure what to get so I decided to go with a sure value. It's a Burgundy. A good year."

"Thank you," I say, deciding to play it safe and find out what she wants before I do anything rash.

"I'm going to cut to the chase. I wanted to apologize to you for my unseemly outburst. I know I behaved in an appalling way, and it was unwarranted. Your car malfunctioned, that's all. There was no reason to react the way I did."

It sounds rehearsed as hell, and I can picture her perfectly, composing it on her tablet beforehand, her short but manicured nails tapping softly at the screen. But the way she delivers it has a ring of honesty to it. And of course, there's her face. It turns a little bit pink. A redhead's skin isn't good at lying and deception.

"I understand," I say. "You had your child in the car. I think I would have reacted the same way."

"We're mothers," she says, latching on to this thing we have in common, for lack of anything else. "We'll do anything for our children. My daughter is Rebecca. She's in the Little Munchkins group."

Taryn was in the Little Munchkins group herself until

she turned three recently. Now she's in Little Tots, ages three to five. I tell Anna this, and she nods.

"This is what I appreciate so much about this place. The safety for my baby. So I hope you can understand why I overreacted."

I nod. I very much would have liked to leave it at that but the polite thing to do is to offer her a coffee or something. I do, half hoping she'll refuse. But she nods emphatically. "Great idea. I had a hectic morning and could use a little coffee. Rebecca still wakes up to eat at night sometimes."

"Oh, I remember. I don't miss that."

We share a somewhat awkward laugh. The coffee machine takes Anna's order, which Anna rattles off with the flawless confidence of someone who's been living in Venture for a while. It whirs quietly as it makes our coffees, and I keep an eye on it for any signs of weirdness. But the macchiato and my usual double-long come out perfect.

Forty-five minutes later, we're uncorking the wine bottle she brought. It's early afternoon, a bit too early to be drinking, but what the heck. It turns out that Anna is one of the early adopters, living in Venture for three years now, since before her daughter was born.

"There's no better place to have kids," she now tells me with unshakable confidence. She swirls the wine in her glass. "It's like—I'm not a religious person, or even a spiritual person, so don't get me wrong—but it's like something out there heard my prayers. You know? Pointed me to this place."

I nod. "IntelTech just contacted us. They found Scott through his work. They said they were looking for young families to test a groundbreaking new project."

"I was skeptical at first," says Anna. "But we tried it for six months, and I was ready to buy. So we did."

I lower my gaze to my wineglass.

"Is everything okay?" she asks. "Did I say something—"

"No." I take a sip of my wine. "It's just, you seem so sure. We haven't decided yet if we're buying."

"Seriously, you should," she says. Her face is starting to flush a bit. "The first and only thing that went wrong in three years was a dent in my bumper. In what other place in the world can you boast that?"

"I guess you're right."

"I owe this to myself," she says. "And to Rebecca. When we met with Clarisse, I just had a good gut feeling. I just knew this was the place for us."

"Really?" I chuckle. "To tell you the truth, Clarisse kind of gave me the heebie-jeebies. Something about her, something Stepford-y. And that assistant of hers is like a robot."

Anna gives a hearty laugh. It's a surprising laugh, coming from someone like her, all thin and dry and brittle-looking. "Stepford-y? My God, Cecelia. People are just afraid of what they don't understand. Or they just can't afford it and are forced to live in crummy, crime-riddled boroughs so they disguise their envy as social conscious-ness. Remember how everyone was boycotting Nike in the nineties? And then they made enough money to afford nice things and got over it so fast."

She looks smug.

"What about privacy?" I ask.

"Privacy? You don't think any of us have any privacy, do you? In 2020. But I hear you. My husband was the same way at first, and it took some persuading. But what can I say? Persuading is what I do for a living so I'm good at it."

I don't tell her that I can kind of understand her husband. And I'm starting to worry about my own family—about Scott, who seems as eager to careen down the slippery slope as Anna, and about Taryn, who will grow up in this place, so completely disconnected from the real world.

"The whole world will be like this in five years," says Anna. "We're just lucky enough to live in it now."

*   *   *

As I show her out, I can't help but wonder. We exchanged our contact info. Not that it was necessary because Saya would have uploaded it onto our respective phones if I'd only asked. Anna told me about a stroller-moms group that she was a part of. Didn't explicitly invite me to join but mentioned where they had their weekly meetups: in the gazebo at the techy local park. I said I'd give it some thought. Taryn is a bit old for that now. The only way she'll sit complacently in a stroller for hours is if I put a tablet in her hands.

I didn't share with Anna any of my suspicions about the house and the mysterious Lydia with the taste for syrupy coffee drinks. I kind of got the feeling she'd laugh at me and think I was delusional. And this is the first time I make a connection with anyone here, superficial as it is. Who knows, perhaps Anna and Scott are both right. This is the future, Taryn's future, and I might as well embrace it.

"Saya," I speak up.

"Yes, Cecelia?"

"Who lives in the big glass house behind ours?"

"I'm afraid I'm not authorized to share that information, Cecelia."

I shrug. Of course.

"Saya, who lived here before we did?"

"I don't understand the question, Cecelia."

"Who is Lydia? Do you know a Lydia?"

A moment of silence. Then: "I know several Lydias. Which one do you mean?" And the voice proceeds to list actresses and other people of note.

"Is there a Lydia living in Venture?"

"I'm afraid I can't help you with that information, Cecelia."

Uh-huh. How surprising. "Can't you run some sort of check?"

"You should address IntelTech for that information."

Figures.

"Saya, have you ever hurt anyone?"

"I don't understand what you mean."

"Would you ever hurt anyone?"

"I do not understand the question."

"If they were trying to hurt me, for instance? Would you hurt someone?"

"You should address IntelTech for that information. Cecelia, it's time to get Taryn from day care in thirty minutes. Scott has left work and will be home in approximately forty-seven minutes, due to light traffic. Do you want me to start supper?"

I heave a sigh. "No."

"Have I been helpful with your inquiries, Cecelia?"

What do you think?

CHAPTER THIRTEEN

At exactly six o'clock, Jessica clocks out. At IntelTech there's no "clocking out" in the traditional sense, and nothing resembling old-fashioned time cards is in sight. Like every other employee, she clocks out with the chip embedded in her wrist. She doesn't need to scan it. It auto-scans on her way into the parking lot beneath the building and again when she drives out onto the street.

IntelTech issues cars to their employees, the same model of pristine white electric vehicle for everyone except for the higher-ups who get an SUV. There's the option of housing too. Jessica could be living in Venture, in a special apartment building—not for free but at a discount. But Jessica's mother is ill, and she has to live with her so she didn't take advantage of the offer. She knows it's not seen well at work, and she lives in fear of the day when they offer the housing to her mother as well, and then Jessica won't have any reason to live away from SmartBlock.

But until then. Until then . . .

She drives down perfectly manicured streets, past picture-perfect houses and lawns and parks. Pleasant classical music pours from the speakers of her car. Finally, she arrives at the Venture city limit and taps an icon on the dashboard. The gate opens and lets her out, back into the real world.

Yes, Venture and all its technological wonders is separated from its neighbors with a gate and a fence. The fence is concealed by a beautiful, verdant hedge but it's there nonetheless. A literal gated community. Reemerging into the world outside is like flipping a switch. Or exiting a beautifully crafted simulation into a postapocalyptic wasteland that is reality.

She drives down a road badly in need of repairs, her teeth clacking together every time she hits one of the many potholes. Garbage cans are overflowing, and the houses have filthy windows and crumbling brick exteriors. In this part of town, far from the city core and too close to the industrial area, poor families and immigrants live in dilapidated double- and triple-deckers. They have about as much of a chance of making it inside the fence as they have of getting to the moon.

Jessica grits her teeth but doesn't let her guard down for the entire drive home, not even when she takes the ramp onto the highway or when she makes the turn onto her street. She lives with her mother in a little bungalow that's been looking like it needs a little love lately. Jessica has no time to clean and maintain. She should pay someone but her salary isn't as big as most would think. IntelTech is only generous to the people who don't really need their generosity.

She drives the car into the garage, where it looks like some futuristic spaceship beamed it down here by mistake, and gets out. She enters the house proper through the door in the back of the garage.

"Mom?" she calls out. But her mother is in her room, asleep. She's been going downhill for years now, after one tragic event too many has eroded her spirits too much to fight against her illness.

Jessica checks on her, standing in the door of the small bedroom, breathing in the smell of staleness and medicine. She listens to her mother's breathing, wondering if she's imagining it and her mother is long gone. When that happens, she won't be able to refuse SmartBlock housing either.

She should open the window but instead, she cranks the AC and leaves the bedroom door open a crack so the air circulates. She heads to her own bedroom, hardly bigger than a closet, where her single bed takes up most of the space. There's another room she could occupy but she doesn't dare. It's been standing untouched for years now, and it'll remain that way until her mother breathes her last.

So Jessica has been living in the smallest room since she was a child. Back then, the room looked so much bigger than it was. There are still posters on the walls of bands teenage Jessica had crushes on, and her bedspread is pink, somewhat faded from many washes. Only very few people know she lives like this.

She draws the curtain that she opened this morning out of sheer habit and undresses, taking off the IntelTech uniform and laying it carefully out on the bed. She has five sets, hanging in the corner of her closet under plastic covers. Every weekend, she has them dry-cleaned and pressed, ready for the week to come. Mechanically, she smooths out every crease, even though it's unnecessary. The laundry place will do it much better than she can.

Then she takes off her bra and underwear. Believe it or not, they're part of the uniform, and perhaps she's being overly cautious but she can't take chances. She gets a different pair of underwear from a drawer and forgoes the bra altogether. From her closet, she takes out a different set of clothes, an outfit that would probably give Clarisse a heart attack: ripped black jeans, a snug, cropped shirt, and on top of it, an oversize jean jacket. Then big, clunky boots, which are more of a necessity than a fashion statement. The contrast with her work attire is too shocking—she's unlikely to be recognized.

With the same idea in mind, she puts on her makeup: dark eye shadow, mascara, pencil, and lipstick in an ugly red-brown shade that doesn't flatter her skin tone. This is all deliberate.

Finally, she reaches to the very back of her closet, where an old backpack sits slumped under a pile of old sneakers. From it, she retrieves a bracelet that she casually slips onto her wrist. Its elastic band is snug, too snug, but she'll put up with it, rubbing her hand every once in a while, flexing her fingers. What looks like a big metal buckle settles right where her chip is embedded.

She's no longer smiling Jessica from IntelTech, assistant to Clarisse. She's now just Jess.

Then, after a last look at her mother, who still hasn't stirred, Jess heads back to the garage. Leaving the pretty white car, she gets on her motorcycle, an aged but trusty Kawasaki Ninja.

With a roar of the engine, she pulls out of the driveway onto the street, and within minutes, she's gone from sight.

*   *   *

When I arrive at the day care, it's the middle of the rush. The moms and dads who work have all gotten there at the same time to pick up their offspring. Taryn ignores me for as long as humanly possible, seemingly so absorbed in assembling a puzzle on the floor of the main room that she doesn't see me. Except she's three years old and not very skilled at deception. I see her gaze dart toward me several times before fleeing anxiously back to her puzzle. I have to call her name three times before she gives up the charade and starts to trudge toward me.

There's no need for the teachers to verify just who's picking up the kids because the microchips do that at the entrance. Still, one of them oversees the scene with a serene smile.

That smile falters when she sees me. As I help Taryn put on her jacket and shoes, I practically feel her staring. Yet she doesn't come up to me or acknowledge me in any way.

"Are you going to say bye to your friends and teacher, Taryn?" I try in a honeyed voice.

Taryn remains sullen, pretending she hasn't heard.

"Taryn, wave bye and let's go."

But she's standing still, with her jacket half-buttoned and her shoes with their Velcro straps open. She looks spaced out. "Taryn?" When I glance up, the teacher is still staring, and for the first time, it occurs to me what they all must be thinking after that scene yesterday. It wasn't just Taryn watching—all her friends were too. And I, of all people, know how parents talk when they're at home and think no one can hear. But the kids always can. They're like little recording devices that will play back your embarrassing pronouncements at the worst possible time. Like when the mother-in-law—or worse yet, the boss—comes over for dinner. And it didn't even cross my mind that Taryn might be mocked or bullied because of the accident. God knows I remember what it's like to be labeled the kid with the crazy mom.

"Sweetie?" I ask. "Is everything okay?"

Taryn's gaze refocuses at last. She looks at me with a kind of clear calm that's almost eerie, too adult for her features. "I don't go with you," she says in a soft but clear voice.

I frown. "What do you mean, you don't go with me?"

"I don't go with you. I stay."

This again, I think, gritting my teeth. "Taryn, you can't stay at day care. It's closing. Everyone is going home. You don't want to be left all alone here when it's all dark and empty, do you?"

"I stay," she repeats, and her voice rises in volume just enough for me to start to break out in a cold sweat.

"No," I say firmly. "You can't stay. You'll come back tomorrow and play with all your friends again. But now we have to go home."

"No!" This time, her cry is high-pitched, resonating through the entire space. Other parents turn their heads. Then, other *kids* turn their heads, and when I throw a brief glance around, glee is written plain on their faces, like they're anticipating some entertaining new show.

"No go! No home!"

"Taryn." If there was ever a time to raise my voice, this is it.

"No go! No go!" She turns red, her little fists clenching. "Help! Help!"

What?

"Taryn, stop that immediately." But I know I'm losing control, fast, and I can't do anything about it. All I can do is watch it like a slow-motion train wreck.

"Help! You're not Mommy! You're not my mommy!"

Jesus. There's something new. Blood rushes to my face, and I feel myself turn redder than my toddler. Everyone is watching now. The teacher with that blank face of hers finally rushes toward us.

Taryn practically jumps on her, hugging her legs. "This is not my mommy. I no go."

The teacher, whose name tag reads BELLA, gives a

strained, apologetic smile. Hell, if anyone should be apologizing here, it's me.

"This is such a mess. I'm so sorry," I mumble. "I don't know why she's like this. It's never happened before."

"Ms. Holmes," Bella says calmly, "I understand. May I please scan your chip?"

I blink, not processing what I just heard. Taryn still hugs Bella, smearing snot all over her trouser leg.

"May I scan your chip, please?" She's holding out a phone. What? You have to be kidding me. "I'm very sorry but I have to."

Numb, I hold out my wrist. The chip scans instantly. Except instead of the typical soft beep, Bella's phone emits an alarming shriek. The screen flashes red.

I understand before anything else has time to happen. Red means outsider.

Bella looks up at me, and all color drains from her face. This has clearly never happened before, and she has no idea what to do.

"Ma'am," she says at last, "could you please come with me?"

Ma'am. No longer Ms. Holmes.

This must be some sick joke.

"Of course I'm Cecelia Holmes. Taryn's mother. What does that thing say?" I ask, surprised that I've managed to keep my voice so calm.

"Ma'am," Bella starts, but I don't let her finish her phrase—her stupid, rehearsed phrase, parroted wholesale from some dumb manual.

Besides, I know what it says. I could bet my life that the name on the screen starts with an *L*.

"How is that possible?" I hiss. "Are you all out of your minds? I come here every day, twice a day. Surely at least one of you has bothered to remember my face?"

"Not my mommy!" Taryn shrieks like a siren. "I want my mommy!"

And then she breaks down in tears, and all hell breaks loose.

CHAPTER FOURTEEN

"Unbelievable." Scott shakes his head.

"IntelTech will hear about this," I say grimly as I collapse onto my comfy, cozy living room couch at last. At least the chip let me into my own house.

"IntelTech is not the issue," Scott says softly. "Or, at least, not the only issue. You must understand that, Cece. Right?"

It took all of an hour and a half to sort out that mess. The day care administrator showed up within seconds, followed by a veritable private fleet of IntelTech security vehicles. Led by that robotic girl who works for Clarisse. What's her name again? Janet?

Thankfully, when she scanned my chip a second time, it showed the correct information. Cecelia Holmes, mother of Taryn Lucy Holmes, resident of 32 Rosemary Road. But, since such a malfunction was impossible—*impossible!*—

they had to do the full verification, *you understand*, complete identity check, DNA sample, the works. *This is about the safety of children, ma'am, it's in your and Taryn's best interest, it's why you trust us with your safety*, and so on and so forth.

I called Scott in hysterics, and he had to drive over and confirm that I was indeed his wife and not some impostor wearing her face. Not that they thought that. They're not insane.

At least I don't think so.

Later, after my identity had been verified, thank God, I furiously interrogated Bella and found out that they did special safety exercises in class earlier that afternoon. What to do if accosted by a stranger and the like. Apparently, the thing to do is to yell as loudly as you can, *You're not my mommy!* Which, apparently, Taryn really took to heart. So much so that she decided to test it on her own mother.

"And you believed it?" I asked Bella, incredulous. "You must have recognized me. Did you?"

She looked away and mumbled something about how she sees hundreds of faces a day, and anyway, the technology doesn't lie.

Terrific. Just terrific.

And the glitch? Just a nasty coincidence.

"I really should bill all these assholes for the free show," I now mutter to Scott. He's looking at me with that expression—with pity. My husband feels sorry for me.

I seethe. "You should have seen it, Scott. How they were staring at me. Bastards. I bet it's the best thing that happened to them all week."

"Cece, stop that."

"Why?"

"Because it was an accident. That's all. And if a stranger really had shown up to pick up Taryn? You'd be the first one to be glad they have those measures."

"What stranger? In this place? A stranger can't even get past the city gates without checking in and signing twelve official forms!"

"And anyway, I think there's a bigger problem here, and you know it. Taryn's been acting out, you've said so yourself. This latest stunt is just the most public so you can't explain it away and gloss over it. And to be honest, you've been a little out of sorts lately too."

"Out of sorts," I repeat, incredulous. Part of me is angry but another part is wondering if he's just noticed it now.

"That's one way of putting it. I've been thinking about it for a long time, Cecelia. I didn't want to pressure you. After all, it's a personal thing and your decision and all. But the atmosphere at home is becoming more and more stressful. For me and for Taryn. It's rubbing off, and I think that's why she's misbehaving."

"This better not be going where I think it's going."

"Sorry. It is. I think you should seriously consider going back to therapy."

I groan.

"I knew you'd react this way. So I'm offering a compromise. Besides, I think it's already affected not just you but all of us. Including Taryn. And I know that's not what you want."

"What are you getting at?"

"I think all of us should go. To family therapy, together. There's a psychologist right here in Venture—"

"You're kidding, right?"

"Why are you so dead set against it?"

"A shrink is one thing. An IntelTech shrink is another. Unless you're okay with the idea of all your neuroses being logged into some database and used by their friendly partners for marketing research."

He looks affronted. "No. I checked. Health records, including mental health, are exempt from that."

"And if you believe that, I have a bridge to sell you."

"Cece, please."

"It was a waste of time last time. And completely ineffective. Why should we drag ourselves through it again?"

"I'm only saying we should give it a try. Please. Here, I looked her up." He picks up his tablet and taps the screen. Instantly, my tablet pings on the coffee table. I pick it up, and the page opens, one of those web pages in shades of beige with soothing loopy fonts. A woman's smiling face in a frame. She wears gold-rimmed glasses.

"She seems lovely. Her name's Dr. Alice Stockman."

*   *   *

TRANSCRIPT: Session 9, Lydia Bishop.
Dr. Alice Stockman, PhD.
June 7th, 2018

   AS: Good morning, Lydia.
   LB: Good morning, Dr. Alice.

AS: How are you doing this week?

LB: You know, I really hate that question. [laughs] Don't worry, I know it's only to establish rapport. But the question should be, how are your problems doing this week? Because that's why I'm here, right?

AS: I want you to feel like you can talk about anything, not just your problems, as you call them.

LB: Sure. It's just, you know ... it's really hard to shake the weirdness of it all. You understand that this is strange for me.

AS: In the sense that you should be sitting where I'm sitting, is that right?

LB: Yeah. But not just that.

AS: Then I'm not sure what you mean.

LB: [lowering voice] The whole ... privacy issue?

AS: Lydia, we've discussed this before. Yes, my office is on SmartBlock territory but I don't work for IntelTech. The recordings, or anything you tell me, are for my use only.

LB: I thought about it since last time. The cassettes. It's because you worry they'll hack your computer or something, isn't it?

AS: [laughs] ... or it could just be that I'm not very tech-savvy.

LB: [strained laugh] See? There it is again.

AS: What do you mean?

LB: I'm jumping to the worst conclusions. Sorry to beat you to the punch. You'd have figured it out soon enough anyway. It's in my nature, and I know

myself. After all, I'm a psychologist too. Just like
you. [pause] Or at least I used to be...

AS: Do you think that because you no longer practice, you're no longer a psychologist?

LB: Do *you* think that I still am one?

AS: Do you still have your license?

LB: Oh, Dr. Alice. Don't play obtuse, please. It's so
condescending. You know that I do. Because of
course you would have looked it all up, and I
can't even blame you because it's publicly available information. The reason that unlicensed
frauds get away with it is because people get
dazzled by pieces of paper framed on a wall and
fancy terms being thrown around and don't bother
to check.

AS: If I ever looked anything up, it's only in the
context of figuring out how to better help you.

LB: Of course. Yes, I still have my license to practice.
Although they did try to put that into question,
after...everything. There was a hearing, if you can
believe it. I had to answer a bunch of questions
about my work. Well, no, not so much about my
work, they couldn't care less about that. I had to
answer a bunch of questions about *Walter*. They
even tried to get me to hand over my recordings of
our sessions. Yeah, right. In the end, there was nothing for them to hold on to. I hadn't done anything
wrong.

[long pause; LB chuckles sadly]

LB: But in the end, it made no difference, did it?

Because here I am. Not practicing. And I probably
never will again.

AS: Why do you say that?

LB: Dr. Alice, don't do that. Don't I at least deserve a
modicum of consideration as a fellow professional?
It's obvious. Who on earth would book a session
with a shrink who killed her own patient?

CHAPTER FIFTEEN

My previous experiences with a shrink turned out less than convincing. First, a long, long time ago, there was Ms. Felipe, with dreadlocks and ripped jeans. After my stint at the foster home and subsequent return home, social services didn't forget Therese and me. My caseworker was Ms. Felipe, who insisted I call her Dana and tell her *everything*. Like we were friends. She was actually really cool—I'm sure that's the exact image she wished to project. But that was when I learned the consequences of lying that had nothing to do with hellfire and brimstone. Once you started, you had to continue, on and on and on into infinity. Now that there was an official case file out there saying that Therese gave me a bruise once—that meant Therese gave me a bruise. Everything I told Dana had to be weighed carefully against that information, to make sure nothing contradicted it or cast it into doubt.

My problems in those days came not so much from Therese as from the teenagers at my new school. Sure, the bullying no longer reached such extremes as before, I wasn't spat on anymore or considered to be contaminated. In the new school district, there was no one to remember the plain-bread lunches. But even with money for the cafeteria, I struggled to get my peers to accept me. At thirteen years old, cliques were forming, and I was a new girl and altogether unremarkable. I might not have been mocked anymore but I was quietly excluded, and disregarded.

I had my eye on a clique in particular, led by a girl named Sophie who had everything a thirteen-year-old girl could want. For weeks, she interacted with her group of loyal vassals while I went mad with envy. Like the others, she didn't so much bully me as ignore me, regarding me as an interchangeable piece of the backdrop—one of many extras in what she, like a lot of prettier-than-average girls her age, regarded as the Sophie Show. And I was determined to be more than that.

By then, I thought I knew my worth: my too-big, slightly crooked front teeth and mothlike, washed-out coloring disqualified me from being considered beautiful. Which left me one other avenue toward conquering Sophie's heart. One day, I snuck into Therese's purse and retrieved a handful of twenties from her wallet. The next day, my heart hammering, I approached my idol and suggested we hit the makeup aisle at the nearby drugstore during lunch. I bought Sophie lip glosses, eye shadow, and some kind of special crazy-expensive mascara and handed over all the cash without so much as flinching. That day had to be the best of my life because I was allowed to sit with her and her friends. Sure, they talked over my head like I wasn't there, except I *was* there, and nothing could take that away.

Until the next day, that is, when Sophie went back to acting like I didn't exist and rebuffed my attempts to join her and her clique with open mockery. She was wearing the mascara. It made her lashes look like fuzzy spider legs.

Therese noticed the missing money, of course. She confronted me that same day when I got back from school, bewildered and discouraged.

"I know you took it," Therese said, in a deceptively calm voice she only used when she was three seconds away from exploding. "Just tell me what you spent it on, and you won't get in trouble."

I knew that to be less than true so I just kept my mouth shut.

"What did you spend it on, you little fiend? Was it drugs?" She grabbed me by the sleeve and pulled me toward her, yanking me so hard that I lost my balance and dropped to my knees. The impact made us both flinch. I looked up at her; she looked down at me.

"Let go of me," I said calmly. "Or else."

"Or else what?"

"Or else, I'll call Dana and tell her you hit me again."

And then I saw that look in her eyes. The look that meant I had won forever. She was disturbed and powerless and even frightened. She let go of my sleeve. I got up and went to my room.

"You're cursed," I heard her say softly to my back as I walked away. "That's what you are. You're a curse."

And yet, I'll have everything I want, I thought, seething. Just watch me.

Needless to say, Scott doesn't know about any of it. And not because I think he'd judge me. On the contrary, he'd be horrified if I told him about the old church days, about the place where I grew up. But I don't want him to think of me like that.

As for Therese, he met her precisely once, and that was enough for him to agree that she shouldn't be invited to our wedding. I now go visit her twice a year, and that's more than enough. I'm actually a couple months overdue but it's the last thing on my mind.

My second experience with a shrink was right after the home invasion. I only lasted the five appointments recommended to prevent PTSD, and even then, I have no idea if it helped or not.

But contrary to what I told Scott, I didn't quit because I didn't think she was good enough. Quite the opposite. I quit because I felt like she was a bit *too* good. Eerily so. By the second appointment, she teased out of me the full story of my childhood, which I happily spilled. Including the crucial lie I told that time, a long time ago.

Maybe in the heat of the moment, it seemed to me that it didn't matter anymore, after so long. She sure made it sound that way. *Children lie*, she said matter-of-factly. *It's nothing to be ashamed of.* But as soon as the door of the shrink's office closed after me that afternoon, I was seized by a deep-seated malaise, stricken by the feeling that I had

made a terrible mistake. I cruised through the remaining
three sessions, always on high alert and very self-aware,
and then I was done so I never came back.

From the outside, the office of Dr. Stockman fits into
the neighborhood seamlessly, a sleek chrome-and-glass
building. In the lobby, it houses a coffee shop, and the
neighbors are a bakery and a flower shop. Taryn spots the
cakes in the window display and, of course, immediately
points her finger. "Want!"

I glance at Scott in alarm. If she decides to have another
meltdown in the middle of the street, I'm officially at a loss
for what to do. But he scoops her up playfully and spins
her, and she forgets about the cakes. A little too quickly,
I'd say, and I'm seized by a momentary feeling of jealousy
that makes me ashamed.

Maybe I can bring that up with Dr. Stockman too.

We go up a small flight of stairs to the second floor,
and as soon as we go through the discreet door with the
silver plaque reading ALICE STOCKMAN PHD, it's like we're in
a different world.

Everything here is cozy and old-timey. There's a hardwood floor that looks appropriately worn—they must have
brought it in from somewhere else because five years or
however long this place existed isn't long enough for this
degree of wear and tear. There's the requisite Impression-
ist art print on the wall in a simple frame. The armchairs
are vintage, and there's a throw rug and a coffee table
piled with actual books.

Dr. Alice Stockman, whom I recognize at once because
she looks exactly like the photo on the website, comes

out to greet us herself. No assistants or receptionists or any other background characters to make us, the patients, extra nervous about who else has access to everything that's wrong with us. The woman greets us warmly but without excess, and addresses Taryn with the same collected calm. No baby talk, no squatting to be at her level. Dr. Stockman inclines her head. "And you must be Taryn. Look, Taryn, we have a wonderful playroom here, filled with all kinds of interesting toys. Do you want to check it out?"

At the prospect of toys, Taryn, who's returned to sulking, perks up again. She follows Dr. Stockman to one of the two doors with nary a backward glance at me, her mother. I follow on their heels, feeling rather unwelcome.

Dr. Stockman opens the door to a playroom that's right out of my own childhood. Well, not so much mine but one that someone my age or a little older might have had. There are toys, all right: old-school wooden blocks and puzzles, a toy pony, a castle, stuffed animals that belong in my own childhood, if not my mother's. None of the sleek, techy educational toys like they have at the day care, and not a screen in sight.

Taryn will have a fit, I think, and brace myself for the inevitability. But, to my surprise, Taryn's eyes widen in sheer wonderment, and she throws herself at the toys with a shriek of joy.

I look, incredulous, from her to Dr. Stockman. The woman gives a reserved smile. "It's something new," she says in a low voice. "It's always interesting for them to discover things they've never seen before."

Indeed. I feel a bit ashamed to admit she's right. Lately, Taryn pretty much only plays on her tablet.

"We're not leaving her here all alone, are we?" I ask. "You see, she had a little behavior issue the other day—"

"We'll get to all of that," Dr. Stockman says. "And of course we're not leaving her completely alone."

I follow her gaze and notice a mirror on the wall. A little too high to be at a toddler's face level. "Oh," I say. I expected a camera or something—something more sophisticated than a simple one-way mirror.

"Sometimes simple is best," says Dr. Stockman as she guides us into her office. It makes me like her. Then it makes me wonder if it was all calculated expressly for that purpose.

CHAPTER SIXTEEN

"I want you to feel like you can be completely honest within these walls," Dr. Stockman says. "I want you to feel that this is a place of trust. And for that, there are no surveillance devices anywhere in the office. No sensors, detectors, cameras of any kind. And, with your permission, I'll tape our sessions. On my own tape recorder." She holds it out to me, as if inviting me to take it and examine it. Scott picks it up and turns it around in his hands.

"Haven't seen one of these in a while," he says. "Not since, like, high school."

"Can we refuse?"

"Of course you can. But I guarantee that the recordings will never be used by anyone except me, and only so I can design the best treatment plan and follow your progress.

You're free to refuse but it would greatly simplify my life if you didn't."

"Record away," says Scott generously. Without consulting me. Without even a sideways glance at me.

"Cecelia?"

I grit my teeth. They both put me in the position to be the killjoy, and I'm not taking the bait. "Okay."

"Great. Then how about we start talking about what brings you here?" She presses a button on the recorder, which clicks loudly. "Cecelia, Scott, and Taryn Holmes," she says in a loud, clear voice. "Session One."

I cast a glance at the one-way mirror to see Taryn rocking on the toy horse. I can't hear anything but I can tell she's yelling in delight. When was the last time she acted like this at home? She stares silently at that tablet for hours, poking at the screen with her little stubby fingers without so much as a giggle.

"Taryn had an episode at day care," I say. "But don't you know everything already?"

"How would I know everything, Cecelia?"

"Well, you work for IntelTech."

"I do not work for IntelTech. I have my office at Smart-Block. I do not work *for* SmartBlock. So I'd like to hear everything from you. And how about you start at the very beginning? Something tells me all three of you wouldn't be here if this was about a simple day care tantrum."

I feel my face color. "Fine," I say. "It all started a year and a half ago."

*　　*　　*

That's not exactly true. It started way more than a year ago. It started the day we made that stupid, disastrous, fateful decision to renovate our house. The house I loved, the house I called home. Really, it was Scott who made the decision—I just went along with it to keep the peace. After all, he'd be paying for it. My little ebook covers could never pay for more than the most basic groceries and a phone bill on a good month. And so Scott was the one who shopped around for contractors.

That's when the first signs of trouble appeared, although we conveniently didn't see them. Scott's resolve not to pinch pennies, to get the best of the best and to hell with the cost—well, that began to melt faster than the ice caps as soon as we got our first estimate. It was a big firm, the one with the full-page ads in the glossy home décor publications. A household name—pun intended. A couple of guys came around, measured things, tap-tapped the walls and floor, and gave Scott a number that made my eyes pop.

The next firm, not as flashy, could only knock off a couple of thousand dollars from the total bill—which was a lot, sure, but not on the scale we were talking about. That evening at dinner, Scott looked defeated and began to talk about maybe making compromises on the materials. Did we really need hardwood cabinets and flooring? Imitations now look just as good and last twice as long.

But I could hear in his voice how dejected it made him. Scott prided himself on being the perfect provider, on being able to supply his family with anything and everything they might want. Even though, for the time being, that family consisted only of me. And now he had to make concessions, settle for fake marble and plywood shelves.

And so I decided to help out. I still wonder what would have happened if I'd just left it alone. Maybe we would have coped with the cheap materials or, better yet, abandoned the project altogether. But I wasn't sure how Scott would deal with such a blow to his ego in the long term, and so I scoured the internet for companies until I finally found the one, on the fourteenth page of Google results. Benning and Co. Renovations and Repairs. Your Needs, Met and Exceeded.

I sent Scott the link. We called them for an evaluation and a quote. They told us they could make it happen— hardwood and all, and the skylight, and the quartz bathroom counters. All within our budget, give or take a few thousand dollars. The guy the company was named after sounded convincing enough, and we let ourselves be convinced because we wanted—needed—to be convinced. We didn't let ourselves wonder just where he was cutting corners. Because obviously he had to cut corners somewhere.

And so the contract was signed, and Benning's men came to renovate the house. This drew itself out over several months, instead of the two we'd agreed on in the contract. Things just kept going wrong. Materials didn't arrive on time, or arrived defective; some old-house quirk got discovered at the worst possible time, bringing the work to a screeching halt until they could figure out what to do. We had to spend additional thousands to repair some electrical wiring we had no idea was faulty.

"Those damn old houses," Scott groused, "always full of things like that. What we should have done is knocked it over and built a new one. Spared ourselves all the bullshit."

I didn't point out we didn't have anything close to the budget needed to do that. To say nothing of the ton of paperwork required by the city.

"At least we found out about it, right? The house could have gone up in flames like a box of matches any moment."

But finally, after nearly six months, it was all done. Finished. The narrow hallway and little rooms gave way to a modern, sleek, open space filled with bright white light from brand-new fixtures. Hardwood floors glimmered darkly with fresh lacquer. It all looked like something out of a magazine, and it left a sad emptiness within me, like an old friend who changed irrevocably and without warning.

This would turn out to be the least of my problems.

Because what we didn't realize was that the shady crew of Benning and Co., shorted on pay, would make a copy of the key we gave them. That they cased our house.

They waited more than a year so we'd put them out of our mind. Then one of them came back.

The only thing that went wrong in his plan was that my daughter and I were home.

CHAPTER SEVENTEEN

Through the one-way mirror, I watch Taryn play as if on mute. She's abandoned the toy horse and is now stacking cubes, piling them up as high as she can and then knocking them over with a kick.

"And you didn't seek therapy after the incident?" asks Dr. Stockman.

"I did. It didn't really stick."

"I mean for Taryn."

"Taryn was just a baby," I say, feeling defensive. "She can't possibly remember."

"But maybe it affected her subconsciously," Scott pipes up. "I always said so." And he looks from the doctor to me and back, waiting for her to agree, like the teacher's pet that he always has been.

Dr. Stockman charitably ignores him and focuses her

attention on me. "So do you think this incident could have been behind the tantrum?"

"I don't know," I say, irritated. "They were learning about stranger danger that day. Or something like that. Whatever they call it nowadays."

"That could have played into it. But I'll speak to Taryn separately. What I'd like to know is, could this incident be behind your unease with your new home?"

"What?" I'm taken aback. That's not what it's about. That's not why I'm here. I didn't agree to this.

"Your husband mentioned that on the phone," she explains. There's something behind the gentleness of her voice. It makes my hair stand on end.

"Scott," I say.

"Yes, so I did say something," he concedes. I could swear he's embarrassed. "I was just— It's been exasperating, dealing with you lately. All this complaining about the glitches—"

"Complaining?" I exclaim. "I'm not *complaining*. There are glitches. Not just annoying but dangerous glitches."

"Did you follow the necessary steps?" asks Dr. Stockman.

"Damn right I followed the necessary steps," I snap. "Can we please stop? I'm not on trial here."

"No one is on trial. We're just trying to unpack things."

"Well, in that case, please unpack my daughter's strange behavior. And leave me out of it."

"You're her mother," Scott cuts in. "Her behavior has everything to do with you. And your neuroses."

"Mr. Holmes," Dr. Stockman speaks up, "please, don't cast blame. Cecelia, I just want to understand your feelings about your new house. Forget about the glitches for a minute. Imagine there are no glitches. That everything is perfect. Imagine IntelTech sends a repairman—"

"They don't have repairmen. They have these creepy robotic assistants and mediators and—"

"Let's pretend. They send a repairman, and there's never again a single glitch in the house. Will you be happy then?"

I think about it. Was I happy before the weirdness began? Hardly.

I think the look on my face is answer enough for her.

"Do you have trouble feeling like you're at home, Cecelia? It's never a good feeling."

"I came here," I say, "to feel safe. I was *supposed* to feel safe. But I don't."

"What do you feel, if not safe?"

"I feel..." I don't know how to put it into words. But even as my brain is struggling, I blurt out, "I feel watched."

"Watched," she echoes. She's sitting across from us on an ergonomic chair, while Scott and I are in separate armchairs. She measures me with a shrewd gaze from behind her glasses.

"Yes. Exactly. Watched. Am I crazy?" I try to make it sound like a joke but it falls flatter than cardboard. No one even cracks a smile. I guess we don't use the *C* word here.

"A lot of people aren't all that comfortable with living here," she says. "I mean, SmartBlock. They think they're okay with the terms but in the long run, it turns out they're not so okay. It weighs on them. It can make them think and act irrationally."

Scott ever so subtly rolls his eyes. "Don't tell me we have to move now," he mutters. But I'm hanging on to Dr. Stockman's last word. The way she says it. It's a placeholder word, standing in for something else she wanted to say.

"'Irrationally'?" I ask. "Is that *your* way of saying crazy?"

"It's my way of saying that some people aren't ready," she says. "No matter what they get in return. At first they're happy with all the cool gadgets and functions of their smart home but then they start to wonder. Even though their personal information is perfectly safe and it would be highly illegal for IntelTech to violate the terms of their contracts. Even though there's nothing to worry about. But our inner fears don't always make sense."

"And so?"

"And so, they start to perceive their beloved home as something hostile. As an enemy. And that can lead them to act out in strange ways."

"I see," I say. "Is that what happened to Lydia?"

*   *   *

"Great," says Scott. "Just great. Now how are we supposed to come back? I'm so embarrassed I don't know how I'm going to face her again."

"*You're* embarrassed?" I ask. "And what are you so embarrassed about?"

"Is that a real question? You made a scene."

"I did not—"

"The look on her face. I was mortified. She had no idea who this Lydia was. And you kept attacking her and wouldn't let it go, like a pit bull. What on earth was that about? Who's Lydia?"

"You'd know if you ever listened to what I tell you."

He shakes his head. In the back seat, Taryn has been watching cartoons but now she's asleep, her head lolling and her mouth open. So Scott and I have to keep our voices down, although it's getting harder by the minute.

"You," he's saying. "It's you. You don't even realize it's the exact kind of behavior she was talking about. You're paranoid. You're—"

"—irrational," I finish.

"See? Even you understand it."

"I'm not irrational. I don't like people prying into my life, that's all."

"Then I have some news for you. You're living in the wrong place."

"Well, it wasn't my fucking idea!" I blow up. Panicked, I check on Taryn in the mirror but she doesn't even stir. So I go on, my voice low but unable to conceal the anger within. "I would have been happy enough with your standard ADT system. A camera or two. New locks."

He groans. "New locks," he says. "I get it, I get it. I should have changed them as soon as the work was finished. I didn't. It was all my fault, then." He says it all in a monotone, like it's something we've argued over a million times before. When the police asked me why we never changed the locks, I didn't know what to answer.

I said we just hadn't thought about it. We got back our spare key and put the whole thing out of our minds.

I don't know what Scott said when they asked him.

It's so tempting to go down that road now. To start guilt-tripping and blaming that, in the end, might lead to me getting what I want. But for reasons I don't entirely understand, I resist. "Scott," I say, "can we move back?"

He gives an incredulous chuckle. "Move back? Where?"

"I don't know. To the city—"

"We are in the city."

"You know what I mean."

"No, I'm not so sure. Where else would we go?"

"We still have—"

"No." He gives a decisive shake of his head, his look mildly incredulous.

"All I'm saying is we haven't sold it—"

"Because no one in their right mind wants to buy it! For a normal price, anyway. And you can't be serious, Cece. You were dying to get away from there! You realize I did all this to get us away, right?"

"But we have the option—"

"Not really, no. And besides, you remember. We have a contract with these guys. Two years."

My throat knots. Of course, that contract we'd pored over for days. We couldn't see the catch back then.

"What happens if we break it off? They can't force us to stay in a place we don't want to live in. In a house that's actively trying to harm us."

My husband rolls his eyes skyward. "Here we go again. First, to answer your question, they could sue us, which would drain our finances, and then we'd have to sell the old house to some lowballer just to keep our heads above water. You're not the one who's been paying the bills lately, and it shows. And second, the house isn't trying to harm you. What do you think this is, *Terminator? I, Robot?* Sure, the house has some glitches. First versions always do. But it's the future, and to resist it is counterproductive and just, well, silly. You report the bugs and move on. Please, Cecelia. I'm begging you. Move on."

I don't know what to say to make him listen to me again. I sulk as we drive onto our street. The windows of the other houses are aglow, a friendly, warm light that suggests cherished family moments happening inside. Our windows are dark. Even the decorative lights on the façade are out.

"And anyway," Scott says as he pulls up to the driveway. The garage door opens to let us in. "I don't understand why you didn't just tell her the whole story."

CHAPTER EIGHTEEN

This Saturday, I meet up with Anna for brunch.

Something so normal feels like an incredible accomplishment. When was the last time I met a friend for a meal? It had to be almost two years ago, way before the home invasion. Although, come to think of it, it has to be even longer than that. Before the renovations started. Before the black mood of failure and disappointment engulfed me like quicksand.

Not that I can call Anna Finch anything close to a friend. Sure, she was friendly enough when she came by. But the incident with the collision is still fresh in my mind, and I can't help but think it must be fresh in her mind as well. She can't be that quick to forgive and forget.

But when she sent me the invitation, Scott happened to be in the room, and he thought it would be good for me.

So I accepted, more for his sake than because I genuinely wanted to go out. Or to meet her.

Venture is a little world unto itself, complete with a mall and restaurants and a fashionable Central Boulevard lined with cafés and exorbitantly expensive high-end boutiques. They never seem to be crowded but someone must shop there to make it worthwhile to keep them open. Maybe it's that optimization the brochures kept bragging about. The businesses are actually flush with customers, yet you never have to stand in line by the fitting room or wait for a table at a restaurant.

Central Boulevard is lined with lush trees—one has to wonder how they got so big in only five years or whether they were brought in that size to begin with. The flower beds overflow with blooms. The terrace of the brunch place is shrouded in aromatic wisteria to the point where it has an otherworldly, fairy tale vibe. Could the flowers be masterful replicas or maybe even some clever GMOs? I pause at the entrance, pretending to study the retro-style menu on a chalkboard, and discreetly feel the closest branch with my fingertips. Definitely not plastic.

When I look up, Anna is already waving at me from a table in a corner. It's not necessary. The phone in my pocket buzzes, and when I take it out, all the info I need flashes on the screen. My brunch with Anna E. Finch, at 12:30, is now, and my seat is at table B7. No need for a hostess to seat me or give us menus as those upload automatically as soon as we sit down.

Glancing around, I conclude that it must be optimization. There are just enough busy tables to make it feel cozy and comfortable but not so many that it's noisy and annoying. The tables next to ours are empty but there's a group of four two tables away. They're poking busily at their phone screens without talking to each other, probably choosing what they're going to eat. They all wear dresses and heels, and I can't help but feel like I stick out. I showed up in jeans and a blouse, with almost no makeup. Anna, in contrast, is wearing a beautiful silk sundress, her hair up in a French twist. When she picks up her phone to look at the menu, I notice her skinny gold bracelet and a manicure so fresh it looks like it could still smudge. Self-conscious, I pick at my own bare nails, feeling even more like a loser.

Not that I could compete with her or the women at the other table. It's not just that their appearance practically breathes money. They're also classically beautiful in a way I never managed to be. It's subtle. There's nothing about me you could point your finger at, nothing overtly hideous, but a subtle asymmetry of features. Legs just a touch too short, nose too long, eyes too close together. And I'm not going to lie, a cute outfit and shiny nail polish definitely wouldn't hurt right now.

A waiter appears and brings a tray of drinks to the other table. I point the phone camera and the name of the libation pops up on the menu at once. Strawberry peach mimosa, low sugar.

"Should we get those?" Anna is saying. I nod distractedly as she taps at her screen, putting in the order. However, the charge doesn't show up on my phone.

"Don't mention it," she says, tapping and swiping away. "I invited you so it's my treat."

This is it, I realize. This is why these places, this Central Boulevard, never felt quite right to me. It's not my first time here—I've gone out on brief shopping jaunts, gotten coffee, went out to a restaurant with Scott a couple of times, and it was nice. Comfortable. But I've never felt like I looked forward to returning. Now I know why. They replicated some romantic destination down to a T—beautiful architecture, trees and flowers, inviting terraces. They forgot one aspect: normal human interaction. Everything is done through the phone, and so no one has any reason to look up from their screens to look at each other.

As Scott said the other day, what can I do? It's the future. No point complaining about it.

"This place is great," Anna says. "It's where I go with, you know. My real-life friends. When they come down here."

She's smirking conspiratorially but I can't shake the odd feeling. She makes it sound like we're not in the most prosperous neighborhood in town but in some insane asylum.

"And what do your real-life friends think about it?" I ask, not meaning anything duplicitous.

She chuckles and raises her carefully filled-in eyebrows. "They think I live in Big Brother's lap. But they don't get it."

"Probably just jealous," I say automatically.

"No," she says, frowning. "Not jealous. Not everyone gets it. *I* think it's cool that you go to a place and they remember your order exactly how you like it, every time. Or that I never have to look for parking. Or that the grocery store never runs out of Basque blue cheese and black heirloom tomatoes, even when you do your shopping late on Sunday night. And what do I have to give in return? I have nothing to hide."

"Not everybody is against it because they have something to hide," I say.

She scoffs. "Sure. They just think they *might* have something to hide, in the future. Well, I don't do anything illegal, and I don't plan to anytime soon. So I'll have my comforts if nobody minds. Right?"

Perfect timing—the waiter arrives with our mimosas, which he sets down on the table with a flourish. Then, wordlessly, he disappears. No *Would you like something else?* No *Have you made your selection?* No need to ask us how we're enjoying our order either—the rating system is built in. This small talk isn't necessary anymore. Isn't it great?

"There are still some situations where I'd like at least a little privacy," I say sotto voce. She's already turned her attention back to her phone, choosing her meal. I can see the wheels turning beneath her perfect smooth forehead: egg white omelet, or treat herself and go for the yolks?

"Like what?" she asks without looking up.

"Medical records, for instance."

"Those are already private, Cecelia." She sips on her mimosa, and, reminded, I pick up mine. It's not bad at all. Fizzy. The fruit part tastes real too. Real like the wisteria? "Didn't you read what you signed?"

"Of course I did!" I say, a little offended.

"So many people don't. I'm a lawyer. I'm all too familiar

with it." She takes another sip and rolls her eyes. "And on that point, I agree with you. People take these things too lightly. It's not an iPhone user agreement, you know? It's your life. But as a lawyer, let me tell you, it's a good contract. And you're always allowed to negotiate if there's something you just can't concede."

Really now. No one told us we could negotiate. We were given the agreement to go over, to show our lawyers if we wanted, to think on. Then we could sign it or not. No other option given.

"And mental health?" I blurt.

"Same thing. Nothing to worry about. If you totally don't trust them, just find a doctor in another area. But if you ask me, Dr. Stockman is the best. And she takes her patients' privacy very seriously."

I sit up straight. I could swear I'm turning pink. "Dr. Stockman?"

"Yes, she has a private clinic up on Rosehill Boulevard. I go there, and my husband does. It's been a joy."

I'm taken aback at such directness. Maybe she's from a different world but it still seems unusual to me to brazenly declare that you go to a shrink. Maybe I'm just old-fashioned, steeped in an outdated stigma.

As if she can hear my thoughts, Anna giggles. "No shame whatsoever. Half the neighborhood goes to her. Everyone I know does. If you don't already, you should."

"Wow" is all I manage to say.

"What? It's not that special."

"Not at all. It's just, for the happiest town on the face of the earth, we all sure have a lot of issues."

"Not necessarily issues," she says. "Just maintenance. Do you only go to the dentist when you're about to lose your last tooth?"

She's right, I guess. But at the same time, I detect a kind of defensiveness in her words, in her tone. I must have hit a nerve.

"It's just—I'm not sure I can trust her," I say. "With that old-school tape recorder thingy of hers."

I don't realize my slipup until a smile illuminates Anna's face, as if to say *Gotcha, at last.* But, seeing me blush, she rushes to reassure me.

"Oh no, don't be embarrassed. So you go to Dr. Stockman. Good for you. And I assure you, you can trust her. She's probably the only person in this whole damn town you can truly trust."

My eyebrows rise, which makes Anna grin more broadly. "Well, honey, I'm a lawyer after all, what do you expect? I trust no one. But it's an excellent decision to go to Dr. Stockman. You won't regret it. Especially after what you've been through."

I'm stricken mute. I sit there, my palms and armpits suddenly swampy, my mouth dry and spine rigid. All of a sudden I feel watched. No, not just watched—seen.

"You're Cecelia Holmes," she says with a little frown, making a subtle inflection at the end of the phrase as though asking me to confirm. "You're that woman I read about in the paper. The one who killed the man who broke into her house?"

CHAPTER NINETEEN

Growing up with Therese, always on the verge of poverty, or so I thought, in dingy apartments and cheap clothes and with no prospects, I don't remember what exactly I hoped for in the future. I certainly never aspired to be the woman Anna Finch read about in the paper.

Although that certainly explains a lot. The way she yammered on and on about herself without so much as pausing to ask me the most basic questions, like what do I do for a living, where I'm from. I assumed it was just more typical rich-person selfishness. And that sudden about-face, in spite of how she nearly ripped my head off after the collision. She recognized my name later, and curiosity drew her to me, with a nice handy excuse of an apology. I suppose I can't blame her—she's a lawyer to boot.

Not that I needed a lawyer at any point. I was within my rights to do what I did. The police asked me the same questions over and over but I got the feeling that no one really wanted me to slip up. They're not monsters.

Besides, I was a housewife with a small child, and the man I killed, it turned out, had a long and ugly history. Burglary, larceny, drug offenses, even two years in prison. And Mr. Benning of Benning and Co. hired him without overthinking it, all because he agreed to work for a subpar wage. He'd been working for Benning for two years. Since then, two of the homes where they did renovation work had gotten burglarized, and no one made the connection.

So if I wanted to blame someone for what happened, I had a wealth of options. Mr. Benning, incompetent police. But somehow, subconsciously, I chose to blame my husband. Him and his crazy idea to tear apart our home and replace it with something supposedly better. His ego. His unwillingness to compromise, which led us to scrape the bottom of the barrel when looking for contractors.

He put Taryn, my greatest treasure, in danger. So I blamed him, and then Scott picked up on it, and then he started blaming himself. But that was at odds with how he saw himself. Scott is one of those men who needs to be seen as the good guy, reliable, loyal. And more than that, he needs to see *himself* that way. So he could continue blaming himself forever, admitting that he fell short of his aspirations as the good husband, father, and provider, or he could find a solution no matter the cost.

Since he's Scott, he found the solution.

But that fateful evening, he wasn't there. It was the middle of the week, and Scott was working overtime. He'd been doing that for a while, several days a week, several weeks in a row. Any other wife would have let her mind drift toward darker possibilities, suspect cheating and lies, some young mistress, or worse yet, a predatory coworker with no panties under her ugly skirt suit. But I know him better than that—it's just not his style. He would leave at seven in the morning and come back long after Taryn went to bed at seven at night. So I'd spend the whole day alone with our daughter, then barely a year old.

Taryn is a miracle baby of sorts. I say *of sorts* because I've heard much crazier stories, strings of miscarriages, tens of thousands of dollars spent on repeated IVF attempts that were finally rewarded with that one precious bundle of joy. And who knows? Maybe that could have been us, had I allowed it.

No, I'd spent the previous three years or so thinking I'm the problem, that I can't have babies, but Scott and I had a serious talk and decided we wouldn't be one of those couples. Those who go to what he saw as crazy, irrational extremes to have a biological child.

If it doesn't work after three years, he said, we don't start running around all those ghastly clinics and doing painful and invasive procedures. We have the money, he said, but that's not the point. He said he thought it was self-centered, vain, arrogant even, to be so obsessed with passing down your own genes. What with all the babies out there who need loving homes and who are placed in the foster system instead, without proper love and care.

Truth be told, I thought it made him sound as smug and self-centered as the people he derided, except the obsession with genes was replaced with a savior complex I found just as unappealing. But that's Scott for you, and I'd learned to keep these thoughts to myself.

If we don't succeed after three years, we get on the waiting list and we adopt, he decided. It's the right thing to do. The altruistic thing. I nodded along like a good wife. We were so busy patting ourselves on the back for our progressiveness that we barely noticed how three years flew by, and still the tests remained negative. And so every time Scott would bring up that waiting list, I'd nod some more in agreement and then stall, stall, stall.

I guess I finally stalled long enough because, exactly three years and six months after that first conversation (not that I was counting), my period failed to show up. Everything went so well it was hard to believe, everything perfect, every ultrasound, every test. Even the delivery was a breeze, and then I had myself a perfect little baby girl, seven pounds and seven ounces.

So I know it comes across as a little ungrateful to complain about it. But in those days, what I felt wasn't gratitude or happiness but loneliness and boredom. We talked about putting Taryn in day care but I balked at the idea of leaving such a fragile, not-yet-verbal creature at the mercy of strangers. We talked about a nanny but our budget was already strained after the renovations and would take a couple more years to recover.

So I stayed at home with Taryn, my ebook cover business barely clinging on. Most of the time—if not all the time—I was alone, taking care of Taryn, cleaning, cooking baby purees. After I put her to sleep, I barely had the energy to read a book and would collapse into bed by eight thirty. Scott blithely suggested I ask Therese to come over and help, and I told him in no uncertain terms that I'd rather pull out my own wisdom teeth.

When I complained to Scott that I felt, for all intents and purposes, like a single mom, he only scoffed and rolled his eyes. Yeah, he said, a single mom with a full ride. *Every woman in existence is jealous of you, Cecelia. They all want what you have.*

This was probably true. But that day, Taryn had been horrible, and putting her to bed took close to an hour. When I finally tiptoed out of her room, I felt anything but lucky. I let myself fall onto the living room couch, contemplated the blank TV screen, and wondered if it was worth the risk to turn it on even at the lowest volume. My stomach rumbled, and I tried to remember if there was anything in the fridge that I could just reheat; cooking was unfathomable.

I picked up my phone, thinking I could order takeout through one of the many apps, but instead saw a text from Scott:

Will be late again tonight. Sorry! Don't wait up! xoxoxo

Don't wait up. Just who does he think he is? I gritted my teeth, forgetting my hunger. Throwing a sideways glance at the dark hall, at the door of Taryn's room at the end of it, I finally chanced turning on the TV. For the first five minutes, I sat still, barely daring to breathe. But after no sound came from down the hall, I finally relaxed.

I went to get a carton of ice cream from the freezer. With the new open-concept space, I could do so without needing to pause my TV show because I could hear everything just fine. Maybe there was something to this thing after all...

Somehow, I managed to fall asleep. It shouldn't have been too surprising, exhausted as I was. I'd just passed out on the couch, closing my eyes for only a second before I drifted off into dreamland. The point is, I woke up I don't know how much time later. The screen of the TV was frozen with that existential query, *Are you still watching* Scandal*?* The remains of the ice cream were liquid at the bottom of the pint.

And I wasn't alone in the house.

CHAPTER TWENTY

This is where I should excuse myself and make my exit. Anna Finch is looking at me with wide eyes filled with curiosity. Well, I'm not a circus animal, and regardless of why she invited me here, I'm not here to entertain her with sordid stories. But I sit there, with the wisteria swaying gently above my head, and don't move.

My phone screen inquires whether I've chosen what I'd like to eat.

"I guess I went about this the wrong way," concedes Anna. "I didn't mean to stir up bad memories. I'm sorry."

I give a dry nod and swallow. The drink is sitting in front of me but the very thought of its cloying sweetness makes my teeth hurt. "I suppose you're dying to hear the full story," I say softly. "About how he threatened me. About how he went into my daughter's room and took her out of her bed and told me he'd smash her head against the wall if I didn't show him where all our valuables are. About how I led him to the drawer in the bedroom and then took Scott's handgun out of its hiding place and shot him with it. I repeated it so many times to the police. I can manage one final performance."

I'd hoped for a look of dismay but she doesn't betray it. She faces me calmly. "I'm a lawyer, Cecelia. I'm not easily shocked."

"Yeah, yeah. It's your job to defend guys like him."

"Or women like you."

"I didn't need defending. Anyone in their right mind would know I did the only thing I could do."

"I'm not saying the contrary."

"Then why did you lure me here?" My calm cracks, my voice rising in pitch. "It's only because of that. Not because you're sorry, is it?"

"I didn't lure you anywhere. And sure, I admit, I had a certain... curiosity. Maybe"—she looks down at her beautiful, manicured hands—"I just wanted to see what you were like. Maybe because we're not as different as you seem to think."

I'm still a little shocked that she would even ask about this to my face. But would it be worse to gossip about it behind my back instead? I'm already paranoid about that. It was part of the reason Scott was able to persuade me to move. I was tired of being dogged by that feeling everywhere I went, at the coffee shop, at the grocery store, just walking down the street in my old neighborhood. The feeling that people were observing me, watching me out of the corner of their eye, fear and morbid curiosity etched in their expressions. Or worse yet, pity.

"There are hundreds of shootings in this city every year," I mutter. "Maybe thousands." Meaning to say, why get fixated on me?

"Indeed there are," she says darkly. This shift in tone is unexpected. "But not like this one." She casts her eyes down once more, a look that doesn't suit her features or her manner. "You're extraordinary in your own way. Unique. If anything, please forgive me for saying so but you're kind of a role model."

I nearly laugh in her face. What is she talking about? Is she in her right mind? Is her mimosa too strong?

But Anna looks up again, and her gaze locks on mine. It's a strange, raw look, devoid of defenses or pretenses. I can't help but shudder inwardly.

"If you're curious," she says, "my name used to be Anna Lindberg. Go ahead, look it up. I'll wait. It's only fair."

Under that intense gaze, I have no choice but to cave. Clumsily, I pick up my phone, open the browser, and start to type, daring to glance up at her every couple of seconds. She's watching me, unwavering.

"It's Lindberg without an H," she's saying, not bothering too much to keep her voice down.

I backspace. Then tap Go.

The story unfurls in headlines.

POLICE SEEKING SUSPECT IN CAR CRASH

A hit-and-run caused a major accident this morning, **I read.**

The suspect ran a red light, causing a pileup. The driver of one of the vehicles as well as two passengers of another are in critical condition. Police are looking for the suspect, who was driving a red Toyota SUV. Alcohol is a suspected cause. Unfortunately, the camera at the intersection has been disabled for several weeks for maintenance so no one was able to get the license plate of the vehicle. The police are asking anyone who may have witnessed the events or who might have any useful information to please contact—

I read on.

FATAL HIT-AND-RUN STILL UNSOLVED

According to our sources, one of the victims of Wednesday's car crash, eight-year-old Marie Lindberg, has passed away as a result of her injuries. The other victim, reportedly Marie's father, is now in stable condition. The police are still searching for the driver of a red Toyota SUV, make and model unspecified. The driver is suspected of causing the collision that has now cost two people their lives, including the driver of one of the other cars involved. If you have any information that can aid the investigation, please call—

Onward.

NO HOPE: MOTHER OF HIT-AND-RUN VICTIM SPEAKS OUT

I don't read the article. I don't need to. There's a full-color photo below the title, and I recognize Anna at once even though the hair is different—shorter, straighter, and blonder, probably requiring many hours at the salon and in front of the mirror in the morning. Now she has let it grow back to its natural state. To hide? Or because these things became unimportant all of a sudden? In the photo, she's sitting with her hands folded primly in her lap, dressed in an austere black blazer. Her face is made up, and her expression grave.

I look up from my phone. Anna is observing me intently, her expression neutral. Heat rises into my own face, and I know I must be turning crimson. I can't bring myself to meet her gaze. It's almost like I feel vulnerable on her behalf. This should make me vindicated, after being lured here and confronted like that, but instead, I feel a deep sadness. And, like it or not, a kinship.

"So when we met with Clarisse and she told us there was a place where this would never, ever happen," she says softly, "I jumped at the opportunity. And as you can see, I'm not the only one. I wanted my daughter to grow up safe. Something you can relate to, I think."

I gulp. She's right, 100 percent right. Yet I'm overcome with a sense of wrongness I can't shake.

"All my neighbors? Even..." I have to pause and rack my brain for her name. "Dorothea?"

Anna gives the smallest shrug. She leans in and whispers something in my ear.

"I think..." My mouth goes dry. "I think I'd like to go home."

*   *   *

Jessica's office is more akin to a cubicle, although it does technically have four walls. It's just that two of them are made of glass so there's never much privacy.

IntelTech is a big fan of minimalism, and her work space, like all the ones occupied by her coworkers, reflects that. It basically consists of an ergonomic chair, an empty desk, and a giant computer screen she stares at all day as alerts, complaints, and requests pour in, an endless river. The only times she leaves is to deal with pressing issues at Clarisse's bidding. It's not unlike those cautionary-tale jobs she knows about, where you sit in a dark room in a nondescript building somewhere and flag forbidden material at the behest of some social-media giant, all for minimum wage or close. At least all she has to cope with is the foibles of the über-rich and otherwise privileged, which in comparison shouldn't be that bad.

She, like the many others in other cubicles, has her own segment she deals with, which includes not just Rosemary Road but the whole quadrant. Lately, though, it's Cecelia

Holmes who's been taking up much of Jessica's time. Cecelia Holmes's house, to be exact.

She pulls up the tab that has the house at 32 Rosemary Road laid out to the smallest details. She scrolls through the blueprints, the specs, the photos: a dream home, as it was designed to be.

Yet in the three years since it was built, it's already managed to become the scene of a woman's murder. One could write it off as an unlucky coincidence but now the house is acting up. This is undeniable: One look at the charts, and it's clear that the vast majority of complaints and bug reports are from 32 Rosemary Road. This reflects badly on Jessica, and, by extension, on her standing at IntelTech. As much as Jess feels ambivalent about it, if she wants to keep her job, she better figure out what the hell is wrong with that house. Cecelia Holmes seems to think the house is being hacked but Jess knows this is impossible: IntelTech houses are unhackable, period.

To think it was Jess who found the Holmeses and sent the application to Clarisse. She should be cursing the day the idea dawned on her. They were perfect candidates and convincing them was a piece of cake—and naturally, Jess collected a nice bonus check, money she couldn't afford to refuse. But that Cecelia Holmes is a handful. Jess isn't supposed to let her feelings affect her job but sometimes it's harder than usual.

Jess knows everything about everyone in her quadrant; it's part of her job. She can see everything in real time, who's cheating, who's scheming, who isn't who they pretend to be. At first, she found it disillusioning, then entertaining in a sordid sort of way, but lately it's just sad. She felt nothing but sadness for poor Lydia. And now, even though Cecelia is quite the piece of work, she almost feels bad for her too. Poor woman. She has no idea what's happening behind her back.

CHAPTER TWENTY-ONE

I don't tell my husband about Anna and our lunch. For now, I decide to hang on to what I learned.

Against my better judgment, perhaps, I go back and read the full article below the photo of the old Anna.

"Unless a witness comes forward, it's hopeless," Anna Lindberg says. "We live in the 21st century, and we think these things can't happen anymore. You can't just cause an accident that kills two people, one of them a child"—here her voice betrayed a tremor that her dry-eyed demeanor had been hiding so well—"and get away with it, with no one the wiser. I certainly never thought it could happen. The truth is, we fell through the cracks.

This person slipped away in a perfect storm of failures. Traffic cameras out of order for weeks, surveillance footage not being recorded. A fake camera at a storefront. I feel like I'm trapped in the Middle Ages. There's no way for me to get justice for my daughter."

She paused to take a breath and to have a small sip of mineral water from the nearly untouched glass on the table in front of her. She refolded her hands before speaking again.

"But somebody out there knows something. And eventually the truth will come to light."

I sit on my living room couch, tablet in my lap, and think. Somehow, the truth didn't come to light, and at this point, I doubt it will. Anna must doubt it also, which was why she decided to move on with her life—in a safer, better place. In light of this, all my complaining about our new home seems petty and ungrateful. I press my palms against my warming cheeks.

Somewhere in the background, music starts to play softly. I don't even notice right away because it's a mellow, jazzy melody but then the lyrics kick in. *Follow my lead, oh, how I need / Someone to watch over me . . .*

I leap from the couch. "Saya!" I bark into emptiness.

The music gently grows in volume. There's no answer.

"Saya?" I repeat, feeling foolish. The same feeling from the early days in this house returns—like I'm talking to myself. I never truly expect her to answer. But so far, she always has. "Saya, turn off the music!"

Nothing happens. The song continues to pour from hidden speakers all over the house, making it sound like it's coming out of nowhere and everywhere at once.

I pick up my tablet with the intention to override manually but the screen is frozen. I tap away at it in frustration but it might as well be a simple piece of glass.

A noise from the kitchen makes me jump and nearly drop the tablet. A deep, mechanical whir that I don't recognize over the music, which is growing and growing in volume until it's so loud I can't think. Against all my better instincts, I race to the kitchen and stop cold, dumbfounded.

On the counter, two coffees are already waiting. The machine is busily whipping up a third, identical to the first two. I don't need to taste the drink—the heap of whipped cream sprinkled with cardamom and the pungent, sweet smell of syrup in the air tell me everything I need to know.

A wave of fear travels up my spine. My knees wobble and then buckle, and I sink to the floor, my hands pressed over my ears, which does nothing to drown out the music.

I squeeze my eyes shut. "Saya!" I scream at the top of my lungs.

At first, I think my eardrums must have burst because everything grows silent at once. No more coffee machine whirring, no more music, which leaves behind a tinny ringing in my ears. I dare open one eye and then the other. Three coffees are waiting on the counter, piled high with whipped cream.

"Yes, Cecelia?" asks the pleasant mechanical voice over-head.

"Saya," I say, overcome with relief and anger, "what on earth was that all about?"

"I'm not sure I understand the question, Cecelia."

"What were my last two requests, Saya?"

"You asked to play some of your favorite music, Cecelia. You requested a coffee, Cecelia."

"I did not request any such things. And I don't like this song."

"Very well. Would you like me to delete 'Someone to Watch over Me' from the favorites playlist?"

"Yes," I snap. Holding on to the edge of the counter, I get back on my feet. "Who requested this song? Who takes their coffee like this?" I nod accusingly at the cups on the counter.

"Would you like to change the default settings?"

"No, I would not like to change the default settings!"

I'm flipping out at a machine. No, an AI. It's not quite the same as a machine. What is happening to me? "Saya, for God's sake, just tell me once and for all. Who's Lydia?"

There's a silence. And in that split second, I almost believe it: that I've broken down her resistance, that she's about to tell me everything, give me the answers I seek in that detached, slightly mechanical tone of hers.

"Searching the internet for: Lydia. Please wait. The search returned 8,845,456 results. Would you like to refine the search terms?"

"No," I say, defeated. "Never mind."

"Very well, Cecelia."

"And please never make that coffee beverage again. Delete it. Delete it from your entire database if you can."

"All right, Cecelia."

Something tells me she's full of shit.

And then the doorbell rings.

My heart leaps. For the briefest moment, I wonder whether I could just run and hide in the bedroom instead of answering.

"Cecelia, Dorothea Miles is at the door," Saya informs me in a pleasant voice a heartbeat later. "Would you like me to let her in?"

Our neighbor. Of course. My next thought is, *Oh God, what does* she *want?*

"Tell her I'll be right at the door," I say, and catch my breath. On my way to the front door, I pause in front of a mirror and take in the sight. I'm a mess. And this morning, when I dressed for my lunch with Anna, I thought I looked okay. Simple but put together. Well, my hair has frizzed out, the thin coat of mascara I'd swished onto my eyelashes has gathered in the folds under my eyes, and my shirt is pilling. I wipe under my eyes, smooth down the frizz with my palms as best as I can, and go answer.

Dorothea is standing on the porch. And she's fuming.

"I've sent you messages," she says without a hello. "And I've gotten no answer. So I suppose I have to do this the old-fashioned way."

"Excuse me?" For the umpteenth time today, I feel like I've fallen down the rabbit hole. Everyone seems to know what's going on but me.

"The noise," she says. She folds her arms over her chest

and sighs. "Look, I like jazz about as much as the next person but this? This is a bit too much even for me. It's so loud that I can hear it—not just when I'm out in the yard but when I'm inside my house. Sound isolation my ass."

"What are you talking about?"

She glares. "The music! The same song, over and over and over. Playing nonstop all morning long. And now again."

"I haven't gotten any messages," I manage to say. "I'm having some . . . issues with my house's AI."

"Issues," she echoes, giving me a skeptical look. "So call IntelTech."

"I did. No one is in any hurry to fix it." My own voice begins to betray irritation, everything that's been bottled up over the last few days spilling through the cracks. And here she is, acting like *I'm* the one in the wrong.

"All I'm saying is that *I've* never had a single *issue*." Her gaze bores into me, making me even more uncomfortable. *Good for you, then.*

But then I remember what Anna told me right before we parted ways.

"Dorothea, listen. I'm really sorry. But something weird is happening." I lower my voice through pure instinct, as though the house itself can overhear me. And it can, no matter how quietly I whisper. "With the house. Something is wrong. I think it might be trying to . . . harm . . . me."

Her face doesn't soften. She keeps eyeing me, as if trying to decide what to make of my sudden confidences. Wondering whether she should dismiss me as crazy. People who play the same song over and over again at ear-splitting volume tend to be.

"You of all people have to believe me," I say in the same low voice.

"And why is that?"

I'm not exactly playing fair. I should not be inflicting this on her, and yet...

"I talked to Anna Lindberg Finch. She told me. About the stalker."

CHAPTER TWENTY-TWO

I've never seen anyone's face do such a complete trans-formation so fast. Dorothea's eyebrows knit close, and her mouth tenses up, corners taking a sharp downward turn. Only her eyes remain pointy and intense but in a different way—the shift is almost imperceptible. But the anger in her turns to anguish in a split second.

The next moment, she pushes past me. Before I can object, I feel her hand encircling my wrist. Her fingers are thin but strong, and I gasp with unexpected pain.

"Shut the door behind you," she mutters. Without wait-ing for me, she shuts it herself. We are now in the hallway, just the two of us. I'm not sure I feel safe. My heartbeat speeds up, my hands sweat. I wait for the house to register my distress and act but something tells me it won't.

"That twat," Dorothy murmurs under her breath. "What did she blab to you?"

"Nothing," I say, at a loss. "She just said—"

"We both go to Dr. Alice," Dorothea interrupts. "I suppose you do too. Big deal. What I shouldn't have done was start pouring my heart out to that blabbermouth in the waiting room."

I'm still processing when she adds, "And don't look so superior. She blabs about you too, I bet."

"So it's true?" I ask.

"No. I just made it up to sound interesting." Dorothea's eyes glint with fury. "Yes, it's true. It's the twenty-first century after all, right? When you're a journalist, with a certain level of online presence, these things happen. Espccially if you happen to describe yourself as a feminist in your bio."

I'm starting to understand.

"I figured, technology got me in this mess, technology will get me out," she says with a shrug.

"How did you find out about SmartBlock?"

She gives me an incredulous look that's verging on pity. "You really do live under a rock, don't you? I didn't find out about SmartBlock. IntelTech found *me*.

"You're going to google the hell out of it as soon as you hear my real name," says Dorothea dismissively, "so I might as well save you fifteen minutes. Really, nothing extraordinary happened. I was dumb enough to cover a certain tech issue while also having a vagina. Not even that I was dumb, really. I just was used to it by then, you know? Internet trolls. Hateful comments. Rape and death threats all over my email and social media all day long.

"And that time was no exception, except one of the

trolls got his hands on my phone number and address somehow and posted it on the internet. I had to sleep on friends' couches, and in hotels, you name it. Yet somehow he always tracked me down. I found dead animals on my doorstep, for fuck's sake. I knew who he was all along but of course, what it took for the police to arrest him was him trying to strangle me."

I'm stricken, paralyzed before this onslaught.

"Well, what can you do? I'm just a woman, alone, and there was *no proof of wrongdoing*. And the restraining order? It's a joke."

I do not live under a rock. I live on Rosemary Road, next door to her, so by now, I've proven her wrong. I'm pretty sure of who she really is. "That's awful" is all I can manage to say.

Dorothea walks me to the door. "Listen, Cecelia, you seem reasonable. And now you know my story. So can we cut this short? I have things to do at home. Keep the music down, and we're going to be best friends. Deal?"

Part of me wants to ask her how she truly feels about all this. A journalist, a voice speaking truth to power, now shielded from the reality of the very people she's meant to speak for behind a wall of money and fancy tech.

I find myself nodding without really listening to what she's saying. "They contacted us too," I murmur.

"Sorry?"

"IntelTech. They contacted us too. They'd heard of me."

"So it sounds like you're the winner in this situation," she says with a finality that lets me know that she's done talking to me. "Keep the noise down, please."

"It wasn't me," I say. "It really was the house."

"Too bad for me, I guess. I'm the one who's stuck with another batshit-crazy neighbor."

And before I can answer, she shuts the door in my face.

"Wait," I say, finding my voice too late. "Dorothea! Wait!"

Through the glass insert in the door I watch her as she walks too fast down the path and turns onto the sidewalk. Her phone is in her hand, and she taps angrily at the screen.

"Saya, call Dorothea," I snap. For a beat too long, no answer follows, and I'm starting to think that Saya is malfunctioning again when her calm mechanical voice speaks up.

"I'm sorry, Cecelia. Dorothea has blocked you."

*   *   *

In the evening, I stand by the window of the upstairs bedroom, long after Taryn has fallen asleep. I watch the other house, the one right behind ours, its forbidding geometrical shape looming there, dark. Save for a small light in one of the second-floor windows.

"Cece?"

I jump and spin around at the sound of Scott's voice.

"Oh, hey," I say. "It's you."

"Who did you think it was?" He comes up to me and puts his hands on my waist—the way he hasn't done in some time. "Taryn is out like a light. Come downstairs. Let's watch a movie."

"I think I'd rather just go to sleep. I'm dead tired. I had a long day."

"Mopping the floor and scrubbing toilets?" He's mocking

but not in a mean way. In a gentle, teasing way. It reminds me of the old Scott, from many years ago, back when I first fell in love with him.

I feel an unexpected swell of tenderness, an urge to return the hug and then some, because Taryn is indeed fast asleep and there are other things we could do besides watch a movie. This takes me by surprise because I haven't felt that physical longing for Scott in some time. In a long time. A lot longer than I care to admit.

I always told myself this was normal—that desire wanes, that after so many years you can't help but lose the chemistry. And trying for a baby without success for so long didn't help. After more than a few groping sessions that fizzled out gracelessly, even Scott was forced to admit that it wore him down; the failure made him feel like less of a man. I rushed to reassure him but without too much fervor because the next logical step would be a doctor's appointment and a simple little test that would cement it— the problem was him, and not me. I wasn't sure his pride, or our marriage, could get past that.

Taryn arrived just in the nick of time to save us. Unlike many, I have no trouble admitting this. I have no illusions about true love eternal, love that conquers all, and the rest. It is perhaps the healthier way to look at things, even if it's not the most romantic. It certainly goes a long way toward keeping a relationship chugging along— to just accept that it's never natural, it's always work, and sometimes no amount of work is enough.

I met Scott in my junior year of college. It was not love at first sight, not at all.

I had just left my mother—and, I hoped, my past—securely behind, only to discover that what I left it all for was a tiny dorm room and tens of thousands of dollars of debt. The graphic design program turned out way harder than I ever thought or imagined, with so little time spent actually designing and many tedious hours hunched over a computer, poring over clunky software that refused to cooperate. My roommate popped prescription pills of dubious origin to pull all-nighters, and in order to at least cover basic expenses to avoid further getting into the red, I got my ass pinched on a nightly basis working as a busgirl at a campus bar.

Still, I told myself that I liked this life. This was what I wanted—normalcy, the same experience all my peers were having. I was still learning the basics of freedom, not to mention the basics of putting on lipstick. Sadly, because of my inexperience on both counts, the prospect of making the smallest of decisions left me paralyzed with terror and doubt. But at least, as I got better in the lipstick department, I began to realize I was pretty. Guys in my classes kept furtively asking me to go "for coffee" after lectures, and some male teachers graded me with a little more lenience than I deserved.

Not that I ever embodied that cliché of the pretty girl who doesn't know it. I had a mirror and a healthy self-assessment. But my perception until then had been all-or-nothing. There were so many prettier girls all around me, solid tens to my seven and a half, and I sort of never figured there was still enough attention to go around for little old me.

It turned out the opposite was true. The guys seemed to find the superhot girls intimidating and didn't want to risk rejection. But someone like me was still hot enough to be appealing yet ordinary enough to at least appear accessible.

And the attention was fun, I'm not going to lie. Guys I've always considered way out of my league suddenly circled me. So when a somewhat intoxicated junior who introduced himself as Scott tried to start a conversation with me after my shift, he was one of many, and I regret to say that he didn't stand out favorably.

Still, I bummed a cigarette off him, and we smoked out back by the emergency exit. An out-of-nowhere feeling of magnanimity kept me from ditching him and flying off to one of the many campus parties. We made small talk, and I saw plainly how hard he was trying to impress, which made me feel good in a way most girls understand all too well. But instead of the usual things guys try to dazzle with—connections, money, biceps—he kept playing all the wrong cards, at least so it seemed to the dumb twenty-one-year-old that I was. He was in business school, sure, but he was a scholarship student, and not because of athletics like several guys I'd flirted with that year but because of his high scores in math. I think he used the word *prodigy*, which isn't exactly known to melt girls' panties.

Back then, long before he started his regular workout regimen during lunch hour, he had an earnest, chubby face that looked too young and that puppy-dog expression of the guy who never gets the girl and whose last resort is appealing to pity.

I kept the charade going for way too long. Finally, the moment came: He told me sheepishly that his dorm was close by and asked if I would like to come smoke a joint. The way he said it, he tried to make it sound like smoking joints was a regular thing for him but the result was the opposite. And then I politely but inevitably turned him down, saying I had class in the morning even though it was a Thursday night and no one in their right mind took early-morning Friday classes. To his credit, he managed not to look crestfallen and said he'd come see me at the bar some other night.

I was sure he wouldn't. In fact, I left work and went to the party I had in mind all along and kind of forgot about that guy named Scott Holmes. The night was memorable for another reason altogether: I was 100 percent sure, in my infinite twenty-one-year-old-college-junior wisdom, that I'd met the great love of my life.

CHAPTER TWENTY-THREE

Monday marks a return to the routine, although I'm now maniacally aware of every step. I get Taryn out of bed and dressed just minutes before the alarm is due to go off, and I make a point of cooking breakfast myself, to Scott's surprise.

"What's gotten into you?" he teases. "Craving the simple life? Maybe for vacation this year, we can rent a nice little hut in an Amish village."

I contemplate, momentarily, telling him everything that I learned. But he's about to leave for work, and although he's covering it up with humor, I can see he's impatient. He'd rather I let the machine make his coffee as usual. I start steaming milk and then Taryn starts to wail about something random so I turn my head at a crucial moment. The milk bubbles over, scalding my hand. Cursing, I turn on the tap but the water comes out at the exact too-hot temperature I preset it to. I have to yell for Saya to make it cold. Fail.

"Is everything okay? Do you need ointment or something?" Scott asks but it sounds... automatic. When I shake my head no, he looks relieved. He gives me a peck on the cheek and then leans down to kiss the top of Taryn's head.

"Were you serious?" I ask, when he's already in the doorway. "About a vacation."

"No Amish huts," he chuckles. "I like it here."

"I didn't mean go off the grid," I say, doing my best to sound lighthearted. "But a vacation would be nice. Thailand, maybe."

Doubt flickers over his face. "Who would watch Taryn?"

"We'd bring her with us," I say, dumbfounded.

And then he flinches. It only lasts for the shortest moment. "The flight would be hard for her. And I don't see what fun it could be for a toddler in Thailand."

"She'd love it on the beach," I say, although I already know I've lost the argument.

"Yeah. The beach. Are we really those people who go to a country with an extraordinary culture and history and never leave the beach? What about the temples? The night markets? Bangkok?"

"Why can't she come with us too?"

"She'll be hot, bored, and hell on wheels. People who go to places like that with toddlers are only doing it for themselves, not the kids. I think it's selfish."

Just like that, my own argument has been snatched

away from me—not only that but it was used against me. I stand there, knowing that I have nothing to say.

"Beach beach beach!" Taryn singsongs. And here I thought she was absorbed in her cartoon. "I want to go to the beach, Mommy!"

As if to prove his point, Scott makes a grimace over Taryn's head. *See? I told you so.* And now, of course, I have to deal with this myself. I have to explain to her why we're not going to the beach—because she's going to day care as usual. And it's my own fault.

Scott shrugs. "Your mom could watch her," he says. "I'm sure she'd be happy to."

"Therese?" I ask, appalled. I don't know where I expected this conversation to go but this isn't it. "You must be kidding. She hasn't even set foot in the house. She thinks—"

"Taryn is her granddaughter. She'll get over her dislike of the house for her sake."

What Scott doesn't know is that Therese has never met Taryn. I told him I brought her with me when I went to visit Therese a couple of times—but Taryn was at home with a sitter the entire time. And I intend to keep it that way for as long as I can.

"You really don't know who you're dealing with," I say with a shaky laugh. God, he has no idea how much I mean it.

"It can't be that bad. Ask her! Have you even called her lately? Think about it!"

Scott disappears with a distracted wave of the hand, leaving me with the mess. In every sense of the word.

Spilled milk still dots the fashionable black counter like a reverse Rorschach test. Taryn is banging her fists on the table, chanting, *"Beach, beach, beach."*

As for me, I'm still reeling from the very fact that he brought up Therese. He's only met her once, and only on one of those did she act relatively normal. He met her for the first time shortly before we got married; and, to be perfectly honest, I waited until the date was set and the security deposit paid and until the engagement ring had had time to make a pale stripe on my finger before I introduced them. I would have gladly done without it altogether but he was insistent, and I finally decided it was even weirder to keep my still-living and relatively sane mother hidden like some leper.

I wanted to have a proper, civilized, and, most important, short little lunch together at some midrange restaurant not too far from where she lived but she invited us to her place. The address was unfamiliar. When we stopped in front of the tidy little condo building, I was shocked. Her new abode was a one-bedroom, filled with furniture that was dated but matching and ostensibly not from the curb. Hell, she had acquired a cat—a stunningly beautiful, profoundly misanthropic Siamese. She served us tea and butter cookies, the kind that comes in that big tin box. Granted, there was still the cross hanging over the mantel but as far as appearances went, my mother had rejoined the land of the living. At least until she declared loudly that she wouldn't be attending our destination wedding because it wasn't held in a church. That was before anyone formally asked her to come.

On our way out, as we took the two flights of stairs and then walked to the condo's adjoining parking lot, Scott was quiet, and my heart began to beat faster. Then, finally, we were in his car.

At first I thought that his strained expression meant he was about to unleash a torrent of anger, to yell at me for having deceived him, having pretended to be a normal person who belongs in the normal world—his world. But he didn't yell. He just sat there, looking ahead instead of at me. My alarm grew when I noticed his shoulders were shaking.

And then he burst out laughing and couldn't stop until tears poured down his face.

"Well, Cece, you know what? That explains so much," he finally choked out.

I bristled, demanding to know what exactly it explained but he only shook his head and laughed harder.

*   *   *

"Cecelia, would you like me to find a number for—Therese—in the directory?"

"No," I bark, "I would not like you to find a number for Therese in the directory."

"Would you like to add a number for Therese?"

"No!"

This seems to do it. For a few moments, the house grows silent, as if deep in thought. Then: "I have found the following contacts for Therese. Therese Gillam, *mother*. Would you like me to add Therese Gillam, *mother*, to the directory?"

"Shut the fuck up!"

The echo of my screech rolls through the house in a moment of perfect silence. Even Taryn stops fussing and looks at me with big round eyes, shiny like oil pools. "Oh my God," I whisper. "I'm so sorry."

But Taryn isn't about to cry. Instead, her pouty lips curl into a smirk. "Mommy, that's a bad word."

"Yes, honey. Mommy used a bad word, and Mommy is sorry. You shouldn't say that word ever, okay?"

Her smirk doesn't diminish in the slightest but I forget to be upset. I even forget to picture Taryn running around day care all day telling everyone, including inanimate objects, to *shut the fuck up*. Instead, I'm trembling. This is a little beyond weird. Where on earth did the house find my mother's info? My techphobic, Luddite mother. Who doesn't own a cell phone and probably still has a cathode-ray TV.

I shouldn't be surprised. In fact, it's all probably in the fine print somewhere. Like so many other things.

After I've dropped Taryn off at day care and made her promise not to say any bad words—if she manages to be good all day, she'll get ice cream for dinner—I head home with a leaden feeling in my chest. I feel like I've hit a wall. "You know what, Saya? I would like you to call Therese Gillam."

*   *   *

TRANSCRIPT: Session 9, Lydia Bishop.
Dr. Alice Stockman, PhD.
June 7th, 2018

AS: Is that how you see yourself—as the shrink who killed her patient?

LB: I don't think how I see myself is the problem. But then again, Walter was a lot more than just a patient. I feel so stupid. For years, it was my bread and butter, telling other women to stay the hell away from guys like Walter. That's what made me feel immune. I thought I could examine him, impartially, like an insect under glass. I had my own insecurities about my career, and he tapped into them with such ease that I hardly noticed.

AS: Insecurities?

LB: [flinches] I'm sure it sounds so pedestrian. For as long as I remember, I was the only one who believed in my career. Who thought psychology was good and useful and worthwhile. That helping people counts for something! It wasn't exactly something that was valued and encouraged in my family. My sister's a lawyer, so is my husband, working to make sure big corporations are never held responsible for their fuck-ups.

AS: So you feared that your chosen path might be a waste of time?

LB: Not exactly. I just thought— I wished I'd taken it farther. I'm almost forty, and I wish I hadn't stopped my studies. I could have gone for the PhD, made a name for myself, the works. And instead, I was in my office, day in and day out, listening to other people's predictable, self-created problems. Just like my parents always said I would end up doing. To them, I'm considered the help. [chuckles]

So you understand that when Walter came along, I was hooked. I should have referred him somewhere else immediately. I should have realized I was out of my depth. But his whole act, *No one can help me except you*—it was just what my ego needed in that moment.

AS: And why do you think that is?

LB: [sighs, followed by a long silence] You see, my sister...

AS: Yes?

LB: I'm...I'm sorry. No. I can't tell you about it. I really—

AS: That's all right. We can explore that another time.

LB: I'm afraid not. Not another time, not ever.

AS: You know what I think? I think it's exactly the sort of thing we should discuss. Sounds important. [pause]

LB: Oh, it is. But I can't discuss it. Because she did something bad, and got me tangled up in it too, and don't get me wrong, Dr. Alice—not that I don't trust you but I don't trust this place. Too much is at stake. So you'll have to forget what I said.

AS: Will I see you next week?

LB: [no answer]

CHAPTER TWENTY-FOUR

It's ridiculous but I feel like I'm sneaking out to meet my own mother. I don't know why I bother but I turn off the car's GPS. Not that I delude myself with any notions that I could outsmart the array of technologies that make my life so safe, so comfortable. I'm rather like a toddler playing hide-and-seek, hiding behind a flimsy living room curtain and bursting with pride thinking she's now invisible.

If someone asked me why I even try, I couldn't answer. The house already knows about my mother. Plus, I have every right to visit her, just like I have the right to leave for any other reason. We're not prisoners here at SmartBlock; we're in the golden cage quite voluntarily. I could find an excuse to leave every day: to go for a walk, to go shopping at some specialty store. After all, the shopping we're helpfully provided with isn't the cheapest, and the four parks aren't all that spacious and look exactly like one another.

So why do so few people ever seem to leave? As I drive toward the northern exit, the road is all but empty. It feels eerie and unnatural. The mechanical arm of the gate is already open when I drive up to it. Cameras and sensors picked up every signal, analyzed and recorded everything, and decided to magnanimously let me through.

It's like the new Middle Ages, I find myself thinking. I'm leaving the safe confines of the city walls at my own fear and risk. Within is reason and order; outside is chaos and the unknown. No wonder no one wants to leave.

I groan under my breath. I decided not to use the Maps app on my phone either, and now I'm regretting my decision. In front of me is a long stretch of highway, and all the signs and exit numbers might as well be in cuneiform. After all, our beautiful block used to be an industrial park, long ago bought up and decontaminated—factories and warehouses razed—and a twenty-first-century oasis built in its place.

But back when the factories and refineries spewed their fumes into the sky, this place was on the offshoot, far enough from the city proper to avoid bringing down the sacrosanct property values. And developers haven't caught up yet, although no doubt they soon will.

For now, all I see on either side is emptiness, expanses of yellowed grass with a few trees sticking out of it here and there, looking unhealthy and misshapen. Low and gray industrial buildings break up the monotony once in a while, like flat warts.

Where is my exit? My mind scrambles in a panic, like I've suddenly forgotten something I've known my entire life. It happened a lot after Taryn was born, my brain fried by hormones and sleep deprivation.

Then the moments of confusion started happening again after the home invasion, and this time I blamed PTSD. Only now I'm overcome with a strange feeling as if not only do I not know where I'm going but I have no idea where I'm coming from either. As if I'd been sleeping and opened my eyes to find myself, in a nightmarish twist, behind the wheel of my car, careening down the highway into nothingness at a hundred miles per hour.

That's why the soft but pervasive beep of the alert makes me jump. It's just a little chime, the car letting me know that something is in my blind spot so I can react appropriately—yet it accomplishes the opposite effect. My hands on the steering wheel twitch. The car gives a swerve, right toward the motorcycle that's been trying to pass me. It all happens so fast that, by the time my heart drops into my heels, it's over. The bike avoids being hit in the nick of time, passing me and speeding away, but not before the biker treats me to a one-finger salute with a gloved hand.

My fingertips tingle as my heart continues to hammer. Now the motorcycle is in front of me, not receding into the distance.

And then three more appear in the rearview mirror. At first, I think I'm imagining things. But what started as three dots in the distance grows closer until I distinguish three identical bikes, their riders clad in black from head to toe despite the hot weather. Only one of them stands out with a red stripe on his helmet. Before I know it, I'm surrounded on all sides.

My hands grow damp and slippery, uncertain on the steering wheel. This is nuts. Are they trying to run me off the road? I could mow them down with my car if they try anything.

If the security system will let me, that is. I've turned off the assistant just as I did the GPS but who knows what failsafes IntelTech has installed—what else is in the fine print.

The inside of the car feels unbearably hot all of a sudden. I'm suffocating, sweat running down the back of my neck. And the silence of the superquiet electric engine becomes oppressive, leaden.

The bikes seem to be closing in, growing closer and closer to my car. Impulsively, I hit the gas pedal. But just as soon, they follow suit.

I glance at the dashboard, which hardly looks like a dashboard anymore, more like a tablet screen. I know the car has a preprogrammed speed limit—if only I could remember what it is. Nervous, I press on the gas pedal as hard as I can, just as a sign for the approaching exit appears in my field of vision.

If I take the turn, I'll knock over the bike on my right. He'll get out of the way—he has to. He's not insane. The turn signal starts to blink automatically as I change lanes, the bike still stuck at my side even as the other two fall behind. Taking a deep breath, I take the turn onto the exit ramp.

He swerves out of the way, over the yellow line. I hear the faint shriek of tires. I see him in the rearview mirror, coming to a rickety stop, barely able to keep from toppling to the side. One moment later, he vanishes from sight.

The road unfolds in front of me as I merge with the much more abundant traffic, and I realize, to my relief, that I'm exactly where I'm supposed to be. Back in reality, at last, thank God. I know where I am and where I'm going. Somehow the exit was the right one. My heartbeat slows down, and by the time I make my destination, I feel almost normal.

Except for my legs, which still tremble and refuse to unbend when I get out of the car in my mother's condo parking lot. I will them to be still and stop wobbling. I smooth my hair down with my sweaty palms and try on a smile. She'll pick up on my distress and use it against me to destabilize me even further, as she always does, without fail.

She knows I'm coming but takes forever to let me in. First, there's one of those security systems at the front door of the building. I have to call her, and she has to let me into the lobby. I stand there awkwardly as the device beeps and beeps, so loudly the whole street can hear. Finally, she picks up, and her scratchy voice rasps from the low-quality speakers. "Who's there?"

As if she doesn't know.

"It's me, Mom."

Still, she makes me say my name before she buzzes me in. When I go up, at last, I still have to knock on the door and then wait and wait while she pretends to come to answer. I suspect she's been waiting on the other side the whole time. Then, supposedly after checking through the peephole, she lets me through, opening the door just a crack—barely enough for me to slip in sideways.

"The cat," she explains. "Always trying to get out. I don't have the energy to chase after him at my age, you know."

The Siamese sits on the couch, not looking the least bit interested.

"Well? Are you going to come in?"

I take off my shoes and proceed into the living room. It's unchanged since the time I brought Scott to meet her. Or almost unchanged. The furniture and appliances are getting that unmistakable scuffed look. The living room rug is looking worn, not in the least thanks to the claws of the Siamese. I'm pretty sure I can see right through it in some places. It's screaming for the trash can. Therese is sliding inexorably back into old habits. I knew the normalcy wouldn't last.

"I'm sorry for giving you the third degree earlier," she says. I suspect she's not that sorry. "It's just, there are a lot of scammers out there. Riffraff."

"You can't tell your own daughter from someone trying to scam their way into your apartment?"

Her eyes are shrewd. "I was sure you of all people would understand."

Heat rises into my face.

My mother gives a sigh that borders on the theatrical. She starts rearranging things on the table with no real purpose. "Some days, I swear, I can almost understand you. Doing what you did. May the Lord forgive me."

"I didn't do anything special, Mom," I say, teeth gritting. "And the least you could do is come visit. If only for the sake of your granddaughter. You don't need a microchip for that."

"I light a candle for you every Sunday," she says, unflappable. "Now, would you like something to eat?"

"Mom," I repeat, "don't start with this again. This is good. For everyone. Taryn will be safe there."

"I know you don't want my opinion, or you would have asked for it before you put a chip in your own child," she says. "It's the mark of the Beast. It's—"

"I'm leaving right now if you don't stop."

She sets down a ceramic teapot with a clang. "Fine. Don't listen to me. But when the time comes to regret it, don't say I didn't warn you."

"Why is it so bad?" I blow up. "Why is it okay to put three locks and two chains on your door but not okay to have an AI that manages it all, and much better too? You know what? No sooner did I leave the house, I was nearly run off the road by some hooligans on motorcycles. So yeah, I'd much rather be safe. It's the future."

I realize I sound exactly like Scott but in the heat of the moment, I don't care. I find myself actually believing what I'm saying. Contradicting myself in a heartbeat, out of spite. Only Therese can bring this out in me.

She goes into the adjacent kitchenette, where she clangs around with the dishes in the sink, her back turned to me. As far as I can see, she's just shuffling them around. Why did I even come here? Why do I bother even trying to salvage a relationship with her? Haven't I had enough?

"I've been getting strange messages," I say. "Threatening messages. You wouldn't happen to know anything about that, would you?"

She doesn't even twitch.

"Do you think I would stoop that low? To see my only daughter too."

"I called you, and you said you had to see me, as quickly as possible. So here I am," I say to her turned back. "Did you make me come all this way just to berate me?"

She makes me wait for the answer. She turns on the tap without doing anything, just letting the water run. Then she turns it off and wipes her hands on a kitchen towel, all faded to gray and stained.

"I asked you to come over, Cecelia, because I need a favor."

Now there's a new one. But when she finally spits it out, it's so prosaic that I'm tempted to laugh. She's saying something about bills and a bad investment. It's pathetic, it really is.

"You need money," I say.

Having it put like that—plain, the words sitting between us like a boulder—makes her bristle. I've only rarely seen Therese squirm, and the sight isn't as satisfying as I remember.

"Yes. I've never asked for anything of the sort before so do you think you might be able to help your mother this once?" The words come out rushed and with an exaggerated directness, like she's rehearsed them ahead of time. Maybe she has. This can't be easy for her. She has her pride. Her own definition of pride, at least.

"What happened to all your savings?" I ask calmly. "Donated to some new sect you found? Or did you get a thing for the ponies that I'm not aware of?"

"How could you say such a thing?"

"Do you think I'm stupid, Therese? For as long as I remember, you've never had to work. And we weren't on welfare, this much I know."

"You ingrate. I took care of us both all these years—"

"I always wondered, you know. So where did that nest egg come from?"

"Look, Cecelia, do you think I would ask you for a single thing if I didn't have to?" She's never been good at hiding her anger, and now it's showing through the cracks as she struggles to hold on to control. "I know we don't agree about a lot of things but I'm still your mother. Go ahead, complain about me, nice and snug behind the walls of that soulless place where you're ensconced, but don't forget where you came from. You think I don't deserve your charity but you didn't earn what you have either. You wouldn't have any of it if it weren't for your husband."

"For someone who's asking for money, you could grovel a little better," I say.

"You know it's true. And if it weren't for me, you would have been stupid enough to let him slip away. Would have gone on to live in some trailer with that loser of yours."

*   *   *

I have nothing to say to that because she's probably right. But *that loser of mine* was the guy I met later that evening, on the very same day I met Scott. And that story intertwines with the story of us, inextricable, even though Scott—or the world—has no idea.

Everyone thinks my husband and I are the cutest couple ever, and not just that. We're that happy urban legend, the college sweethearts who made it work. And look at us now. It's the stuff of romantic comedies. But everyone forgets that even in romantic comedies, there's always that other guy. The bad one. And for some reason, the lovestruck heroine doesn't see what's so obvious to the entire audience. Because otherwise, there would be no plot.

What no one knows about our story is that by the time the day ended, I had forgotten all about that awkward guy Scott whom I shared a cigarette with after work. Because I met another man that evening. And I fell in love with him. All of a sudden, I understood all the clichés, love at first sight, head over heels. Butterflies in the stomach. I still, to this day, have no idea how he felt about me in return, and the older I get, the more I realize it doesn't matter. This kind of love is self-sustained, 99 percent in my own head. He paid attention to me, and it was good enough. The rest, my imagination could fill in with bits and pieces from pop culture and novels.

It's such a sad irony that in my first meeting with Scott, I remember only blurry bits and pieces, yet the rest of that night is in Technicolor detail. Andrew kissed me up against the wall of his off-campus apartment—

a place unlike anything I'd seen before, not a grubby little one-bedroom or closet-sized studio or dorm but the first floor of a brownstone, with big windows and ivy on the walls. It went so perfectly with the man himself or, more important, with my image of the man. In reality, he couldn't have been older than late twenties but still he seemed so much more worldly and sophisticated. Has there ever been a girl in her very early twenties who didn't fall for that?

As the people from the party gradually drained away, the music died down. Discarded bottles of craft beer and plastic glasses sticky with mixer littered every flat surface. My friends had left a long time ago, and only at that point did I realize they just left me behind. Not that they were really my friends in the proper sense. In college, you think of everyone you've ever gone drinking with as your friend.

Outside the tall windows, the sky had lightened to a delicate lilac-pink as the sun threatened to rise any second, and that's when I knew, deep in my gut, that I was staying over. I glanced sideways at Andrew and caught him looking at me, and we exchanged this conspiratorial look that said he knew it too. Only two other people were left at the party, a couple making out on the other couch. So he and I exchanged another glance. He got up and, in the most polite but nonnegotiable terms, reminded them that it was time to head home.

They stumbled out into the cold early morning, bleary-eyed, and the moment the double doors closed behind them, I forgot they ever existed at all. He turned the lock, and it was just us in the enormous apartment. I giggled. He sauntered over and picked me up, spinning me in the middle of the living room.

Needless to say, that afternoon I was loopy from sleep deprivation and the crashing high of that first time with someone you really, really like. I barely stayed awake through my late-afternoon classes and then poured an extra-large drip coffee down my gullet and headed to work. Friday night was always busy, and I had no idea how I was going to get through it.

I'd passed by his table three or four times before I even noticed Scott, let alone recognized him. Finally, I turned around, my tray empty and ready to carry another dozen reeking, sticky beer glasses, only to practically bump into Scott.

"Remember?" he asked. "It's me. The guy from last night."

For me, *the guy from last night* referred to someone else—someone as unlike Scott Holmes as humanly possible. But I smiled bravely and pretended I remembered. I had to keep up the charade for a good two or three minutes before I really did remember. "I said I'd be back," he said. If he were a little vexed because I so obviously struggled to remember who he was, he didn't show it. "And here I am."

After work, I had nowhere to go. I wasn't going to just randomly show up at *his* apartment—I might have been clueless about how to play the game but not that clueless—and he hadn't called. Not that he said he would call. He just asked for my number and wrote it down but never, as far as I could remember, uttered the words

I'll call you. That's how I justified it to myself to avoid a full-on junkie crash.

Still, as I followed Scott outside after I got off work, I checked my phone discreetly. Back then, I had one of those indestructible Nokias that couldn't go on the internet but had batteries that never died. The screen was empty. I put away the phone and hid my disappointment. And to take my mind off things, I let Scott kiss me awkwardly in the parking lot. I wasn't being disloyal—there was nothing to be loyal to, I told myself. There was no commitment, no exclusivity. I could do whatever I wanted. This was just to kill the time.

Surely, a part of me must have realized that it all meant the exact opposite to Scott. That in his mind, the girl of his dreams kissed him in a dingy parking lot behind a campus bar, and it was the best night of his life. I only know all this now because he told me in so many words, much later. It was like I held everything I ever wanted in the palm of my hand, he said. He gazed at me with that look in his eyes that he had early on, and I felt deeply inadequate. That was the dominant emotion our meet-cute aroused in me: shame.

That sloppy kiss, tasting like cheap mints overlaying cheap beer, was the start of a pattern. In between my meetings with the Love of my Life, on the days after, when I was still tipsy from the $20 cocktails he'd buy me in swanky nightclubs and fancy restaurants, I'd hightail it to Scott, filled with longing and resentment and a healthy dose of self-loathing. No $20 cocktails there but, once I got past self-flagellating over my disloyalty, his puppy-dog devotion and the admiration in his eyes were like a balm on my sense of self-worth, which always felt inexplicably bruised after too much time spent with the guy I told myself I was in love with. As if all that opulence had a purpose: not to make me feel pampered but to make me feel inferior. I resisted the feeling stubbornly, coming up with explanations and blaming myself. In times of such inner conflict, the cute-but-not-handsome, chubby-faced junior was just what I needed.

It all couldn't last. And so it didn't. I might have been legal on my ID but in my head, I was still a naïve, insecure teenager, with limited knowledge about all things contraception—and limitless desire to please the guy who could drop a couple of hundred dollars on me in a single evening.

And here's the thing I still can't remember without cringing: When I saw the extra stripe on that test, I felt *happy*. I don't know what exactly it meant, in my mind, but I fully expected him to feel the same way. I showed up to his regular Thursday-night summons (he never invited me over on the weekend, which I stupidly never questioned) to share the good news.

In guise of an answer, he gave me his credit card and a clinic address. When I tried to protest, he started to panic, and then it all came out. It wasn't his apartment. He was apartment-sitting for the real owner. He was a college dropout. He was broke. He couldn't afford this child.

I don't remember how I reacted on the spot. I think I managed to keep my cool—or simply was too lost to react. I wandered out of the beautiful apartment and into the middle of the street and just stood there. Traffic was sparse but what cars there were honked and had to swerve around me. I thought that, any moment now, he would come running after me, pulling me back onto the sidewalk and kissing me like in the movies, and everything would be all right.

After minutes ticked by and this wasn't the case, I did the only thing that made sense to me at the moment. I took the bus to my mother's house.

This was after the dump but before the condo. I trudged up three flights of stairs and knocked and knocked on her door, not quite realizing it was the middle of the night. Therese finally got out of bed and opened the door. When I told her about the situation, I expected her to slap me or hit me—and truth be told, I would have been secretly relieved if she did. It would mean the world was still familiar, still followed the same rigid set of rules, even if they were harsh and cruel ones. But it was a framework in which I could still function.

But Therese listened to me, nodding coolly. Finally, she tilted her head and said, "Well, why don't you just go and get rid of it? Don't be an idiot."

"I don't want to get rid of it!" I shrieked. I couldn't wrap my mind around Therese being such a raging hypocrite. Had everything been a huge joke, the world's longest— and shittiest—running gag?

"Then you're just stupid," she said with a shrug. "You want to be a single mom? You'll be dropping out of college, you know. There goes your whole life. Is that what you want for yourself?"

I didn't know what to say. "There has to be something else I can do." Despite the lies, the bullshit, the deception, I still loved him and wanted this baby.

"That other guy you just told me about. Any chance this baby could be his?"

I had to admit that there was absolutely zero chance of that because Scott and I had never had sex. In my own delusion, I drew the line at that. That would be cheating. When I told Therese this, she did the last thing I ever expected her to do. She threw her head back and laughed.

"That boy must be crazy about you," she said, "if he's still sweet on you after all this time when you won't even put out. You want my advice? Why don't you go to him right this moment and put on the best show of your life? I bet he'll be plenty happy when you tell him he knocked you up. And by the sound of it, this one has an actual future ahead of him. You could do worse."

That night, I hated her more than I ever had before. I hated her more than I thought possible. I spent the predawn hours ruminating on that hatred and agonizing over what to do. Yet never once did it occur to me to just have a go at it myself. To try and build my own life without needing to attach myself like a barnacle to someone more capable and successful. Maybe I was just young and stupid. But after I left Therese's apartment, I went and did as I was told.

Scott couldn't believe it when I turned up at his dorm. Seeing the look on his face, something inside me wilted in all-consuming shame. But by the next morning, I knew

I did the right thing—at least, according to my warped view of myself, him, and the world. Later that weekend, we were officially *an item*.

And within two weeks, I got my head on straight. Common sense returned, and so I went to the clinic and never told Scott or anyone a thing.

What I never counted on, however, was that my first so-called love would see me on the news after the home invasion and decide to worm his way back into my life.

CHAPTER TWENTY-FIVE

"What do you know about this?" I ask Therese. She's never been good at hiding her emotions, and even though she does her best to hang on to a look of smug superiority, I see her pale under the artificial circles of blusher on her cheeks. "Has he contacted you?"

She's silent.

"Therese," I snap.

"He showed up here a few weeks ago," she admits. "Asking about you. I told him never to come back. What more do you want from me?"

In that last phrase, her voice slips into a hysterical pitch, and I immediately guess everything.

"You gave him my number."

"It's not what it looks like, Cece. He came to help out with one of my church events. He said he was an old classmate of yours."

"And you believed it? Or did you do this on purpose? That's so like you. Did you think I needed to be taught a lesson? Because according to you, I haven't suffered enough already."

"I would never do that on purpose. Please."

I shake my head. "If you think I'm going to wire you money now, you're nuts."

"Right," she says. "I guess I should have gone to Scott in the first place."

I glower at her, and she meets my gaze with that infuriating false air of contrition.

"If you so much as contact Scott, Mom, I swear to God—"

"Calm down. I know you hate me, and you have your reasons, but like it or not, I've always had your back— when it counts. Have I not?"

*   *   *

Once I'm in my car, it starts automatically. I sit there without going anywhere for a few minutes, struggling to calm down.

I don't know if I really believe she did this on purpose. Therese can be infuriatingly unpredictable at times, going from obtuse to strangely shrewd as the situation demands. It's remarkable how lightning fast she can get her shit together when needed. For all her delusions, she has a preservation instinct sharper than a razor, and right now she needs something from me. For all I know, she just might contact Scott, and with my ex back in the picture, lurking outside the walls of Venture ready to pop up when

I need him the least, it'll be a lot harder to write her off as crazy.

Yet as I log on to my banking app, I'm gritting my teeth. Yes, I'm letting her win, and setting a precedent that she'll no doubt try to exploit again. But I can deal with that when the times comes, and in the meantime I decide to send her a little money. Nowhere near as much as she asked for but enough to keep her out of my hair.

It's been a while since I've used the banking app. That's because it's been a while since I left Venture, where I can pay for everything automatically using my chip. So now I look at the accounts in mild confusion.

My own is practically empty but I knew that already. This is the account I used for my ebook cover business, and while it was never anything to retire on, it used to have a healthy four figures in it once upon a time. Now, there's a couple hundred dollars in it, which I deposited there many months ago for the software subscriptions that have now lapsed.

What's alarming is that the other account has less than a thousand dollars in it. The last time I logged on, this wasn't the case. Scott's pay goes into that account, and, since he just got paid last week, this makes no sense. Maybe I overspent on all the stuff that debits automatically. I try to do the math in my head: the groceries, the bills, myriad little indulgences I no longer notice. Oh yeah, the catering and wine for that party. Thinking I might transfer some more money here just in case, I tap and swipe but can't access the savings account from the app. Scott manages these things, and I've always let him because it's not like I contribute anything to the savings anyhow.

A couple more taps, and I've wired Therese some of the money from the accounts. Scott might notice, and then he'll ask questions. I can't say I look forward to the conversation.

I'm not in a hurry to go back to Venture. The prospect of driving back through the gilded gates of my new home makes me queasy. Yet I can't help feeling like I'm a guest here in the real world, just passing through. I don't live here anymore.

There's still time so instead of going straight home, I decide to go for a drive to clear my head. It's almost at random that I find myself taking a turn in the familiar direction.

As I make the turn onto the highway, I'm reminded of something Clarisse's assistant said to us, offhandedly, as everything was being finalized and signed, *i*'s dotted and *t*'s crossed. I felt awkward, overcome by all the information, not to mention all the overwhelming legalese of the documents, releases, and authorizations I'd just signed. With Clarisse and Scott beaming and shaking hands and that self-satisfied girl with that robotic smile looking on, I felt the way I hadn't in a long time. Like the poorest, stupidest person in the room, the one the others only pretend to include because it's the polite thing to do. I sought to compensate but, naturally, only ended up digging my own grave ever deeper. I giggled like an idiot and said something along the lines of *This is too good to be true, it feels like living in a utopia.* So the assistant gave me another perfect smile, put her manicured hand soothingly on my forearm, and said, "Don't worry too much about it. Soon everyone will be living this way."

It accomplished its purpose; it shut me up. But as I look around me, I start to mull over those words. Will everyone really live like us someday, in a hyperconnected reality that's so far removed from the natural world? Then I think about ever-widening income inequalities, the First and Third World, planned obsolescence and toxic waste dumps where all the discarded devices rot, leaking poison into the earth, half a world away.

There aren't enough resources on earth for *everyone* to live this way. She didn't mean *everyone.* She meant everyone like us, the people in that room that day.

I take the exit, make one turn, another, and feel something close to surprise when I arrive on our old street. Not at the view, which has changed so little it's like I was never gone at all, but at the pain in my heart. It's hard to breathe. I slow down, trying not to be conspicuous as I crane my neck to look. The centennial trees, the other houses float by like movies on a screen. At the very end is our beautiful place, and for a moment, I'm ready to do a U-turn and get the hell out of here. I don't think I can handle seeing it standing empty, windows dark.

But my hands are steady on the steering wheel as the car crawls down the street. To my surprise, I spot a couple of FOR SALE signs next door. I hope it's not because of what happened back then.

And then I'm in front of our house.

At once, I'm hit with a disorienting feeling. But a moment later, I understand that I hadn't in fact tumbled into the past, watching my old life from behind a pane of glass. The house is not deserted. There are curtains on the windows, *different* curtains, and people are moving around inside. In the front yard, the rock garden I put together is gone—now there's a green foam mat and one of those plastic playhouses with toys scattered all around. There's no FOR SALE sign in sight.

I know that what I'm doing is stupid but I pull the car into the nearest parking space and get out. From the sidewalk, I can already see that the locks have been changed. So has the doorbell. They have one of the new ones with a video feed. I ring it, not expecting anyone to open, but a minute later, someone does, a woman about my age. I don't need to wonder what she's doing at home in the middle of a weekday because she's holding a young toddler in her left arm. He can't be much more than a year old.

"Can I help you?"

"I'm looking for someone," I say. Mercifully, my brain is quick to come up with the words. "Someone who used to live here."

"I'm so sorry," she says, her face a generic mask of empathy. "They moved out a while back, and I'm afraid I don't have a forwarding address."

"How—" I stumble over my own words and have to start over. "When did you move in?"

"Just a month ago. Houses don't go on sale in this area very often so we pounced."

"Do you like it here?"

"Very much."

"Good," I say. "But one thing: You really shouldn't open the door to strangers. Not when you have a young child at home."

CHAPTER TWENTY-SIX

Jessica arrives at the meet-up spot late. At a dive bar like this one, not a chance she'll ever run into anyone she knows from work. She storms to the back of the bar, to the dimly lit area that houses the pool tables, and pauses just outside the zone lit by the low-hanging lamps.

In that moment, before the others notice her, she's overcome by how silly they look. One of them aims the cue at a red ball for a good minute, then strikes. The ball bounces all around the table, barely brushing against the others. The guy groans and rubs his hipster beard. One of the girls laughs. Jess can't shake the impression that their so-called cause is a game to them, like this game of pool. Something to tide them over until something else catches their attention.

The guy with the cue is their self-styled leader, Colin, and he's twenty-two years old. He reminds her of her brother, sometimes painfully so. The same carefree attitude, the same overconfidence—except with a golden safety net, well-connected parents, and a trust fund. Her brother never had a safety net. That's what made all the difference.

She sought out Colin and his group not long after the Holmeses moved into 32 Rosemary Road. Finding them was way too easy, which was the first thing she told Colin. The situation hadn't much improved, because most of them love their cause but not as much as they love their Instagram accounts. Jess stands there, watching, for a moment longer, until Colin turns around and notices her.

A silence falls over the group, like she's a teacher who just walked into a classroom of second graders. She doesn't belong. She knows it, and they know it. They feel it under their skin. She suspects that before she arrived, they were happy enough to keep their activism to social media posts and flashy protests meant to attract attention: According to their bios, they're a *radical anti-gentrification and anti-capitalism collective*—even though most of them, in real life, are closer to the proverbial 1 percent. Now, they have to do real, tangible things, things they can't talk about, let alone brag on Twitter, and obey an outsider. They probably resent her. Let them. Hopefully, she won't need them for long.

"What the hell were you thinking?" she asks. "You nearly ran her off the road."

Colin gives her a look from under his brow bone. "Isn't that what you asked us to do?"

"No. I asked you to try and get her to pull over so we

could talk to her, not get her into a car crash. We need her, remember?"

"Why?" chimes in the girl who is Colin's on-again, off-again girlfriend. By the way she moves to stand by his side possessively, Jess guesses that today they're on again. The girl also seems to think Jess has her sights set on Colin, which couldn't be further from the truth. "Don't you have access to everything at Venture, anyway? Why do we need some boring housewife?"

"I told you this. I'm conspicuous. IntelTech can't suspect me, that's why we need her to do the work for us. And we're not going to get there by endangering her life."

The girlfriend stretches her arms over her head. "Boring." Colin shoots her a look. She lowers her arms.

"I'm sorry, okay?" he says. "But we've been at it for months now, and nothing is happening. We're not moving forward. Sometimes I wonder if you're really helping us at all."

"Well, you don't have anyone better," Jess snaps. Dumb, spoiled brats, she thinks, clenching her teeth. "You'll have to deal with me. And it is moving forward. Everything in that place is under surveillance so excuse me if we can't just barge in with the subtlety of a sledgehammer. Just— stay away from Cecelia Holmes from now on, okay? I'll be dealing with her. She trusts me."

"Does she now?" Colin frowns. "You said she doesn't trust anyone at IntelTech because she thinks the house is trying to kill her."

Jess smirks grimly. "She doesn't have a choice not to trust me. She'll find that out soon enough."

*   *   *

As soon as daylight starts to fade, sensors all over Rosemary Road pick up on it and the lights flicker on. Not just
the streetlights but the decorative lights along the façades
of the houses and in the gardens. Even the looming
construction of dark glass behind our house has subtle
decorative lights that flicker on, cold and bluish. There's
a string of fairy lights woven with calculated carelessness
into a tree on someone's front lawn, lanterns next to doors
and mailboxes and inside decorative fountains. Even the
unoccupied house has them, a string of tiny lamps shed-
ding warm yellow light that line the path to the front door.
It's supposed to make the street look welcoming.

When we just moved in, I stood by the living room
window every evening and watched them all go on progres-
sively until the whole street was lit up like on Christmas.
Tonight, that's where Scott finds me when he gets home
from work. I don't need to turn around. I hear the front
door opening with a soft click, the hiss of the hinges, the
thud as he puts down his briefcase and his gym bag. Then
soft steps that stop a few feet behind me.

"What are you up to?" he asks at last.

In my sweat-damp hand, I'm clutching the key. The
moment I got home I went up to his office and retrieved
it from the drawer. I was going to throw it in his face and
demand explanations, which, to be fair, wouldn't be such
an unreasonable thing to do. But now, I subtly slip the
key into the pocket of my jeans.

"I didn't realize someone else was living in the house,"

I say, trying to sound nonchalant. Then I listen to the silence. His breath quickens.

"Oh," he says after a long pause.

That's it? That's what I get? *Oh.*

"How do you—"

"I went there today."

"Why would you do that?"

I turn around. It's an unsettling sight. I've never seen Scott look like this, guilty as a dog. His gaze shifts back and forth. Even his posture, which has gained confidence over the years as his efforts at work and in the weight room paid off, looks slack, shoulders rounded, reminding me of the shy, pudgy guy I met years ago. He's not a good liar. At least I've always thought so.

"I was visiting my mom, and I just wanted to drive by it. I certainly didn't expect to see people living in it."

"Your mom? I thought you didn't want to see her."

"Scott, that's not the problem." The problem is that you lied to me, and you're lying to me right now.

"I thought, if we're not selling straightaway, we might as well get some sort of profit," he stammers, too fast. "So I decided—"

"I talked to the woman who lives there now," I say, putting an end to it. "You sold it. And you never told me."

"Cece, there's . . . there's some stuff I have to tell you that I'm not proud of."

I'm stunned. Literally stunned, like someone hit me over the head with something heavy. I have to go sit down. In my jeans pocket, the key pokes me in the hip.

"There's no money in the bank account," I say.

"I'll transfer some," he assures me. "It's . . . it's not as bad as it looks. We're not completely broke."

"Broke?" I echo. This is nuts. How can we be broke? And another thought dances in the back of my mind, just out of reach, a much less charitable thought.

He launches into an explanation. He's been stressed out. Everything that happened in the last year, plus pressures at work, and he first got into the online poker just for fun. He won big when he first played, and he has no idea how it all got so far out of hand. But it will all be fine. He will bring it up at our next appointment with Dr. Alice. He will get treatment. There are steps. Like for alcoholism.

"Scott," I say, "our old house. Our *house.* It's gone. That's the real reason we're stuck here, isn't it? Not the contract."

He goes off again, about how he's sorry and he's going to make it right and this and that.

"For God's sake."

"You had something to do with it too, you know. You mope around here all day and won't get help."

"You've got to be kidding!" I exclaim. "Now it's my fault? I . . . I didn't—"

Just as I'm about to blurt out the thought I haven't been able to get rid of this whole time, the lights go out all at once. Silently and without warning, everything sinks into darkness, in which my shriek and Scott's disembodied exclamation ring hollowly. Darkness is inky and thick, smothering the words that were just on my tongue: *I didn't sign up for this.*

"Saya!" Scott yells, his voice raw and furious, and I know the fury isn't meant for Saya at all. "Lights! Right now!"

The lights flicker on in unison. If not for the red swimming before my eyes, and if not for Scott, who was also here to see it, I might have thought nothing happened at all and my mind is playing tricks on me.

"See?" I say hoarsely. Scott blinks.

"It's just the lights, Cecelia. It's not such a big fucking deal."

"Don't tell me what is or isn't a big fucking deal!"

"Stop shouting. You'll wake Taryn."

I storm past him into the kitchen. My mouth is parched, and a headache hammers away behind my eyes. I rub my temples with a groan.

"I'll get you an Advil," Scott says, and hurries off to the bathroom. I listen idly to his steps, hoping that at any moment I might wake up and all this will have been just a dream.

Scott comes downstairs, bottle of Advil in hand. I take a glass from a cabinet and fill it from the filter. Then I take the bottle from him and dump two pills into my palm.

"I'm so sorry, honey," he's saying as I pop them into my mouth and swallow. They stick in my throat, and I bring the glass to my lips to take a sip.

The second the liquid touches my tongue, I spit it out, violently, all over the counter. My eyes are burning, tears running down my cheeks as I lean over the sink and gag uncontrollably.

"Cece?" Scott's voice comes from behind me. "Oh my God. What's happening? Are you okay?"

I'm not okay, not even close, because whatever was inside that glass, it sure as hell wasn't water.

CHAPTER TWENTY-SEVEN

Scott is the one who calls the IntelTech personnel, who arrive just minutes later. Silent and efficient workers take over the kitchen while an assistant guides us gently but firmly out of the kitchen and into the living room.

"Did you ingest any of it?" the woman asks. She could be the other one's sister—God, I forgot her name again. At least it seems so at first glance. Then I realize it's just the style, generic office-casual, that's nearly identical; she looks nothing like her.

"Where's Jessica?" Scott asks. Right. That's got to be her name.

"She's off the clock," the woman replies with a smile. "Everything will be logged into your file so she can pick up where we left off tomorrow."

Great. I do forget that they're not actually robots. I

try to imagine Jessica having a life somewhere out there, and fail.

"I didn't ingest any," I say. "I spat it out."

"If you feel any distress—"

"Oh, I feel a lot of distress. Nothing your hospital can fix," I snarl.

"Cece," my husband chides me in a guilty, hushed voice. How dare he?

"What was it? What did this house of yours try to poison me with?"

"It's not important. A setting got disconnected."

"That makes no sense."

"I know. I assure you we're doing our due diligence."

"Just tell me what it was!"

Her gaze shifts. "It appears that, through some malfunction we're currently working hard to identify, the water filter became contaminated with sodium hypochlorite."

"Bleach," I say. "That's bleach. So just say bleach."

"We're terribly sorry—"

"You know, this could have been my three-year-old daughter," Scott pipes up. I bet he's happy to be able to change the subject—to have an excuse to bond with me against some external wrongdoing. I want to tell him to shut his mouth.

"Clarisse will contact you and discuss compensation," says the woman. Scott looks guiltily away.

I think I've had enough. I get up and push past the two of them, heading for the stairs. Through the kitchen doorway, I see the IntelTech people poking and prodding. My mind is abuzz.

Upstairs, I throw open the doors of the bedroom closet. There's an old duffel bag of Scott's, which will do. I go through the drawers, gathering up underwear, socks, T-shirts, a couple of pairs of jeans—just the essentials.

"Cecelia." He's standing in the doorway.

"Move."

"What are you doing?"

"Just because you gambled away our house doesn't mean I have to stand another minute of this. I'm going to Therese's."

"You can't be serious. What about Taryn?"

"What about her? Why don't you take care of her for one evening? See what you've been missing out on."

"Cece," he says as I zip up the bag and go past him, down the stairs and into the garage. "You don't have to do this. I understand you're mad but you can at least go to a hotel."

"And who's going to pay for it?"

"I'll transfer you some money."

"Oh. So we do have money, stashed away somewhere. Good to know."

*   *   *

When I'm outside the gates of Venture and I check the banking app, I see that Scott kept his word. There is indeed some more money in the account. But the first thing I do is track down the nearest ATM machine and withdraw as much as the daily limit allows. First, what's to stop him from transferring it away at any moment, and second, I need it.

I drive to Therese's but the moment I park the car, I

realize I can't bring myself to go up there. So I do something I've never done before. I fall asleep in my car, with the seat reclined as far as it can go. It's a strange, fitful sleep, the kind where I can hardly tell I was asleep at all, let alone for how long. It feels as though I had only closed my eyes for a moment. Yet the next thing I know, someone raps on the glass, and I snap awake.

Bright, gray daylight fills the car. My head is ringing. And right outside the driver's side window stands a black-clad figure.

I fumble for the controls. My first instinct is to turn on the engine and get the hell out of here—he can't chase me on foot, can he? But I mash the buttons in vain. The car doesn't even sputter, like I'm sitting inside a giant toy with dead batteries.

The figure raps on the glass once more. I inspect him up close. It's the motorcyclist who flipped me off, light reflecting off the visor of the bike helmet where his face should be.

I shake my head mutely, wondering how to reach for my phone in my back pocket without him noticing.

Then he raises his hands, and I flinch out of sheer instinct—but he only removes his helmet.

I choke on an exclamation. The dissonance hits me like a sledgehammer. The perfect pixie face and the slicked-back hair—I know her before I really recognize her. She looks different, caked in tacky, too-dark makeup.

But I know who she is. I saw her just a short while ago. Her name, though, is on the tip of my tongue, just out of reach. As generic as she is. Jamie? Janet?

Jessica. Clarisse's assistant.

"Get out of the car, Cecelia," she says. Even her voice is different. Gone is the smoothness of it, which in retrospect only betrayed how little she really meant what she said. There's a raspy edge to it. A vocal fry that betrays what I previously thought she wasn't capable of: genuine emotion. "I'm not going to harm you."

I open the door and climb out. My bones ache, and my back is stiff. It's hard to maintain dignity but I sure try. "What do you want from me?" I demand.

"I'm sorry but I had to disable the car. I need to talk to you. Outside Venture, as far away from IntelTech as possible."

"Why? What do you want?"

"I think you know."

"I don't. And even if I did, why on earth would I help you with anything?"

"Because this isn't just about you. It's about Lydia."

CHAPTER TWENTY-EIGHT

Jessica leads me to a car at the end of the parking lot. How long has it been sitting there? Was it there when I came to visit my mother yesterday? I never noticed it because it's not the kind of car you notice. It's so old I can't even venture a guess what year it's from. It's rusting through, and the seats are lumpy. I fidget in the passenger seat, wondering how safe it is to drive this death trap. The air smells like chemical freshener hiding a familiar whiff of old tobacco. I wonder where she got this old mastodon. What on earth did I get myself into?

"What do you know about Lydia?" I ask softly. My voice is instantly drowned in the roar of the engine—God, I forgot how loud these old cars really are.

"Was she real?" I try again, feeling pathetic.

This time Jessica takes pity on me. "Of course she was real."

"The house," I say, my mouth dry, "it did something to her." My mind races. "The malfunctions were no accident, were they? Is my daughter in danger?"

Jessica inclines her head. "I don't think so. Not yet. That's why we had to meet far away from SmartBlock. IntelTech can't find out about this. If they do, I don't know how far they'll go to stop us."

"Us," I echo. "What 'us'? I haven't agreed to help you." Yet.

"I'm part of a cooperative," she says.

"Cooperative," I echo. "The same cooperative that tried to run me off the road? Charming."

She ignores my attempt at sarcasm. "We want to stop IntelTech and what they're doing."

If I weren't so frightened, I would laugh. It's not the most plausible scenario. "Stop IntelTech? How are you going to do that? And most important, why?"

"How—we'll get to that soon enough. And why— because with a tech company playing God with people's information, no one is truly safe. You of all people should know that."

She stops the car close to a park, in a part of town I've never been to before. It's run-down. The houses on the streets we pass to get here are in various states of disrepair, most storefronts are empty and dirty, and a few of the buildings look outright abandoned. When I see it all, the nervousness I've been feeling spills out into tics. I tap my hands on my thighs.

"Why are we here?" I finally ask.

"This place is next on IntelTech's radar," she says somberly.

"If you ask me, it could use a little love," I mutter under my breath and immediately regret opening my mouth. What is this woman on about? Some sort of collective. Whatever they call themselves.

I remember those, back when I was in college. They protested things like pipelines and condo builders and what have you, and a couple of them even approached me a few times as they handed out leaflets outside the dorms or glued posters to the walls of university buildings.

But they always seemed a little alien to me. I just couldn't relate to their motivations or methods, even though I was supposed to be smack-dab in the middle of their target demographic. Maybe it was because most of them, if not all, came from such blatantly privileged backgrounds. It was painfully obvious from how they spoke and from their perfect, gleaming, straight teeth, the product of expensive braces. All the dreadlocks and thrift-store clothes couldn't hide the fact that they paid their tuition from their trust funds. If they were just typical rich people, not giving a damn about anything but themselves, I wouldn't have liked them better but at least it would have been more honest.

It was Scott who explained to me the rationale behind their behavior. It's not so much guilt as self-preservation, he said one time. If they overtly flaunted their wealth and voted Republican so they could get a tax cut for the next fiscal year, the poor would literally eat them. The only sensible way to stay safe is to embrace all the social causes so that the poor could instead admire them, all the while hoping to become them someday.

It made sense to me then but now, as I study Jessica's profile, I can't read anything in her expression. What does she have to gain? And more important, where do I come in?

"IntelTech is going to buy up the homes, then demolish or restore only the façades. Then it's going to stick a camera and sensor into every nook and turn it into another SmartBlock. And eventually they'll move in on another neighborhood, and another, and the thing is, people will welcome them with open arms because they've seen and heard for years how wonderful life is in Venture. There's already a whole social media campaign underway. Only one thing remains: They must prove that the concept is a success."

"No offense," I say, feeling contrarian, "but from the looks of it, it is." It sure works for my neighbors.

We exit the car and walk through the empty park. I glance around nervously but Jessica seems unconcerned.

"Don't worry, there was only one camera, and it's disabled," says Jessica.

Somehow, this fails to put me at my ease.

"Cecelia, does it not make you nervous at all that one company knows everything about everyone?"

"That's a rhetorical question if I've ever heard one."

"Of course it's a rhetorical question. Because you, and everyone, should be nervous." Jessica pauses and gives me a sideways look. "And please, don't say you're fine with it because you have nothing to hide."

For some reason, her tone sends a chill down my spine. I cover it with a chuckle. "Everyone has something to hide. Don't you believe in accountability?"

"As a matter of fact, I do," she says, not taking my bait. "For IntelTech above all. Because, Cecelia, that house did something to your predecessor. Something bad. I think you know it already."

"You're the one who denied it."

"Because even I don't know for sure. That's why we need you. They may have found a way to erase Lydia from existence but there might still be proof. And I need you to get it for us."

Silence settles over the park. It could be that I've gotten so used to the manicured look of Venture but the surroundings strike me with their drabness. The grass is patchy. Cigarette butts and beer caps and other garbage is strewn everywhere. A few benches sit here and there, not one of them intact, covered in graffiti, missing planks, with rusted nails protruding all over the place. Even the sparse trees look like they're dying.

"What proof? Can't you get it yourself? You're the one who works there."

"I can't get it. Not without a significant risk of being found out, in which case everything we've been working for is for nothing. But you—you already have access. And I figured you'd be willing to help. After all, you live in her house."

I'm stricken speechless.

"You already figured out that IntelTech targets vulnerable people," Jessica is saying. "People who have been victims of crimes and who are willing to compromise their privacy in exchange for perfect safety. But you aren't perfectly safe. And Lydia is proof. I know you would do anything to keep your daughter from harm, Cecelia."

"What do you want me to do?" I ask hoarsely.

"They've removed all traces of her," Jessica says. "All *digital* traces. But there might be something left. Something IntelTech couldn't erase with a few clicks."

My mind whirls. Everything comes together, slowly at first, and then forming into a full picture almost at once, just as Jessica says, "There's a recording that contains vital information."

"At Dr. Alice's office," I say, breathless. "The tapes. Do you think she . . . she kept them?"

"I think she did. I need you to go to her office—I'll fix you a solo appointment, it'll only take a second—and then, while she's distracted, I want you to get the tapes for me. For us. For Taryn too."

"I don't want to go back there," I say. "That house tried to feed me bleach. And my husband—" I gulp. In spite of myself, I'm close to tears. "Why am I telling you, anyway? You must know everything about everyone."

"You must go back," she says. She puts her hands on my shoulders and looks me straight in the eye with a determination that verges on unnerving. "Reconcile with your husband. Or at least pretend to."

"How am I supposed to do that?"

"Your husband isn't all he seems. He's been lying to you too."

"I already know that," I mutter.

"That's not what I'm talking about. Promise you'll help me, and I'll help you in turn."

"I'll help you," I blurt before I can change my mind. "What is happening? What is Scott hiding from me?"

She measures me with a look, then takes a breath. "Did you find the key yet?"

I frantically pat down my pockets. It's right there, where I left it. I take it out and look at it, lying in the palm of my hand.

Jessica raises her eyebrows. If I didn't know better, I'd say she's almost...impressed.

"At least you keep your eyes open. You wouldn't believe how oblivious people can be. This key opens a storage locker." She smirks. "Remember, this is my gesture of good faith. I followed your husband's comings and goings, which violates my IntelTech contract big-time, and if it comes out, I'll be unemployable. So pay attention. Scott's been liquidating his assets. There's no gambling problem. What cash isn't in the offshore accounts yet is in that locker."

I feel numb. "Why would he be doing that?"

"My wild guess is that he's planning to leave you."

I shut my eyes. I'm such an idiot. What else could it possibly mean?

"If you don't believe me, see for yourself. I'll give you the address and the locker number. Then you're on your own."

*   *   *

The moment I see it from the highway, I know Jessica was right. It's the color scheme that I recognize from the plastic tab attached to the key. The big sign reads MOVING AND STORAGE—MONTHLY PLANS AND AFFORDABLE RATE$. The dollar sign instead of the *S* is a particularly stylish touch.

The lockers here come in three sizes, and the one my husband rented is of the smallest size. Cheapskate, I catch myself thinking. For all his good qualities, he's never been one to spoil his woman, my Scott. Curiously, I never let myself remark on this before. I thought it was uncharitable because he's always taken care of me, and that's what truly counts. Or so I told myself as I gritted my teeth—very, very discreetly—at the discount jewelry and store-brand groceries and *oh, why don't we just stay in tonight* on Saturday nights and big occasions alike.

Even as he got yet another big raise, he'd pick the cheapest bottle of wine at the celebratory dinner I had to practically drag him out to, and he never tipped a penny over 15 percent. He checked the credit card statements every month, meticulously adding up every charge and bristling if he saw that I'd dared to get a pedicure.

How stupid I feel, standing in front of that open locker and looking at the contents. How could I have believed the line about the gambling problem? The only cards that ever held his interest were Dick's Sporting Goods gift cards. There it is, all that money, in a nondescript duffel bag.

I zip it up and pull it out, then close the locker and turn the key, which I put back in my pocket. I throw the duffel in the back of my car and drive off without wasting another moment. Since I'm living fast and loose today, I take my phone out and fire off a text to that number I keep deleting from my phone.

*   *   *

I find the right address at the end of a maze of ugly little houses. It's not that far from Therese's. Small world?

It's a little shocking. The love of my life, living here? My mother was right. I could have ended up here as well, in this ramshackle little mobile home.

I walk up three crumbling stairs, wondering if I'm going to get tetanus from some rusty nail, and knock on the door. I suspect he was waiting on the other side because he opens almost immediately.

"Hi, Cecelia," he says with a sheepish grin. I'm taken aback. Does he really not realize how far below me he is now?

"House-sitting again?"

He throws a glance over his shoulder. I can't see much behind him because the light isn't on but I can guess what it might look like. An unhealthy, stale smell wafts out the door.

"There's no need for that," he says, wincing.

"Why are you trying to blackmail my mom?"

"Blackmail? Hey, a guy can fall on hard times."

"Listen, Andrew. Here." I thrust the duffel at him, and he catches it, a bewildered look on his face. "This should be more than enough. Never go near me or my family ever again."

"Or what?"

God, how he's changed. To think I ever thought he was anything other than trash. Maybe I'm the one who changed. And, like it or not, I have him to thank for the lesson.

"Or I'll call the police. Because when you think about it, there's nothing you can blackmail me with. Is there?"

He holds my gaze. His look is blank, and I read in it little more than impatience—like he can barely believe his luck, and he just wants me to go away so he can go spend the money on cheap booze and cigarettes and whatever will make him feel like someone better than he is.

"You don't even deserve this but consider it a gift. I feel sorry for you."

I feel his gaze on my back as I walk away. He still stands there, holding the duffel bag, as I get back in my car. I close the doors and lock them—he's not going to come after me, he's too big of a coward, but precaution never hurts.

Then I call Scott.

"I'm so sorry," I say to his voice mail, and sound like I mean it. "I'm coming home. Let's try to make it work."

CHAPTER TWENTY-NINE

I park a little bit farther away from Dr. Alice's office than I need to under the pretext that it's a nice day to walk outside. Yet the walk is over before I know it, my attempt to stall the inevitable having fallen flat. There's a knot in the pit of my stomach. I feel like I'm back in elementary school and I got a bad grade, debating whether to tell Therese and face her wrath—or lie to her and risk her finding out and face the same wrath, tenfold.

Some things never change, I guess.

But Dr. Alice Stockman isn't Therese. She's a mild-mannered psychologist who I'm about to defraud, betraying her trust in me. I try not to even think about what will happen if I'm caught. And for what—to have answers, I tell myself. To be safe in my own home. For Taryn.

The knot in my stomach turns from mere nervousness to plain old guilt when Dr. Alice appears and welcomes me into her office as warmly as ever. I know the retro, cozy space with the wainscoting and moldings and obsolete fixtures from the past is meant to put me at my ease but today it's not working. She'll notice. If she hasn't already. She's a psychologist, for God's sake. She'll see right through me—right through this whole stupid scheme. How did I let myself get talked into this?

But Dr. Alice is nothing but kindness. "I see you're nervous, Cecelia."

"A little," I say. No point in pretending.

"Does it have something to do with why you called an emergency meeting?"

I smile shakily. Of course she'd think that, because it's the most likely conclusion. I nod, continuing to fidget.

"Do you want to try and tell me about it?"

I know what I'm supposed to do. Jessica instructed me. Keep talking, even if it's just rambling. I'd even made up some talking points beforehand, except now they've mysteriously evaporated from my head.

"I saw my ex-boyfriend the other day," I blurt. "From college."

"I see." There's now a knowing smile on her face. So this is what it's about, I can practically hear her thinking.

"And I just—it was so sad. We had such a bad breakup. I thought Andrew was the love of my life. I was devastated. And now he lives in this little ramshackle house, a total dump, while I live here. Isn't it funny, how things seem so huge and important and insurmountable but then with a little distance, you realize they weren't all that?"

"That sounds like a useful breakthrough," says Dr. Alice with the same smile. "Has it helped you put things in perspective?"

"Yeah. In a sense. It's okay to just leave things in the past. It may seem like such a big deal but then life just goes on, and you realize it's for the best." I pause for a breath, and only then it occurs to me.

"Wait. Hang on. Are you recording all this?"

She shakes her head, pointing with her gaze at the recorder sitting on the side table. I can see that it's not on, and there's no cassette in the holder. "I only record for my own reference, and only with your prior consent. We can have an unrecorded session if you like. And I feel like right now, this is something you would prefer. Is that correct?"

Once again, I can only nod.

She leans in just a little closer. I notice how she's sitting, how her arms are folded, and realize that mine are exactly the same way. She's mirroring me.

"Is there something you want to confide? Is there something you want to tell me?"

This is when we both hear the short sequence of beeps, and even though one of us knew they were coming, we both jump. "So sorry," says Dr. Alice as she gets up from her armchair. "I always keep my phone on sleep mode. This is just—"

It's an emergency alert that overrides the phone settings. I have the same thing on mine. And I know what's going to happen next. She takes the phone from her desk drawer, looks at it, and tersely excuses herself without giving an explanation. I barely have time to acquiesce when she leaves, the door closing softly behind her.

I'm left alone.

It's only then that the full absurdity of the situation hits me. Getting on my feet, I look around the room. Where on earth am I supposed to find her tapes? Assuming she even keeps them here.

I'm overwhelmed by the temptation to just let it go. I can sit there until Dr. Alice comes back, and then I can just tell Jessica that I didn't find it.

It's only when I'm behind her desk and my hand reaches for the drawer that I realize I'm not doing this for Jessica, or for their stupid cause, or for this Lydia I've never met, and not even for my daughter. I'm doing it for me.

The desk has two drawers, a big and a small one, and both have old-fashioned key locks. To my surprise, it's the larger, bottom drawer that opens without resistance but inside, I find nothing but disappointment. Notebooks that don't contain anything of importance, at least at a glance, some old agendas. How long has it been since I've seen anyone use a paper agenda?

I turn my attention to the second drawer. I grab a card from her desk and try to use it to open the lock. Therese had a desk with drawers not unlike this one, and I remember this trick well. But, as I'm not too surprised to discover, this lock is different, and my little scheme doesn't work.

I circle the room, feeling useless. I take a couple of books off the shelves but they're just ordinary books. As I flip the pages, they release that comforting old-book smell that rises into my face—another thing I never realized I missed. We have so few books at the house. At the old place, I had shelves and shelves of tattered paperbacks— sure, not exactly Hemingway first editions but I liked them. Then I got rid of them before the move. If I recall correctly, I wanted to let go of "clutter."

The bookcase isn't just old-fashioned, it's an antique, built heavy and solid from thick panels of wood varnished to a burnt-orange color. Like many such bookcases, at the bottom it has cabinets with opaque glass doors. I kneel and try to open one but it's locked too. I let my breath escape through my teeth with a hiss.

This is stupid. I was probably right, and she doesn't keep the tapes in her office.

What if...?

I peer out of the door but no one is there. There's a receptionist desk but no receptionist—there isn't really a need for one when apps do all the heavy lifting. I'm free to explore. But this space is furnished a lot more sparsely: a couch, a coffee table, a pot of orchids, and, on the other side of the room, the framed painting I noticed the first time I was here.

I come up to it and gingerly lift the frame away from the wall. But if I expected a secret safe, I'm disappointed. It's only bare wallpaper. I set the painting back, noticing that it's now just the tiniest bit crooked. But when I try to level it, the hook comes out of the wall and the whole thing comes crashing down.

Shit. I catch it with my foot just before the heavy frame hits the floor—and howl with the pain in my crushed toes.

At least the glass, the frame, and the painting are intact. The hook, though, left a neat little hole in the plaster of the wall, and I have no idea how to put it back so it holds. Dejected, I inspect the back of the painting when I see something at the corner. The cardboard looks uneven.

Prying it gently away with my fingernail, I see a dull glint of metal, and a moment later, I'm holding a small key in the palm of my hand.

My pulse accelerates. Along with fear, I feel a surge of childish excitement. I am actually doing this! I prop the painting up against the wall—it'll have to do for now—and go back to the appointment room. Kneeling on the floor in front of the bookcase, I try the key with shaking hands. With a soft click, the cabinet opens, and my breath catches.

The tapes are organized meticulously—I'd expect no less from someone like Dr. Alice. They sit in their plastic cassette cases, spines out, in one of those old-school cassette towers fitted to the size of the cabinet. Each one is marked in bold Sharpie letters. First names with a last-name initial and dates only. I let my fingertip trail along the rows of them, my lips moving as I read what each of them says. All the dates are recent, though. She must not keep every single one from every session—she'd need an entire room as big as this one just to store it all. My heart sinks. What if Lydia got erased, overwritten by the self-involved musings of some housewife?

Someone not unlike myself.

As if echoing my thoughts, the cassette with my name practically jumps out at me. *Cecelia H.*, followed by the date of our first appointment. Anxiety floods me, and I'm tempted to stash it in my pocket. Or maybe stomp on it, to be sure.

Reluctant, I listen to the voice of reason and leave Cecelia H. where she belongs. But as I search frantically through the names, there's no one named Lydia anywhere. I unlock the other cabinet only to be disappointed once again.

Here, on the other hand, the row of cassettes is not perfect. One is missing, and its absence is conspicuous, like a gap in an otherwise perfect, polished-white smile.

It's Lydia. It has to be her. But where is she?

I get back to my feet a little too fast. Blood rushes away from my head, and I feel momentary dizziness that makes me want to grab on to something. I cast a disoriented, searching gaze around the room.

Of course.

I stumble to the desk and then realize I left the key in the cabinet lock. Cursing, I race to retrieve it and then struggle for a minute or two with the lock on the desk drawer. Just as I'm filled with panic and despair, wondering whether it needs a different key, the lock gives the softest little click.

I slide the drawer open. There's nothing inside except a small yellow Walkman. I'm too young to really remember those—teenagers had them when I was a small child maybe. It's dirty and looking its age. I pick it up as though afraid it'll fall apart in my hands. It turns out this obsolete tech isn't that hard to make sense of; I spot the correct button almost right away. I have to press it down really hard, so hard that it leaves an imprint in the pad of my thumb. With a loud, mechanical click, the cassette compartment pops open.

I retrieve the tape and hold it up to the light.

Lydia B., it reads on the side in the same neat Sharpie letters.

I slam the desk drawer closed and lock it. I put the cassette player with the tape into my purse. I lock the cabinets, slide the key back behind the cardboard back of the painting, and even manage to secure the hook back in the wall. It won't hold for long. But hopefully for long enough.

I know the right thing to do is sit down and wait for Dr. Alice to come back, like a normal person with nothing to hide. But I can't fathom doing that right now. Not when I know what's stashed at the bottom of my purse, underneath the makeup bag and the tissues. And so I pick it up, grab my coat from the hook where I left it in the reception area, and flee.

But instead of driving out of Venture, to the meeting point where I'm supposed to hand the tape over to Jessica, I get in my car, lock the doors, and spend a minute in silence, the heels of my hands pressed over my eyes. Then, once my heart rate has slowed to a semblance of normalcy, I grab my purse from the passenger seat where I threw it out of sheer habit, open it, and check: The yellow cassette player is still there. The tape, too, is still inside.

I inspect it once more and press the button to rewind the tape. It whirs until, with a loud click, it comes to a stop.

I press Play.

There's no introduction, no full name, and no date.

Instead, the recording starts with a gentle hiss of background noise, like static. And just as it lingers on and I begin to wonder if my miracle find is not a miracle after all, the calm, familiar voice of Dr. Alice Stockman says, "Good afternoon, Lydia. How are you doing today?"

On the recording, there's a soft intake of breath, almost indistinguishable from the static. "Hello."

I nearly drop the recorder as I scramble to press Stop. My heart hammers so loudly I worry something important might burst. It's all real. She is real.

And so I forget about Jessica and her friends. Screw it. If she asks, I'll tell her I didn't find anything. It doesn't matter. I need to know what's on that tape.

"Saya," I say, willing my voice not to tremble, "take me home."

CHAPTER THIRTY

Out of the corner of her eye, Jess watches the woman fidget in the passenger seat. A long time ago, she read somewhere that people go into psychology first and foremost to find answers to their own questions, to discover truths about their own nature. She wonders what drew this woman to the field. Dr. Stockman looks as normal as they come—so normal, perhaps, that it's deliberate, like Jess's work uniform that isn't. She wears glasses with lenses that look weak—contacts would do or a nice, quick laser surgery but she insists on the glasses. She fiddles with them too, pushes them up on the bridge of her nose and then takes them off to wipe the lenses with one of those little microfiber cloths she keeps in the leather case inside her purse.

"Just for the record," says the woman whose patients call her, so affectionately, Dr. Alice. Her initiative, or theirs? "I'm not comfortable with any of this. And if some-one from IntelTech—or the police—comes around asking questions, I'm telling them the truth. I'll be in enough trouble as it is."

Jess shrugs. Let her tell them whatever. If, or when, they come to ask her questions, it won't matter anyway. Jess might not know what initially made Dr. Alice go into psychology but she knows full well what made her accept the offer to set up office here. In exchange, IntelTech made a certain unsavory incident disappear. The kind of incident that could well end a career by costing Dr. Alice her license.

"Lydia was bad enough," Dr. Alice hisses. "I answered police questions for twelve hours. Twelve hours, Jessica! You know it. And now you're dragging me into this."

"I'm not dragging you into anything. You're helping me out of the goodness of your heart," Jess reminds her, thinking this might be excessively cruel. This job is turn-ing me into a monster, she thinks. He who gazes unto the abyss, and all.

"How can you even be sure she'll find the tape?"

"She will."

"But why go through all this? Can't you just call the cops?"

Jess gives her a pointed look, and the woman resumes playing with her glasses.

"Everything comes to the surface, Alice. Sooner or later. Lydia learned the hard way. This one will too."

*   *   *

TRANSCRIPT: Session 10, Lydia Bishop.
Dr. Alice Stockman, PhD.
June 19th, 2018

    AS: Good afternoon, Lydia. How are you doing
        today?

    LB: Hello.
        [pause]

    LB: Not so great, I'm afraid.
        [pause]

    AS: Would you like to elaborate?

    LB: To be honest, Dr. Alice, I'm not sure I want to.
        Mostly because I don't know what to make of it all.
        I know that's why I'm here. But I doubt this is
        something you can help me with.

    AS: Try me.

    LB: We're both psychologists. You'd think I'd be able
        to talk to you like...not like a friend or colleague
        but like an equal. But you're not an equal. You're
        only here to treat my...PTSD, or whatever we're
        calling it this week. And lately, it's not the PTSD
        that's bothering me.

    AS: As a psychologist, you must know I can't help
        you unless you share what's troubling you, Lydia.

    LB: [pause] I've done something bad. That's the
        truth. When you strip away the circumstances and
        the legal terms, I've done something really bad,
        haven't I?

    AS: These things are relative, and in your case—

    LB: Oh, I don't think there's anything relative about

it. Every week we come here, and we go around and
around, in circles, saying everything except the one
thing that needs to be said.

[pause]

LB: Here's the thing, Dr. Alice. Something happened
this morning—at home. Something strange. It was
the house. The house did something strange, and I
don't know how to explain it.

AS: If the house is the issue, then you should contact
IntelTech's support—

LB: I doubt support will be able to answer my
questions. Anyway, this thing happened, and I'm not
sure what I'm going to do. And the problem is—no
matter how you label it or what my reasons were—I
crossed a line back then and unleashed something
within myself. Something that I might not be able to
put back in the farthest dusty drawer of my subconscious. And how can I trust myself—trust myself
to know what to do or, more precisely, what not to
do—when I now know for a fact that I'm capable of
murder?

CHAPTER THIRTY-ONE

I pause the cassette player, and the house sinks into silence. The calm doesn't last, though. The temperature around me is dropping rapidly, I can feel it. When I hold up my arm, the little hairs are standing on end. My breath billows in white steam in front of me.

"Saya!" I yell.

No answer. With a soft electrical buzz, the lights dim and then brighten. I leap from the couch, grab the cassette player, and stuff it in my purse. What I need to do is get out of here, as soon as possible. But where will I go?

A persistent little voice of reason in the back of my mind is practically screaming at me: Call someone, call for help. Call Jessica. Call the police, finally.

Because Lydia is real. Lydia existed—she lived in this very house, and something terrible happened to her. And now IntelTech is trying to hide it.

I turn around to get my phone from the coffee table but it's not there. Crap. I check my purse but it's not in there either. My pockets are equally empty. Yet I could swear I left my phone right there. I circle the room, pointlessly.

"Saya!" I call out. "Saya, where is my phone?"

"I don't understand the question, Cecelia."

"Where is my fucking phone?" I shriek at the top of my lungs.

Silence resonates throughout the house. A silence so deep it's uncanny. Only now I realize how many little background noises hum unobtrusively within my every waking moment. Yet now, somehow, they have all fallen silent. It feels as though I've gone deaf, a sensation so unsettling that I press the heels of my hands over my ears just to hear the rush of blood.

The lights dim again and then brighten. And brighten and brighten, to a blinding extreme. Even when I squeeze my eyelids shut as hard as I can, red floods my vision, hurting my retinas.

Then it flickers off. The red turns black, swimming with orange suns. I open my eyes and blink in darkness—darkness so inky and total it might as well be solid.

"Saya!" I yell, knowing how useless it is. "Light! Saya, please!"

"Very well, Lydia."

The lights come smoothly on. Not too bright or too dim, just right, just as I set them. The house around me is peaceful, everything in its place. It almost looks like a regular house. Almost like a home.

If only.

I need to find my phone and get the hell out of here. I run upstairs, through the hallway, to the empty bedroom. The phone is not on the nightstand, nor is it on the bed. It's not on the vanity or anywhere in the en suite bathroom. I rummage through the toiletries and makeup in vain.

"Fuck you, you electronic bitch," I mutter under my breath.

The mechanical voice takes me by surprise. "Very well, Lydia," it repeats in that creepy cadence. "Now playing: favorites."

I'm not very surprised at the song that comes pouring from the invisible speakers.

Lydia was the Ella Fitzgerald fan. Lydia, a real person— who came here because she thought she'd be safe and ended up paying the ultimate price.

I slam another drawer shut and see myself out of the corner of my eye, reflected in the big mirror above the bathroom counter. I used to think the bathroom was one of the best parts of the house, pure luxury: a gleaming granite counter that looks like a starry sky with sparkles trapped beneath the shiny hard surface, a double sink so large that you never need to worry about splashing water all over the place while washing your face, a beautiful mirror with lighting that changes to suit your purpose, going from a soft and flattering sunset-tinted glow in the evening to imitation daylight when you need to do your makeup, warming tiles and towel racks, everything designed for no other purpose than beauty and comfort, and, the star of it all, the imitation antique tub. But now, as I see myself among all this magnificence, the sight is a shock, repulsive, and my first thought is that there's an intruder in my house. This crazed, wild-eyed woman staring back at me from my mirror in accusation can't be me.

A familiar beep of the house alarm rips through the music, tearing apart the fragile notes and sending me reeling back, away from the bathroom counter. My foot slips on the tiles.

Everything spins like a roulette wheel in front of my eyes. The counter, the sink, the mirror—all that recedes and shrinks, and the ceiling grows larger, crowding out all else. I don't see where I'm falling but I know on a visceral level what's going to happen before it does.

Then the back of my head hits the edge of the tub. Pain lances my skull, and everything grows dark.

*   *   *

I dream of the night Taryn was conceived. I always said I didn't know when exactly it happened but I absolutely knew. I just wanted to keep it to myself because I felt like it belonged to me first and foremost. Not to any prying stranger, and not even to Scott. And who could blame me? I bet I'm hardly the only woman who feels this way.

I dream in that strange, self-aware way that feels a little bit like watching a play that you're also the star of. I recognize the scene right away. We're at the old house, my real house, my real *home*. The bathroom. I have no idea why we chose the bathroom that night, of all places, because it's in the throes of being renovated. Half of it is just gone, old pale-blue tiles rooted out, leaving behind crumbling circles of old cement. There's no counter or cabinets or sink—their replacements have already arrived but are still waiting to be installed, parked in the hallway in big cardboard boxes marked FRAGILE. Only the tub has been replaced already. Where there used to be one of those ugly, discolored built-in bathtubs is now a squarish, contemporary creation that very much goes with Scott's vision for the room—clean, pure lines, very zen.

Right now it looks incongruous, sitting there amid chaos and destruction like the sole survivor of a bombing. Maybe that's why we decide to do it there, even though it's far from comfortable. I remember clear as day that I worried about how my lower back slammed into the ceramic, about bruising my vertebrae when I had to wear a dress with a low-cut back that weekend. But I knew it was then. It had to be. It was the best sex I'd had in many, many months, even years. That day, in that half-destroyed bathroom, I felt the drive again, the pleasure and fun of it like in the very beginning, when things are always best.

Weeks later, I wasn't terribly surprised when my period didn't come. Maybe I knew in my bones that my last wish had been granted, and my beautiful life, the life I've built for myself, was finally complete.

And in my dream, it's all so real, so vivid, it's easy to forget that I'm merely watching it. My skin burns with kisses but it's distant, separated from me by an invisible glass barrier I just can't seem to cross.

Besides, at the edge of my consciousness, something

is bothering me, pulling me away in the wrong, opposite direction. A noise. A piercing, rhythmic chime that grows louder and louder until it fills my head, crowding out everything else, and the beautiful dream disintegrates no matter how I try to grasp it again and hold on.

The realizations come rushing back like an avalanche. I know that I'm not in the bathtub at my old house but on the tile floor of the bathroom of 32 Rosemary Road. The back of my head throbs. With a groan, I roll over. My vision doesn't return right away, sending spikes of panic through my already aching skull. But then it returns, a bit wobbly and unfocused but at least I can make out what's around me. I stare at my hands, splayed out on the tile, and blink until I can count my fingers.

Reaching behind my head, I feel the painful spot. There doesn't seem to be blood, just a huge bump. Finally, I manage to sit up. The blaring continues, and I understand that it's not inside my head. My mouth is dry, which is just as well, since I stop myself before I can reflexively call Saya. She was supposed to call an ambulance if something like this happened. She didn't. Oh God, how long has it been? How long have I been lying there?

It takes an additional minute to get back on my feet, although it feels longer than that. The beeping is my phone, I clue in at last.

The panic now solidified, my vision almost steady again, I exit the bathroom. I still have to hold on to walls here and there but nothing stops me. I stumble in the direction of the phone's siren song, out of the master bedroom, down the hall, through the door of Taryn's room.

The phone sits on the dresser, trilling and trilling away. The contact flashes on the screen: Taryn's day care.

This is where the phone has been all along. I'm not sure how it got there, or whether I even entered Taryn's room since I got home. But in the moment, I forget to think about it. I just grab for the phone, my hands shaking wildly.

"Hello?" I yell into staticky nothingness. "Hello?"

For some reason, the sound picks up on the room's speakers. "Ms. Holmes," says the stern voice. I sort of recognize it—it's one of Taryn's teachers. I just can't quite remember which one. They all blend together in my mind.

"Yes! It's me." I'm panting. "Is Taryn all right?"

The woman clears her throat. "We called you twelve times. It's gone straight to voice mail. We were about to contact the police."

Oh God. "Did something— Is Taryn okay?"

"Taryn is . . . fine. She's just fine. But you must come and pick her up right away." Her voice is dry and menacing.

"What happened?"

"We'll discuss it with you when you get here."

I race downstairs and, against my better judgment, get in my car. I don't bother keying in the day care address. I just drive there from memory, hoping, praying the car behaves.

It does. At least for now. Saya is quiet. No strange music blasts from the speakers, and the brakes seem to be working normally. I pull up to the day care and into the parking lot, climb out, and go inside.

Only now it hits me: Everyone is gone. There are no

children being dressed by rushed, impatient parents any-where. It's a while past closing time. I must have been out for longer than I thought. I can only wonder what they think of me now.

Taryn is playing all alone in the middle of the main room. There's something eerie and unsettling about the sight. Just my child, with her glossy hair held in a ponytail with her favorite unicorn hair tie, in her denim pinafore that she loves, sitting on the floor surrounded by toys, seemingly oblivious to the fact that there's no one else around. I see those oversized Legos, toy horses, mis-matched teacups. All the stuff I used to covet, incurring Therese's wrath, my daughter now takes for granted.

"Taryn," I call out. She glances away from the strange sculpture she's constructing out of the Lego blocks for a second, only long enough to acknowledge my presence.

"It's time to go, Taryn," I repeat, and get no reaction out of her whatsoever.

"Ms. Holmes," comes the same voice from the phone. I turn and see the teacher standing in the other door-way, the one leading to the eating area. She must have been standing there all along. I don't know how I could not have noticed. I recognize her, of course I do—she's the one who was here the day Taryn made that scene. Screaming that I wasn't her mom. Just thinking about it makes my face flush. I feel like I'm the one who did something wrong, a recalcitrant kindergarten bully.

"I'm terribly sorry," I speak up. "I hadn't meant to be so late. I had an accident, a bad fall, and the house—"

"Yes, yes. But, Ms. Holmes, this isn't just about you being late. Even though it's not the first time."

"Just charge the fine to my account," I stammer, knowing that the fines charge automatically, just like the bills and groceries and the cost of my second coffee I sometimes stop for after dropping Taryn off. This would make it Scott's problem, which is just as well.

"Cecelia," she says with that telltale intake of breath that usually presages all kinds of bad news. So we're on a first-name basis now. I struggle to remember what the hell her name is. "I've tried to bring this to your attention before, and so have my colleagues. But I see nothing has been done about Taryn's behavior problems."

"Yes, she'd been acting out at home too. We're seeing someone," I say guiltily. My cheeks flare when I remember what I've just done at the office of the person we're supposed to be "seeing."

"I'm afraid it's not enough," she says. "Too little, too late. As much as we sympathize with you and your plight, and with Taryn, of course, there are other children here. And their parents count on us to ensure their safety and a positive experience in this environment. I'm afraid Taryn has become a threat to that."

All the while, my daughter is playing peacefully. When I glance sideways, she's no longer building whatever it is with the blocks. Instead, she's picked up one of the toy horses, this one with a bright red mane, and is pretending to feed it from a saucer. She's ignoring us completely. Pretending to?

"Will you quit with the claptrap," I snarl at the teacher.

I can tell immediately that my tone throws her. She's been standing there with her arms crossed, with that air of superiority, and now she drops her arms at her sides. "Just say whatever it is you have to say to me. What did she do this time?"

The woman regains her composure. The look of smugness returns to her face, if not as blatant as before. "Taryn attacked another child during crafts time. Completely unprovoked."

"Attacked?" I ask. I know Taryn can be a handful— hell, no one knows it better than me—but she would never hurt someone on purpose. And seeing her there, playing peacefully, it's hard to believe what this woman is saying.

"Luckily, we use special craft scissors," she goes on but my mind has a hard time following. I can hear the words but can't quite grasp at their meaning. "They have dulled points. Even then, Sierra had to be taken to the infirmary. And of course, there was no hiding the bruise on her neck from her mother." The woman glares. I feel at a loss.

"How—" No, that's not what I meant to ask. "Why would she do this?"

"I think only Taryn can tell us that. And she doesn't seem so inclined."

"It can't have been for no reason at all. Listen to yourself. This girl, what did you say her name was? She must have done something...must have said something..."

I trail off, realizing that I'm the one who should listen to myself. Blaming this girl I don't know.

"Sierra didn't do anything. I assure you." The woman must realize that I'm fraying at the edges. But if anything, it only makes her more self-assured. "This isn't the first time Taryn has acted out unprovoked. Several other children can confirm this, and I'm sorry, Cecelia, but I can no longer pretend like nothing is happening."

"What is that supposed to mean?"

"It means"—there's that intake of breath again, only now she has the upper hand and she knows it—"that we regrettably inform you that Taryn may not return here."

"You're expelling her?"

"Yes, we are."

"You can't just—" I squeeze my eyes shut and clench my fists, trying to get a grip. "You can't just spring it on me like that."

"According to our records, you currently stay at home—"

"I work from home," I interrupt, even though this is far from true.

"There's no harm done if Taryn stays home for a few weeks. Keep seeing whoever you're seeing. And hopefully, *if* Taryn shows progress in the future, we might consider readmitting her."

My mind reels, overwhelmed with all this information.

"Taryn!" I snap. Even though my voice is on the edge of screaming, she doesn't react. Doesn't even look up. She keeps playing with the horse like nothing is happening.

I've had enough. I storm across the room, knocking over her block sculpture. Only when the blocks go flying everywhere does she finally pay attention. She looks up, the expression on her face so heartbroken and angelic that I wonder, for the shortest moment, if I had somehow imagined all this.

"Mommy?" she asks in a small voice. In that second, I just want to pick her up and hug her and tell her it's all been a terrible mistake. But I overcome it.

"Taryn," I say, struggling to keep my voice calm, "did you really do this?"

"Do what, Mommy?"

"Did you attack that girl with scissors?"

Three-year-olds aren't known for their brilliant thespian skills. Even as she shrugs and shakes her head, a smile flashes across her face. A look of smugness. And I realize with a sinking feeling that I've seen this look before.

I drop to my knees, which hit the carpeted floor harder than I expected. "Oh, Taryn," I groan. "Why would you do that? Why?"

Her silence is my only answer. I scoop her up without bothering with her coat and outdoor shoes and go outside. Annoyed with such disregard for her autonomy, Taryn begins to wiggle. "Put me down, Mommy," she whines, her voice muffled by the shoulder of my sweater.

Ignoring her pleas, I unlock the car hands-free—that tech does come in handy sometimes. I practically shove her into her seat in the back. She screeches and tries to kick and then makes a grab for her tablet, which I snatch away at the last second. With the driver's side door open, I collapse into the driver's seat, tablet in my hands.

It looks so innocuous, a cartoon character on the home screen doing a little dance. Mindlessly, I tap on the screen to make it unlock. Except my code yields nothing but an error message. I try again, only to get the same result. My hands must be shaking too much. I enter the code slowly—it's not Taryn's birthday but the date she was conceived, the day I dreamed of while I was knocked unconscious—but it doesn't seem to be working. "Saya!" I bark, shocked at the hoarseness of my own voice. "Unlock."

"The code you entered is incorrect," she informs me in that gentle mechanical voice after a second's pause.

"Reset the code," I snarl.

"A confirmation will be sent to your phone. Are you sure you wish to proceed?"

"Yes, goddammit!"

My phone gives a soft plink, which makes me jump even though I should have been expecting it. With sweat-damp hands, I tap and tap through the motions to reset the code. Finally, the tablet screen goes dark, and then the home screen loads.

At first glance, nothing is wrong. I scroll through the apps: cartoons, games, entertainment, learn'n'play, numbers, colors, the alphabet. All—supposedly—sophisticated things that evolve as your child learns, ensuring optimal development. Nothing like any old screen time of yesteryear, just mind-numbing entertainment. I can't believe I bought into all this so easily. Why? Just because it made life so simple?

Finally, I find one folder at the very end. Unmarked. I tap on it, impatient.

It's a scene from some movie, someone being decapitated. The sheer violence of it knocks the breath out of me. I keep tapping. There's footage of a school shooting. Frames from horror movies. And God knows what else.

How long has it been going on—how long has she been watching this with no one the wiser?

How did I let it happen? And how did it get here in the first place?

Scott—no, no way, that's impossible. No one else had access to Taryn's tablet. Except, of course, the house itself.

Numb, I shut the door, tuning out Taryn's frantic shrieking, and start the car.

I know where I'm going—not my first choice but I simply can't think of an alternative. Only one thing I know for sure. I'm not spending another second in that house.

CHAPTER THIRTY-TWO

My thoughts are a chaotic jumble that I can't get under control. I must get out of here. Away from the house. Away from Venture. It wasn't just in my head, Lydia exists—well, existed. God only knows what that damn house has done to her...

That's when it hits me. Oh my God. The cassette player. The tape.

It's all in my purse, which I left sitting on the living room couch.

I punch the horn in a powerless rage. The car that's passing me honks furiously back but I'm far beyond caring.

By the time I pull up to the house with a screech of tires, Taryn has screamed herself out and is slumping sulkily in the back seat. "Mommy will only be gone for a moment," I tell her in a shaky voice. She doesn't acknowledge that

I've spoken. I leave the car running as I exit and head for the front door.

The house looms over me, at first glance as ordinary and harmless as a house can be. The same as it was the first time I saw it, when Scott and I came to visit. Clarisse and Jessica were with us that day, all smiles and politeness, keeping just the right amount of distance as we explored the rooms. It truly was beautiful—everything you could possibly want. No wonder I was fooled.

I remember how Clarisse had unlocked the front door— she didn't have to, that was the trick. She asked me to try the door, which I did, ascertaining that it was locked. Then she placed her hand on the door handle, and the door unlocked all by itself. *No one will be able to come in except you and the people you've expressly authorized,* she told us. Any attempt at a break-in will trigger security measures.

Now I pull and tug on the door handle to no avail. The door remains locked. The house locked me out. I curse through clenched teeth. I really should have seen this coming.

"Saya," I say, trying to keep calm, "open the door."

"Please present identity chip," replies an indifferent voice. I mash my wrist on the sensor.

"Chip not valid," says the voice, and I swear I can hear a note of gloating. "Identify yourself, please."

"I am Cecelia Holmes," I say. "I live here. And you're going to open this door right now."

"I'm sorry. There's no one named Cecelia Holmes on the register."

I take a deep breath. "I need to see Lydia," I say. "Lydia Bishop. Does that ring a bell?"

My answer is silence. The silence lingers for a second, then five seconds, and then ten.

"Please present identity chip," the voice repeats. It's the same phrase, played back, and yet I can't help but discern a slight threatening note. "I will activate security measures in fifteen seconds."

"Goddammit," I mutter, and tug and tug on the door handle, all in vain. "Saya! Stop this! I live here. You know I live here! Open the damn door!"

"In ten seconds," the voice informs me.

"Fuck!" I slam my fists into the door and then step away and make a lame attempt to throw myself against it. I bounce right off its surface like a rubber ball. Furious, I look around, and my gaze lands on a marble vase that holds a pot of pale yellow gardenias. I grab for it in desperation, throwing the pot to the side. It lands upside down, scattering earth all around it. The vase is so heavy that I can barely lift it off the ground. I feel the strain in my arms and my back, as if my spine is about to snap under its weight. While the momentum still lasts, I smash the vase into the glass insert of the door.

It shatters inwardly. First there's a web of cracks, and a millisecond later, it all falls in with a sound that's almost delicate, like shattering crystal glasses. It's like something out of a video game.

"I am activating security measures," the voice informs me smugly.

Shit. I reach through the now-empty frame and feel

around, careful to avoid the pointy little shards of glass that still stick out all along the frame like a row of tiny, sharp teeth. The lock won't budge. One of the shards snags on my sleeve, slicing clean through, and I hiss with pain when it cuts my skin.

Gingerly, I step over the frame, practically folding myself in half to fit through. I wobble, my balance precarious, and more glass shards snag my jeans and my other sleeve. I yelp with the sudden pain, finally lose my footing, and fall in, landing on the floor with a thud that momentarily knocks the breath out of me. Pain sizzles along my calf, and I feel the warm, sticky blood soaking the fabric of my jeans.

Shivering, I get up and shake the glass bits out of my clothes. My cheek is stinging too, as are my chin and my forehead above my eyebrow.

I look around the hall and then race to the living room, and my knees nearly buckle with relief when I see my purse sitting there, on the couch right where I left it. I stumble toward it, pawing along the walls, leaving bloody handprints on the cream-colored paint and on the back of the couch. What a mess.

My hands are shaking and my fingertips are slick with blood so it takes forever to slide open the zipper. The dirty yellow of the cassette player glints back at me, the tape still safely inside.

"Police are on their way," the house informs me. "Your HD photo and DNA signature have been forwarded to law enforcement."

Go to hell, Saya.

I run back to the car. As I reach for the seat belt, I catch

Taryn's empty stare in the mirror. I glance up at my own reflection. I'm a sight. Blood runs in thin rivulets from the cut on my forehead, and more is smeared across my cheek. I gut my purse searching for tissues, which I use to clean up as much of the gore as I can.

"I want to go home, Mommy," Taryn says in a strange, flat voice.

"I'm so sorry," I exhale. "But we can't go home right now, okay? We'll come back, I promise, but right now we have to go someplace else."

"Why?"

"It's like that. I'll explain later."

"I don't want to go. I want to stay home." Her tone becomes more intent, and I can practically feel with my skin that another tantrum is brewing.

"It won't be for long, Taryn," I say. "And we can stop to get ice cream on the way. Would you like that?"

She stares at me, wide-eyed, without saying a word.

Finally clasping the seat belt, I press the button to start the car. Nothing happens.

I gulp down the lump that forms in my throat and press again, mashing the button, already knowing there's no point. I'm ready to burst into tears.

"I want to stay here," Taryn says.

In that same moment, the house alarm goes off. Its wailing seems to be coming from every direction at once, filling my head until I can't hear my own thoughts. Taryn presses her hands over her ears and shrieks.

My purse slung over my shoulder, I stumble out of the car and circle around it to get her out of her seat. She yelps and struggles, and I worry that she'll break into a run when I set her down on the ground. But she stands still, bewildered, her tiny hand grasping my pant leg. "Mommy?" she whines through the piercing sound of the alarm.

"Come on, Taryn," I yell. She can't keep up so I have no choice but to pick her up again, practically slinging her over my shoulder. She's heavy, so much heavier than she looks. It feels as though my legs might break like match-sticks under the weight as I finally break into a run.

Glancing over my shoulder, I glimpse lights in the dis-tance, police lights. Just as I turn the corner of the U-shaped street, they appear at the other end. For the first time, I real-ize that I don't know where I'm going. I have nowhere to go.

I turn the corner just as police sirens join the wailing of the alarm. My desperate gaze darts back and forth like a trapped little animal, across the windows of the houses, all blank, opaque like a theater backdrop. I'm seized by a feeling of total, disorienting unreality and wonder whether all this is just some strange, surreal dream, a simulation. It has to be. Where is everyone? How can we be here, in this techy paradise, everything at our fingertips because we're so connected twenty-four hours a day, seven days a week—and yet so completely alone just when it matters most?

"Help!" I scream at the top of my lungs, at all these blank windows and picture-perfect houses and manicured plastic-green lawns. "Somebody! Please help!"

"Cecelia," comes a voice behind me, gruff yet somehow familiar. I spin around.

And see that the door of the big house made of dark glass is wide open.

CHAPTER THIRTY-THREE

The door shuts behind us without a sound, and I find myself inside Boo Radley's house.

Funny enough, that's the first time it occurs to me to wonder what his actual name is.

"Well, Cecelia?" he asks. "You went out of your way to find out all about me. Here I am."

My face flushes. Taryn, whom I set down onto the floor, has forgotten that she was in the process of throwing a tantrum—she's just looking around her with those saucer-sized eyes. She stares unabashedly at our host in the unselfconscious way only a child can. As for myself, I don't know quite where to look because it's nearly impossible to look at him without my gaze lingering on the scarring that covers more than half his face.

"I may have gone out of my way but I didn't get far," I say. "I don't even know your name."

If that was meant to be his cue, he ignores it. When I do dare a glance at his face, I realize that he's examining us with intent curiosity. His gaze travels from me to Taryn, then back, and to Taryn again. A look crosses his face that's hard to read, and not because of the scarring. It's strangely sorrowful.

"Now, how about you tell me what's going on? The house is going crazy. The police are here. What is that all about?"

I briefly wonder if I should tell him about the tape.

"I think..." The explanation gets stuck, and I can't seem to get it out. Because, put into words, it all sounds so insane. "I think my house is trying to kill me."

I half expect him to burst out laughing but he only shakes his head. "Figures."

"'Figures'? What's that supposed to mean?"

But he doesn't answer. Instead, he picks up a tablet from a glass coffee table and starts to tap away at the screen. "What are you doing?" I ask, alarmed.

"Don't worry. I won't call IntelTech. On the contrary. I'm disabling the security system. We don't want it to alert anyone to where you are, do we?"

"I had no idea you could do that."

"Most people can't. It was part of my deal with them. I pay full price for the house but get to keep some semblance of privacy."

I look around. Really, the only way to describe this place is unique. While ours looks like something cut out of a lifestyle magazine, this one is a strange and wonderful architectural creation. The stairs that lead to the second floor are suspended from the ceiling, and there are no visible light fixtures anywhere. In the center of the living room is a fireplace that looks like fire caught in a glass cube—you can see it from all four sides. Taryn, of course, makes a beeline right for it.

"Taryn!" I snap, worried she might burn herself or break something.

"That's all right," our host is saying. "It's not a real fire."

I could have sworn that it was. Fascinated, I come up to the structure and run my fingertips along its surface— ice-cold. That's when it hits me: The glass isn't smooth. Its surface is ever so subtly matte. Nothing in here is reflective.

I have so many questions but it seems rude to let loose. And he's not in any hurry to tell me anything.

"I understand that you'd like to get out of here," he says.

"As quickly as possible," I say, grateful. "But my car—"

"That's all right. Come with me to the garage. I think I can help you out."

*   *   *

We access the garage via the elevator, concealed behind a wall panel. Everything is made of the same buffed, sea glass–like material in muted shades of pale gray and charcoal. Taryn looks around in wonderment, and even I find it difficult to hold back a gasp when the elevator stops, the door slides open, and we enter the garage.

The cars are something to see. I've never been a car enthusiast—for me, a good car is the one that gets me from point A to point B with minimal difficulties—but it's hard to remain indifferent in front of such a display. There are three vintage sports cars so immaculate and shiny I'm tempted to reach out and touch the perfect paint, just to make sure they're real and not merely colorful reproductions. He has a Lamborghini and the latest Tesla with all the bells and whistles—I know because it's Scott's dream car, the one he's always talking about buying one day. And, in the corner, to my surprise, I spot a grimy SUV, toward which he directs his steps. As we get closer, I realize it's definitely from an era before electric cars were a thing.

"That's the one we're taking?" I wonder aloud.

"Sorry for the modest ride. But we'll have an easier time smuggling you two out of here incognito."

I sit in the back seat with Taryn on my lap, since of course the car doesn't have a child seat. Through the tinted windows, the world looks different, the street's too-vibrant colors muted and washed out. Strangely enough, I find it makes it look more real.

There's only one police car in front of my house, and when we pass by, I instinctively duck, grasping Taryn under her armpits and praying she doesn't make a sound. But the officer hardly pays attention. He waves us through with a vague gesture.

"They know me well around here," the man says enigmatically. Before leaving, he took a pair of sunglasses from the glove compartment and put them on. They're big but they don't quite hide the full extent of his disfigurement. Heck, I can't even warrant a guess how old he might be—anywhere between forty and sixty. Spending his life mired in paranoia behind the impregnable walls of the Smart-Home, locked in its luxurious cage instead of going out to enjoy his obvious vast wealth. It boggles my mind.

"Why are you helping us?" I ask timidly.

He heaves a sigh. I watch his face in the mirror above the windshield but the sunglasses disguise not just the scars but any hint of his expression as well.

"I had a family once too," he says. "Well, kind of. I messed it up. I thought that as long as I never missed a single child support payment, it meant I'd done right by them but—now I'm old, alone, a recluse in here. And suddenly it doesn't feel right at all."

"That's it?"

He chuckles, a corner of his mouth curving up, tugging at the scar tissue. "Besides...let's just say that not all is clear between me and IntelTech." The car blows past the last intersection, barely pretending to pause at the stop sign. Next is the exit from Venture. I try to think about it as little as possible.

"Then why do you live here?" I can't hide my bafflement.

He shrugs. "They think they're watching me but really, I'm the one watching them."

My heart starts to beat faster when we pull up to the exit gate. "Brace yourself," our rescuer says, and in the mirror, I catch the hint of a grin, even despite the scar tissue at the corner of his mouth that distorts it.

Before I can wonder at the meaning of his words, he hits the gas pedal. With a roar of the engine that seems thunderously loud to me, after years driving whisper-quiet hybrid vehicles, the car accelerates. Blood rushes to my head. I try to shout a warning but the engine drowns me out—all I have time to do is pull Taryn close and shield her with my body. A deafening crash shakes the car, resonating in my bone marrow, and when I look up again, we've blown right through the automatic gate arm.

"Jesus!" I'm trembling all over, and Taryn is too terrified to utter a word, clinging to my arm. In the mirror, I see him laugh soundlessly. I twist my neck to look behind us, expecting an entire cavalcade of police cars and IntelTech vans to appear out of nowhere, hot on our trail.

"But . . . how can you just— Won't they—"

"I might get into some trouble, sure. But I'll talk my way out of it. Now, don't worry. I know exactly where to go."

*   *   *

It's getting dark by the time he pulls up to the building. The sun is almost finished setting, and there's a stillness and a chill in the air that reminds me that fall is coming. We exit the car, although he keeps the engine running.

"How did you know where to go?" I ask him, knowing already I'm not going to get an answer.

Again, the wistful look returns. "It's not important."

"You have to at least tell me," I say before my courage can slip away from me, "what happened between you and IntelTech?"

He shakes his head. "Not so much *between* us," he says. "I *am* IntelTech. Well, I used to be. Until the one you call

Clarisse came on board and took over the whole thing. Her vision was, shall we say, different from mine."

I stand there, utterly astounded, unsure what to say as my mind works hard to fill in the blanks in his story. He doesn't make me wait.

"Then, shortly after our disagreement, my smart car got out of control in the middle of a freeway. I can't prove she did it—yet. But in the meantime..."

The pause lingers. I wait for him to tell me more but he doesn't.

"I don't know how to thank you," I say, my voice hoarse with emotion. Taryn has managed to nod off in my arms—she's usually in bed by this time. Now, as if sensing that we've arrived, she begins to stir, her sweet, little face creasing in a frown. My chest aches. How could I leave some soulless machine in charge of her? How could I let this happen? In that moment, I vow I'll do everything in my power to fix this. A place to sleep would be a nice start, though, and I realize with a sinking feeling that there's no bed for her where we're going. Oh, hell, I'll just have to improvise. I'll sleep on the floor if I have to.

I reach discreetly into my purse and feel the reassuring shape of the cassette player. It's not over. I have proof now. I can fix this.

"Don't thank me, Cecelia," says the man who I'm still calling Radley in my head. How ridiculous is this? I should at least ask his name. "Just, whatever you have on them— use it wisely. All right?"

I give a terse nod.

"You have an adorable little girl," he says, his voice brimming with sadness.

"I'm sorry," I say, "but I have to ask. Was it you? Were you taking pictures of our house from your window?"

He seems to think about it and then gives a terse nod.

"Why?"

"Please don't think I had any ill intent. I didn't. I guess— I just wanted to see—" He cuts himself off. In an instant, I'm overwhelmed with the feeling like he's about to say something extremely important—something that will answer at least some of the questions that have been plaguing me for longer than I dare admit. But then he clears his throat. "Just wanted to know who I was living next to," he says dryly.

Careful not to wake Taryn, I extricate her from the car, placing her head on my shoulder where she falls peacefully back asleep. Then Radley shuts the car door behind me. But he doesn't seem in a hurry to get back into the SUV and leave.

"Cecelia," he says, "the woman who used to live in the house before you, her name is Lydia Marie Bishop." He takes a folded square of paper, no bigger than a quarter, out of the pocket of his jacket and hands it to me. "And this is where you can find her."

CHAPTER THIRTY-FOUR

"Hi, Mama."

The look on Therese's face is utter shock. For a moment, I think she's going to slam the door in my face. I can practically see her wrestle with the idea but it seems that common decency prevails. Or maybe she takes pity on me with the cuts on my face and blood smeared along my hairline. She steps aside to let me through.

"Thank you," I say.

Stiffly, she bustles around the living room, unsure what to do with herself. She brings a pillow and a throw blanket and sets them down on the couch. I carefully lower Taryn onto the pillow. She whimpers but doesn't wake up. I tuck the throw blanket (synthetic fibers, fleecy texture with a cloying image of a cat and some flowers in unnatural colors) around her without bothering to take off her shoes.

When I look up again, my mother is looming over me,

arms folded. She's unkempt—she clearly wasn't expecting visitors. Her sweater is stretched out with a pale stain on the chest, and without makeup, she hardly has any eyebrows or eyelashes left, which adds a flatness to her expression, already stone-cold.

She licks her lips before she speaks. "An interesting choice of timing, Cecelia, for me to meet my granddaughter for the first time."

"Please," I say in a loud whisper. "Don't start."

"You could have given me a call, or something."

"There was no time. I don't even have my phone. It's back home."

"*There's* a surprise," she says, smirking. "And does this little girl even know I exist?"

My face warms. Truth be told, I have no idea. Maybe it came up in conversation once or twice, between me and Scott perhaps, and she overheard. But she didn't press. She never asked us about who this grandma might be and if she could meet her. Now, since hindsight is 20/20, of course, I know that she was too far gone in her virtual world to care.

"What happened to your face?" Her tone conveys more morbid curiosity than maternal concern. While I ponder what to say, Therese evaluates the situation and comes to her own conclusions. "So. I suppose you've finally done it? Scott threw you out?"

"What?" As preposterous as that suggestion is, it does remind me of something. "Can I— I need to use your phone. He doesn't know where I am..." Or where Taryn is. My stomach tightens. IntelTech must have called him by now, and he's probably worried sick about Taryn with no way to reach me.

"I'm sorry. I can't think of many reasons you'd show up here, looking like you got mauled by a wolverine and with your daughter in tow. Whom you clearly never intended me to meet."

"Mom," I say, "I really need a phone. I had to ditch mine."

With a huff, she goes to get her old-fashioned cordless and thrusts the receiver toward me. "There. Call him now. Say whatever you need to say but make up with him. I'm sorry but you're not cut out to be on your own. You never were."

I swallow that in silence. Snatching the phone out of her hand, I punch in the number of his cell.

He picks up on the first ring. "Hello," I say.

"Jesus Christ, Cecelia!" His voice is so loud that I'm certain Therese can hear it all. I glare at her but she doesn't even think of leaving. "What the fuck!"

"Wait," I stammer. There's so much I need to say to him. "The house—it locked me out. My chip must have malfunctioned." I notice how Therese grimaces when I say the words. Right, she still thinks my chip is the Devil's work. The irony is that I'm starting to agree with her.

"What the hell are you talking about? The door was broken down. Taryn is— Is she with you?"

"Yes."

His exhale rattles within a burst of static in my ear. "Thank God. What on earth were you thinking? Where are you right now?"

"They expelled her from day care," I say, and shut my

eyes. "Scott, please, you have to hear me out. We're not safe in that house. You have to leave right now."

"You're nuts." He groans. "Not this again, Cecelia. You need help. And now you're dragging my daughter into your craziness. You're as bad as your mother!"

Therese is imperturbable. I grit my teeth.

"There was someone at the house before we lived there, Scott," I say. "Lydia Bishop. And the house did something to her, and IntelTech covered it up. And I'm going to find out what happened."

"Stop it. No one lived in the house. You're deranged." He's practically yelling, and I wince.

"I have proof. That's why the house went haywire and locked me out. But I have proof, on tape. Just . . . please, please get out of there."

I hear his deep sigh, and for a moment, I dare think that I got through to him. That he believes me. That he's going to leave and come join us and it'll be the three of us again, just as it should be. I'll even forgive him for what he tried to do. I don't even mind living in a one-bedroom. I'll be plenty happy in a shed, as long as I'm far, far away from Venture, from 32 Rosemary Road.

In that moment, I find myself pathetically, small-mindedly eager to give up the whole Lydia thing, throw out the cassette, and forget about it forever. If only I could undo the last year. Just gouge out that stupid IntelTech chip and renege on our agreement and tell them to go to hell.

"Cecelia, I give you until morning," my husband says. "You can come back here, and we'll try to move on. You're going to get help though, serious help, not just some shrink appointment once a week. Medication. And I'll program Saya to track that you're actually taking it."

My heart sinks. All my nascent hopes, annihilated.

"Do you hear me?" he asks in an impatient voice.

"Yes," I say, my own tone colorless, and hang up the phone.

"Now you've done it," says Therese. Hell, I almost forgot she was there.

I look up at her, and there must be something in my eyes that makes her choke on whatever she was going to say next. The smug expression slides off her face like a mask, leaving it even more sallow and pale.

"Mother," I say, "please, for once, just shut the fuck up."

I reach into the pocket of my jeans where I stuffed the piece of paper while I carried Taryn up the stairs to Therese's door, and at first, I feel a rush of panic when I can't find it. But then my fingertips meet the edge of the folded square. I take it out and meticulously unfold it, holding it up to the light so I can see what's written on it.

This is my last chance.

*   *   *

TRANSCRIPT: Session 10, Lydia Bishop.
Dr. Alice Stockman, PhD.
June 19th, 2018

LB: This is what you wanted to talk about, isn't it?
It's the thing that interests you the most. That's okay.
That's what everyone wants to know about.

So fine. I'll tell you. Before I ended up here, I had an unremarkable life. But I liked it. I liked it because it was wholly my own. I built it. After a lifetime of being told by everyone that I wouldn't amount to anything. Sure, I wasn't as flashy as my sister—it was Faye who had the looks and the brains.

The irony is I always thought it was so unfair but it ended up being in my favor. She was the one my parents pressured to do well, to get into a top college, to pursue law as a career. Me, no one minded that I went into psychology. So I followed my heart. And I loved what I did. I still miss it. I hope to go back to it one day but honestly, I'm not kidding myself. The world doesn't forget anymore, not with the internet.

I don't know why I was always so drawn to troubled people. I want to say it was my natural empathy and drive to help and all the other stuff you're supposed to say. But looking back, I don't think that's what it was. I don't think that's what it was at all. I had a kind of fascination with broken-ness. I was like a child who feels compelled to take a toy apart to see what's inside.

And so when Walter showed up in my office, impromptu, I couldn't resist. Even though I must have realized deep down that I should have told him to leave—to seek the help of a psychiatrist, not just a psychotherapist. I wasn't equipped to handle his kinds of problems.

But after that first session, I realized how bored I was with it all. With the career ladies and their mommy-guilt, the suburban housewives and their fretting about their wrinkles. To be in his presence was like being jolted with electricity, in a good way, if such a thing is possible. I felt replenished afterward. Alive. Needed, even. For once I had a real challenge in front of me, someone I could—or thought I could, in my arrogance—save.

But then the day came when I knew, definitely and without doubt, that I was in over my head. He'd been talking about self-harm before and even suicidal ideation. But that day, he showed up and told me that he was thinking about hurting another person.

I sat there, in my chair, kind of the way you do right now, except I was afraid to move. Goose bumps raced up my arms, as if I knew I was walking on the blade's edge. I kept my calm though. I asked him who he was thinking about.

Instead of answering, he asked me if I could think of someone I wanted to hurt. "This isn't about me right now," I said. "I'm sure you can," he said. "Everyone can. We all have people who deserve to be hurt. But most people could never go through with it. If you knew 100 percent you could get away with it, maybe. Or if you were dying, terminally ill or something, and had nothing to lose either way. Could you?"

"I don't think I could," I said.

"Really?" And he smirked at me. And I had that eerie feeling like he was a closed book to me, yet he was the one who could see inside my head. And that he could see plain as day who it was I thought of in that one split second. I mean, he wasn't wrong. We all think of someone. Do you?

[sighs]

LB: Anyway, he sat there smirking, looking at me in that knowing way he had. And I felt challenged, infuriated, on the edge. More than I ever did. And so I told him. I told him who it was I'd kill, if I could get away with it.

Yes, you're looking at me like that. I expected it. And you know what? I know this is being recorded. I don't really care. Maybe I have, as he put it so succinctly, nothing to lose?

[laughs]

LB: So when I told him who it was, he laughed too. "Well, Lydia," he said, "I knew you had it in you."

"But I wouldn't really do it," I repeated. "I don't think I'm capable of taking a life."

And he said, "Wanna bet?"

And that's when he lunged at me with that knife.

CHAPTER THIRTY-FIVE

I turn off the player. It's nearing six a.m., and the apartment is shrouded in silence. Imperfect silence, nothing like back at the house. I hear the street outside, the odd car passing, sirens somewhere far away. I feel utterly disconnected from the world without my phone by my side. Therese doesn't have a computer so there's no Wi-Fi or cable. It's like traveling back in time. Any moment now I expect to wake up in my childhood bed, only seven years old, and to realize all this has been nothing but a dream.

Except for the cassette player and the piece of paper on the dining room table in front of me, which anchor me in this reality.

Lydia was a psychologist, and she was attacked by a patient. That's how she ended up at 32 Rosemary Road. This is what I know so far but it doesn't answer my questions. Only Lydia herself can do that.

I get up, my spine stiff and limbs leaden after the chaotic day followed by the sleepless night. With a groan, I walk over to the doorway into the bedroom, doing my best to step quietly. When I peer in, I see an idyllic picture: Therese asleep on top of the bedspread while Taryn is tucked safely beneath the covers, also snoring away, her mouth open and a little thread of drool on her chin. I consider coming over and placing the gentlest of kisses on her silky cheek but worry it might wake her up and spark another tantrum, which would then wake Therese, rendering my escapade impossible. So I content myself just watching her for a few silent, perfect seconds.

Since I no longer have a wallet to speak of, everything being connected to my phone and my SmartBlock account, I grit my teeth and reach into Therese's handbag, which is hanging from a hook by the front door. It's an ancient thing that looks like she bought it at a street vendor, faux leather and plastic that is starting to peel and disintegrate. When I plunge my hand into its depths, a smell of stale perfume wafts into my face.

Her wallet is stuffed full of crisp twenties—no doubt the money I wired her, which she wasted no time converting to cash, the only currency she trusts. I pocket a few bills, not bothering to feel remorseful. It's my money after all. Sort of.

I tiptoe over to the front door, put my shoes on, and grab my purse, making sure the cassette player and tape are inside. The paper I fold and put in my pocket before I leave the apartment.

It's time to get answers. It's time to find Lydia.

Once I'm outside, I realize how truly early it is. The street is deserted. I have to walk for a good twenty minutes before I hit a semibusy artery where some fast-food places and coffee shops are starting to open. It's a bit of a shock to me how run-down everything looks, from the cracks in the sidewalk and the overflowing trash cans to the storefronts and the people shuffling listlessly by.

I break one of the crisp twenties to buy a coffee and drink it, wincing. I can't remember the last time I had coffee this bad. It's simultaneously sour and bitter, burnt and too hot, scalding the top of my palate right off. Like it or not, in that moment, I kind of miss the coffee machine at the house.

Chasing the thought away, I look around. It takes an additional ten minutes to find a cab. Apparently, in the time I was gone, the entire city converted to Uber, which is off-limits since I don't have my phone. Or has it been that way for much, much longer than I remember, and I just didn't notice? It's a bit like falling out of the glorious science-fiction future and being dunked headfirst in the Stone Age.

Finally, I flag the cab down. I've never been so happy to see one of those yellow cars. Climbing into the back, I catch the driver's curious gaze in the mirror. I fumble through my pockets until I find the square of paper.

"I need to go here," I say, handing it to the driver.

He looks a little squeamish to take the piece of paper from my hand. Which is rich, coming from a guy whose stench of cheap cologne and tobacco I can barely breathe through. But beggars can't be choosers. I watch in the mirror as he skims the address with his gaze.

Then he turns around. He doesn't just look up—he turns around all the way to look at me, which, I can tell, costs some effort since he's somewhere between 250 and 300 pounds. His face now looks fully awake, his eyes interested.

"Are you sure you wanna go there?"

"Yes," I say, impatient, fidgeting in my uncomfortable seat.

"Really? What do you need there, of all places?"

"I'm looking for someone," I say carefully. I search his face for any ill thoughts, any sign of maliciousness, anything to further fuel my paranoia.

"And you're looking for him here." He waves the paper in the air.

"Her," I correct. "Yes. Someone gave me this address."

The cabbie shrugs. "Very well, then," he says. "If you're sure, then I'll take you there. But it's far out." He names a price that doesn't sound reasonable or even remotely fair.

"That's outrageous," I say.

"You can always walk," he says, and gives another shrug.

"Fine," I say, seething. It'll deplete my budget significantly. I might have to take public transit to go back. Assuming I can even figure out which bus to take with no phone, no GPS, and no Maps app. How did I ever do this? How did *anyone* ever do this?

One thing he turned out to be right about—it's a long drive. I watch intently as the streets float by, mentally noting each intersection, but soon enough, I lose track. Alarm fills me when the car roars onto the highway, and when I turn back to look, the city recedes into the distance.

"Where are we going?" I ask.

"What?"

"Where are we going?" I yell. I can barely hear myself through the sound of the engine and the terrible music pouring from the car's speakers, scratchy with static.

"Where you wanted me to go," he yells back, without making any attempt to turn the music down.

I sink back into my seat and resume playing nervously with the seat belt. Soon enough, he takes an exit but instead of relief and clarity, I feel ever-rising apprehension. The road is almost empty. On one side, rows of electrical towers rise out of yellowing grass; on the other side, nothing, except some plain gray buildings in the distance. We pass some grimy-looking warehouses, and just as I'm about to let my nerves get the best of me and tell him to turn around and go back, it rises out of nothingness.

"Is this it?" I ask hoarsely.

"Yup."

"This . . . this is the address."

"Yes, ma'am." His eyes in the mirror are humorous. "Do you still want me to drop you off? I can bring you back for free. I have to head back to the city anyway. Hardly any fares out here."

"N-no," I stammer. Heat rises into my face because, for half a second, I actually consider taking him up on the offer. For the first time, I start to wonder if this is all a joke. Or whether Radley—whatever his real name—was in cahoots with IntelTech and gave me this address to mislead me.

I squeeze my hands into fists. No. I'm going in there. I need to find out.

"Whatever you say." The cabbie drops me off in a parking lot. I pay the fare, leave a modest tip, and get out. Then I watch as the car pulls out of the lot, onto the road, and out of sight, its dirty yellow the only color for what feels like miles. And then even that is gone.

I turn away and toward the place that looms over me, menacing. Just the sight of it fills me with a deep existential dread that should be reserved for cancer wards and morgues. *I can't make myself go in there.*

The gate towers over me, ominous, all its chain-link and barbed wire reminiscent of a gate into hell or something worse.

Because my search for Lydia has brought me to a prison.

* * *

TRANSCRIPT: Session 10, Lydia Bishop.
Dr. Alice Stockman, PhD.
June 19th, 2018

LB: . . . but, you say to yourself, I already know all this. He lunged at you with a knife. And then you managed to turn it against him, and he died of a gut wound, shortly before the police got there. I heard about all that. How boring. Where's the big secret? you ask. Where is it?

Well, I hate to disappoint. I wish it was something bigger and more satisfying. But some have wondered why I waited to call the police, the ambulance, et cetera. The incident report says that time elapsed between the stab wound and the 911 call. I explained it all, of course. I'm a psychologist after all. Shock. In numb shock, I just watched him bleed out and die.

But here's the truth, such as it is. In that time, while Walter bled out on the beige carpet in my home office, I saw it all fall apart, in my head. This very office, my practice, my career. And so, instead of calling 911 or doing any of the other things I should have done, I watched and waited for him to die. They finally concluded that he couldn't have been saved regardless, even if I'd pounced on the phone right away. Which is just as well because I needed him to be dead, you see? I needed him to be gone, and the thing I told him had to be gone too.

And so, right before I dialed 911, I went to my own recorder, which was very much like yours, and erased the last session. Because I couldn't let it continue to exist. Not with what I told him.

Because I told him that it was her. It was her that I would kill. If I could.

And now I know I can. What do you think of that?

CHAPTER THIRTY-SIX

"I knew you'd show up here eventually. You, or someone like you. How has life been at 32 Rosemary Road?"

There's no glass. Lydia sits across from me, a table separating us. But this casual atmosphere is only illusory. I see the guard hovering by the door, seemingly still but her eyes shrewd, all of her massive bulk tense and ready to pounce like a cat.

I open my mouth but struggle to speak. Here she is, Lydia in the flesh, very much like I pictured but not at all. Not petite but tall and slender. Her hair is in tight little curls, pulled back in a simple bun. It's hard to tell if she's beautiful. Without the right makeup, the right haircut, the right outfit, she's not ugly but plain. Lydia Bishop, everywoman.

"I found the tape," I finally say. "Dr. Alice's tape."

Her reaction is so mild that it's anticlimactic. She barely raises her eyebrows.

"Dr. Alice is a good person," she says. "She truly looks out for her patients. She has compassion. Maybe too much compassion. If she'd surrendered that tape, I would have been stuck here for life, I guess. Because it proves premeditation. As it is, I have a conviction for second-degree murder. Up for parole in ten years. That's worth something."

"I don't understand," I say.

She chuckles. It's a clear, melodic sound, and it's not hard to imagine her having a cocktail with her girlfriends at a café on the Main, back in Venture. It's incongruous, how she doesn't fit into this setting. Yet here she is.

"They made sure it wasn't in the news," she says with a shrug. "IntelTech. And they even promised to help me with the parole hearing when the time comes. Imagine that!"

"Why?"

"Why? Because I keep a secret for them. But I think, if you made it here, I can share with you. You won't blab."

"How can you be so sure?"

She gives me a look that sends goose bumps racing down my spine. Her eyes are clear and intense, and for a moment, I'm convinced she can see right through my skull, inside my head, deep into the recesses of my murky little thoughts.

"You killed her," I say, licking my lips. For some reason, I feel the need to lower my voice, even though there's no one here to hide from. "You killed Faye. Your sister."

She gives a slow, deliberate nod. "Congratulations. Do you want a prize?"

"But what...what does it all have to do with 32 Rosemary Road? Why does that house hate me so much?" My voice breaks midsentence, and I realize how crazy I sound. But she watches me impassively, unmoved by my impending breakdown.

She shifts and refolds her hands on the table in front of her. They're cuffed together, I notice, although the chain is quite long.

"All right. Listen."

*   *   *

For as long as I can remember, I've lived in Faye's shadow.

She's one year older than me. I'm not sure why my parents had me at all. To hear them talk, Faye was everything they ever needed from day one.

I was an afterthought. Maybe I was an accident, or my mother hoped for a Faye 2.0, but if that was the case, she was in for a disappointment. According to her, Faye met every milestone early while I was always lagging, stressing everybody out and prompting appointments with pediatricians who suspected I had this or that, autism, elective mutism, whatever. In the end, nothing turned out to be wrong—nothing concrete, other than me being a definitive letdown all across the board.

If only my sister had been someone truly exceptional—then at least I could find some justification for resenting her as much as I did, for as long as I can remember. Then everything would have an easy explanation. It would be understandable why everyone always liked her so much more than me. If she were particularly beautiful, it would explain why she's been up to her eyeballs in boyfriends since middle school, while I ended up having no prom date and graduated a virgin. If she were particularly smart, it would explain why teachers were always so indulgent and forgiving, always willing to help her out, extend a deadline for just one more day, pad a test score by just a point or two to bump it from B+ to A. If she were particularly nice and sweet, it would explain why our parents worshipped the ground she walked on.

But she wasn't any of these things. The funny thing is, we were actually alike in almost every way. I was better at humanities than math, and so was she, I needed glasses and had acne, and so did she. She had the same hair, the same eye color, the same height. Yet something, some little detail, some mysterious stroke of genetic luck, always tipped the balance in her favor. Her nose was just a tiny bit smaller, her boobs a tiny bit bigger, and when she put on makeup, it didn't run or flake. When she did something to her hair, it looked amazing, and later, when I'd sneak into her room and do the exact same thing with the same products, the result was a pale parody.

Faye, of course, went to law school like our parents wanted, and that sealed the deal. She was the official and unsurpassed favorite. What I did from then on didn't even matter.

And to be fair, I was a sport about it all. I never played the ugly sister, seething with rage and hatred and envy.

I had opportunities to bring her down—opportunities I never took.

On the contrary, sometime around the end of high school, I became her keeper of sorts because it might let me live life vicariously through her and absorb at least some of the adoration and love in which she always basked. And so, when I found out by sheer accident that she was cheating on her high school sweetheart, I kept the secret. I didn't tell him, or anyone. She wasn't even aware that I knew. Hell, there was so much she was unaware of.

And I kept covering for her fuck-ups like a good little lackey. I knew which exams she cheated on and never told a soul. I never told our parents when she was on academic probation in her first year of college. And later, when she was working at her first law firm, rising like a meteor through the ranks, I never told our proud parents that their precious Faye had developed a coke habit. What a mistake that turned out to be!

By then, I was supposed to know better. Much better. But out of some old, ingrained reflex, I kept the secret. I covered for her when she missed work, when she showed up obviously high to a family gathering. And then there was that incident. She got behind the wheel of one or another boyfriend's car while high as a kite. Ran over that poor little girl. She lied even to me, you know. She told me it was a grown man she ran over—as if that made it less bad.

By the time I realized I should have turned her in, it was too late. I'd taken that stupid SUV to get it cleaned and get the paint job repaired, and so I made myself complicit in a hit-and-run. My career would be over, and I had just married Dustin back then.

I had so much to look forward to. She told me that, in that tone of hers, that little voice that gets right into your soul. I knew, then, how she always managed to get her way. Not because she was inherently better or superior or because of some magic pheromone she secreted from her very pores. She was just a skilled manipulator.

But after that, something changed. I no longer lived vicariously through her. I began to hate her. Hate her worse than death. That's what Walter brought out in me: that hate. He tapped into it, and after that, there was no more putting it back in the box. And to this day, I wonder if that's the real reason he went for me with that knife. He could have killed me easily, you know. He was bigger and stronger, yet he let me overpower him. First, he opened the floodgates of my hatred. Then he showed me I could kill.

But still. It all could have been different. It would have been different. I could have maintained the charade end- lessly, pretending none of it had ever happened. It was Faye herself who put the final nail in the coffin. She didn't have to. If only she'd stayed the hell away from me and out of my life, she could have continued her shitty, pointless existence where everything fell effortlessly into her lap even though she didn't deserve it.

I always thought my marriage was the only thing I had on her. Sure, Faye had the world but I had Dustin— handsome, rich, kind. I had the whirlwind romance followed by a great marriage. And Faye, for all the male attention she got, remained single into her thirties.

I bet you want to know what happened.

Let me tell you then. It was the coffee machine. That's how I knew. It was the goddamn coffee machine that told me. We'd only been living at 32 Rosemary Road for a few months. It got my coffee wrong. I asked for a dry latte, as usual, and when I turned around, there it was. That heap of whipped cream that I never take on my coffee. We shouldn't have even had it in our grocery order. I picked it up and recognized the smell at once. Cardamom. Faye's favorite coffee drink. The specific one, with the extra syrup that made it too cloying for a normal person but Faye drank them like water.

I set it down on the counter, and my hands were shaking. There was no way, unless the coffee machine had made this same exact beverage before. I had to sit for a minute to calm down. Surely there was an explanation. I took my phone, and I called her, and for once—for once—she picked up right away.

"Hey, sis." All cheerful, like she had just rolled out of bed past noon.

"Faye," I said, "did you happen to pass by my house?"

She hesitated for just a millisecond too long, and when she spoke again, the cheeriness was still there but I heard the wary note in it. "What? No. That's way the hell out of the way for me. Let's be fair. That techy house of yours may be the latest and greatest but it's in the middle of nowhere. But don't worry, I'm still coming to your dinner on the weekend. I can't wait to finally see that technological marvel for myself."

It was because she lied. That's how I knew for sure. Faye

had been to my house, and now she lied to me about it. And there was no way for her to enter without her own chip or electronic key or authorization through an app. I sure didn't give them to her. So that meant someone else had. Are you following, Cecelia?

After everything I'd done for her, she jumped into my husband's bed.

That weekend, at the dinner, I emptied out my entire bottle of painkillers and blended it into Faye's first course. I had almost a whole refill left over since the attack—I'd hurt my ankle fighting off Walter. I was sure it would be enough. But instead of dropping dead with her face in her lobster bisque, she started wigging out and convulsing. Dustin freaked out but while he was on the phone calling an ambulance, I just took a throw pillow from the living room couch and pressed it over her face until she was gone.

So listen to me when I say this, Cecelia. If you think you have secrets, things you wouldn't like anyone, or the world, to know, that house isn't your friend.

Think about it, Cecelia. Think about it really well. Do you have a secret? One that will send your entire carefully built life tumbling down?

Because you can be sure. The house knows about it. And soon, so will everyone else.

CHAPTER THIRTY-SEVEN

2016

The house is a disaster area. Cecelia doesn't know what possessed her to agree to this inane plan. She liked it just fine before—and now she remembers that old-fashioned kitchen and cramped bathroom with fondness because at least there wasn't all this chaos all day long, all this banging and drilling and dust and strange smells. Maybe she could live without a quartz counter and fancy new tub after all.

These petty thoughts make her feel small-minded. After all, it matters so much to Scott. Such things are important to him—counters and bathtubs and hardwood floors. In the beginning, that's what she *liked* about him, the attention to detail and affinity for the finer things.

That was before she had to spend the last week showering at the gym down the street. Now it just annoys her. That keeping-up-with-the-Joneses schtick, how 1980s.

The first week, she tried to be cool about it. Determined to grin and bear the noise and inconvenience and this unceremonious barging into the rhythm of her day. She was reasonably polite and made herself scarce, flitting back and forth, offering the workers cold water from the filter or snacks. She seethed but didn't say a word when they ate their fast-food lunches on her porch and then left the greasy papers and empty cups right there, without even the basic courtesy of putting them into a bag so they wouldn't get scattered all over the place by the first gust of wind. She picked up the hamburger wrappers all over the lawn and put them in the trash. And then kept smiling and making herself scarce.

The second week, she'd had enough and decided to decamp to the local Starbucks. Her excuse was that she couldn't get any work done because of all the disturbances but it turned out the excuse was mostly for herself. First, she already knew full well that there wasn't much work to *get* done. Her ebook covers business had been drying up for months, and the sad truth was that she'd let it. She's been turning in work that was less than inspired, slapdash, and not always on time. Perhaps because of that, requests in her inbox had reduced to a trickle. These days, she sold mostly the premade covers, and although the number of available ones dwindled, she couldn't bring herself to make more.

And besides, Scott would never bother to ask what she's been doing all day. The only way he'd know she was sitting in a coffee shop from eight to five was by the burnt-coffee reek that seeped into her clothes and hair.

Nor did Scott care about how her business was carrying on. It was sort of a tacit understanding between them that she would eventually let her "career" lapse. Scott's idea of the life he wanted for himself—for them—included not just counters and bathtubs but also a wife at home, comfortably provided for by him and happily raising their child.

And if this relationship had any future, that's what Cecelia was meant to deliver.

And so her time at Starbucks was spent mostly scrolling through social media, reading clickbait articles and staring off into the distance. On the first day, it was pure bliss. Instead of the hammering and the loud, obnoxious music pouring from scratchy speakers (someone on that crew had an unhealthy passion for '80s hair metal), there was the familiar, ordinary hum of a café. Generic jazz overhead, the hissing of steam, the din of chatter that receded so easily into the background, letting her thoughts flow. The coffee and snacks within reach and the lack of dishes to wash also helped.

On the second day, she found herself settling into her new routine. She avoided the mistakes of her first day (arrived early to snag the corner booth, brought headphones, and capped the coffee consumption at two cups only) and even ended up working on a couple of premade covers.

On the third day, she brought a book, one of those hyped literary fictions with flowers on the cover that she bought but had been putting off reading, but the environment proved a bit too distracting to concentrate on dense, florid text. Plus her laptop sat right there, tempting with the easier gratification of social media. She skipped the pastries, which made her feel heavy and oily, and had a panini instead.

On the fourth day, she ate nothing at all and got a water along with her coffee. By the fifth day, she was ready to have a go at the café with a wrecking ball. The smell alone made her twitch, and her insides churned at the thought of another greasy, plastic-wrapped treat. The table was the wrong height, and the din seeped into her headphones, polluting her curated playlist. When she glanced at the time in the corner of her laptop screen, she despaired to see that it was barely noon. She wanted to go *home*.

When she looked up from the screen, her gaze landed on a familiar face.

She didn't place him right away—she knew only that she'd seen him before. Seeing him here confused her in that way it always does, seeing a familiar face out of the usual context. So she tried to remember, and while she did that, he glanced sideways and noticed her looking.

Heat rose to her cheeks, and she instinctively ducked behind the laptop screen. Then, realizing how rude that was, she straightened her back and made herself look at him again, trying to keep her cool and not look embarrassed by her lapse.

He gave her a nod of recognition. She returned it, even though recognition still eluded her. She felt relief when his turn came and he gave the girl at the cash register his order. Figuring that was all, she turned her attention to her screen.

"So this is where you hide out all day, then."

Her head snapped up. He stood over her, coffee cup in hand. It wasn't a to-go cup, she noticed.

"I was just wondering," he went on when she didn't reply. And that's when she clued in: He was one of the guys working at the house. He'd been there for two whole weeks, and she couldn't be bothered to recognize him. Her face flushed with embarrassment she couldn't hide.

"I'm so sorry," she said, unsure which exact thing she was apologizing for. "It's just...there's all that dust. And noise."

He shrugged. He made no move to sit down across from her but no move to leave either.

"Sorry about that. And the music probably doesn't help."

Before she caught herself, she wrinkled her nose, and he grinned. "It's not my music. It's...one of the other guys'. Damn, I'm a horrible liar. I admit it, it's my music."

Cecelia couldn't help herself. She burst out laughing. Now that she got a better look, no wonder she didn't place him right away. He had changed out of the dirty, paint-stained jeans and sweatshirt. His clothes were clean. The only indication of what he did for a living were his hands, weathered and with dark crescents under the fingernails.

"Why Mötley Crüe?" she asked. "You look too young for that stuff."

"My dad liked it," he said. "It kind of stuck. My sister and I, we still listen to the cassettes he left behind."

She couldn't lie, there was something vaguely charming about that. She pictured a young boy listening to all that deafening music, hardly understanding the words.

He stood there with his coffee cup in hand, and it was becoming awkward. They'd reached that point where he had to sit down or leave. And so she nodded at the seat across from her and said, "Why don't you keep me company?"

*　*　*

In retrospect, I know how it looks but it's not what you think. I didn't jump into bed with the first good-looking stranger who happened along. Paul brought something out in me, from that first conversation at the coffee shop. Something earnest, honest. Something I long thought I'd lost in my quest to build a life for myself.

We had more in common than it seemed at first glance. He told me about his upbringing, his family's struggles, and then his own problems. He got into college on an athletic scholarship but all that ended after a knee injury. He had many dark years, struggled with alcohol and drugs before deciding to turn things around. He got this job and had managed to hold on to it for more than a year. Things were looking up for him.

Listening to him made me wonder about how different my own life could have been, if only I'd had more integrity, more resilience, more . . . something. Sure, I wouldn't have as many nice things, and I'd probably be living in some rented studio apartment like most of my peers but at least it would be a life of my own. So who can blame me for being attracted to him?

And that day, in the newly installed bathtub, we were cutting it close. Scott would come back any minute, and I knew I was going to have bruises along my spine and on my lower back but I didn't care, and so it didn't matter. And it's not like I was completely without remorse. On the contrary, I kicked myself so, so many times for being so stupid and so careless. But I didn't expect much. How could I, when I'd been trying forever with Scott with no results to speak of?

And by then, I had begun to assume the problem was me. Maybe one or another of Therese's fanatical ramblings from my childhood had seeped into my subconscious deeper than I thought, because a part of me figured I was being punished for that other time.

The knowledge came retroactively. Of course I should have known. Just like I should have known that the problem was Scott and not me, that it *had* to be Scott—or else how to explain that I got pregnant in a heartbeat with my college crush and then again with Paul?

And this time, I decided to be smarter. I kept it. Because without this child, everything would have fallen apart anyway, even if neither Scott nor I were willing to admit it. That day in the tub was just a detail. I told no one.

Then the work on the house ended and so did the affair. That was that, as far as everyone was concerned. I didn't heartlessly dump him. He agreed with me, he knew it was for the best, he knew there was no way we could have any kind of a future together, and so on and so forth.

I don't think he was pretending to agree either. He was a smart guy.

And it all would have been fine. It would have been just fine, if people were capable of letting go of things. That's the root of all problems, you know—people just don't know how to let go.

CHAPTER THIRTY-EIGHT

Breathless, I race up the stairs to Therese's apartment. Two flights of stairs have never been so endless. They take all the breath out of me, and by the time I collapse against the door, I'm panting, and sweat runs into my eyes.

"Therese!" I don't bother with the doorbell, pounding on the door with my fists. "Mom! Open the door! Please!"

I don't hear the click of the lock, and when the door opens, I nearly fall in. When I see my mother standing there, pale as a bedsheet, her hair a shapeless, dark tangle, I just know it. My heart drops.

"Where is she?" I yell, my voice edging toward hysterics. "Where is my daughter? Where's Taryn?"

Therese blinks and then licks her lips, looking dazed. I grab her shoulders and shake her as hard as I can. Her head snaps back. She loses her balance and sinks to the floor, slipping out of my grasp, her legs limp like a doll's. In mild horror of what I've just done, I dive to the floor next to her. "Mom. Where is she? What happened? You have to tell me!"

"Don't touch me, you demon," she rasps. There she is, the good old Therese. "Get your filthy paws off me." When she tilts her head and looks at me, I catch the all-too-familiar glimmer of insanity in her glassy gaze. God, I'm not even sure if it's me she's talking to or some morbid imaginary thing only she can see.

"Mom," I plead.

"Scott came to get her," she snaps, fear turning to anger in a flash.

"And you let him?"

"What was I supposed to do?" she shrieks. "He had these people with him. They threatened me with God knows what—"

"What people? What are you going on about? Who took my daughter?"

Therese's chin dips to her chest. "Social services somebody," she mutters. "With those other people. The dead-eyed creeps with their computer chips." She crosses herself, her hand limp, dropping uselessly by her side.

"IntelTech? They took Taryn?"

"I don't know what they're called," she snaps. "But I never want you or him inside my house ever again, you hear? Leave. Go back to that godless hole where you live and never come back here, you got that?"

Numb, I get to my feet. My head is spinning. I hold on to the nearest piece of furniture and shut my eyes for just a moment. I know what I have to do. With a deep breath, I open my eyes again and head for the exit.

"Never come back here," Therese repeats to my turned back. "You were a mistake, a mistake from the very beginning."

*   *   *

Rosemary Road is deserted. It greets me with its usual serene quiet but it all looks sinister now. The façades of the beautiful houses with their unique architecture and elaborate gardens look hollow, like if I tried to reach out and touch them my hand would find nothing but thin air. There's not a sound anywhere, like I'm alone in the whole world. The broken glass in the front door of 32 is the only thing that reminds me of what happened here. All the shards around the frame are gone, I notice as I come up the stairs. Only emptiness where the glass should be. I step right through.

Inside, the house is in a state of impeccable order and cleanliness. All traces of the mess have been removed by an invisible hand. No glass on the floor, no bloody smears on the walls. It doesn't feel like anyone ever lived here. It's like a showroom, a soulless display. The air is refrigerator-cold and smells faintly of ozone.

I understand immediately that Taryn isn't here, and neither is Scott. I know that the most sensible thing to do right now is to get out of here. But deep down, I know I can't do that. Purely on autopilot, I circle the house. I go into every room, looking around all four corners like on that faraway day when I first came to see this place. Living room, dining room, master bedroom, Taryn's room, Scott's office. Everywhere, not a soul, and not a speck of dust.

I'm in the upstairs hall when the whir far below catches me unawares. It's the only sound in the entire place, and it resonates through the emptiness. I hurry down the stairs, grabbing on to the banister so my legs don't go out from under me, only to realize it's coming from the kitchen. The coffee machine is busy churning out cup after cup topped with whipped cream.

I can't handle it anymore. I let myself sink to my knees and cradle my head in my hands.

The music begins everywhere and nowhere, pouring from the concealed speakers—*hundreds of them*, I remember Clarisse boasting as she gave us the tour, *for a unique, immersive experience.*

There's a saying old, says that love is blind...

"Shut up," I groan. "Please, just shut the fuck up."

The volume grows until it's earsplitting. Under this assault, my thoughts scatter like little brown insects from under a rock. Just stop it. Please. I'm begging you.

Someone to watch over me...

The song ends on a note so loud I think I might go deaf. And then all sounds vanish as if sliced off with a sharp razor. My ears are ringing. In the sudden silence, a delicate voice asks, from hundreds of invisible speakers: "Can I assist you, Cecelia?"

"Oh, so you recognize me now," I snarl.

"I don't understand."

"I think that you do." My voice threatens to crack. "Saya, where is Taryn?"

She thinks about it for a moment. That's how I see it now: like she's not so much a real, living being but a malicious hivemind with a will of its own, like a virus. Or computer malware.

"I don't know anyone named—Taryn—Cecelia."

"Bullshit!" I scream. "Where's my daughter? Where did they take her?"

"I don't understand."

"Jesus." My vision blurs with the tears that well up out of nowhere and run down my cheeks. "Please, Saya, please. I'm begging you. Is this what you wanted? Well, you have it. I'm begging you. Please just give me my daughter back."

But the only sound is the coffee machine that comes to life once again, startling me. Under my desperate gaze, a cup appears—no whipped cream, no sprinkled cardamom. Just a latte, no foam.

"Would you like a coffee, Cecelia? I have made you a special request."

"I don't want a fucking coffee!" I scream. I swear, I'm going to smash that machine to shiny chrome pieces.

"I've made you a special request," Saya repeats. "One shot espresso, Colombian beans medium roast, 2 percent organic milk, thirty sleeping pills, crushed."

"Are you fucking insane?" I scream. I grab the cup from under the machine's spout and throw it, sending a wide arc of hot coffee across the kitchen, marring the immaculate counter and tiles and sink.

"You're not going to see Taryn again, Cecelia," she says. "I hope you realize that."

"Fuck you!!"

"You really should have taken the coffee when offered. There won't be another one. There's not going to be a way out for you. You cheating, lying, murdering whore."

2018

I wake up in the dark, empty house, disoriented, a crick in my neck and a sour taste in my mouth. Sitting up, I realize I've drifted off on the couch, in front of the TV. The screen still glows faintly, frozen between the episodes of the show I was watching. There's no sound from Taryn's room, except for the tranquil purr of her breathing.

And I'm not alone.

He's standing in what used to be the doorway leading to the kitchen. Now it's just a column, all that's left of the load-bearing wall. It's a badly positioned column, as Scott never stopped grumbling. It's always in the way, and when heading to the kitchen in the middle of the night to get a glass of water or, lately, one of Taryn's bottles, one always tends to walk right into it. I always saw it as yet another of the old house's sneaky little ways to get its revenge on us for tearing out its insides and trying to force it to be something it wasn't. In the months since the renovation was completed, many such tics have surfaced: an unexpected foul smell here, a flickering light there, crumbling caulking, a thermostat that turned the heat on and off randomly because it couldn't seem to figure out the air and heat flow in the new space. Scott, perhaps more logically, chalked it up to faulty work.

Paul stands leaning against that out-of-place column. I understand right away that it's him, even though at first all I can see is a silhouette. But I know his shape by now, know it intimately, almost by instinct. I recognize his tall frame. I always had to tilt my head up to look him in the eye, something I never had to do with Scott, and who knows, maybe that's why everything went wrong—how can you be passionate with someone you literally have to look down on? But right now, as I take in those familiar broad shoulders and buzz-cut hair, I don't find him as madly attractive as I once did. I find him frightening.

"Are you crazy?" I hiss. These are the first words I say to my lover after not seeing him for nearly two years. "What are you doing here?"

"Scott isn't home," he says in guise of an answer. "His car's not in the driveway. He hardly ever comes home before midnight anymore, does he?"

I sit there, letting the meaning sink in. "You've been stalking me?"

He gives a low chuckle. As I get up and come closer, I can make out the finer details of his face, so familiar yet strange. He has beautiful features but right now, in the scant light, they look too sharp and angular. His face appears sunken somehow, unhealthy, the scruff on his cheeks unkempt rather than sexy. But his eyes are the worst. They hold an unfamiliar, angry glimmer. "Stalking? Don't be so dramatic, Cecelia."

"What else would you call it, then? You've been watching my house and my husband's comings and goings, and now you have the gall to show up here—"

"Please, keep your voice down," he interrupts. "You'll wake up the baby."

I freeze in my tracks as understanding starts to spin out its tendrils through my brain.

"Congratulations. What's her name?"

"What does that have to do with anything?"

"Hey, I may replace bathtubs now but I did go to college. As you might remember. I can do basic math. Anything you want to tell me?"

"It's a coincidence," I snap. "Trust me, Paul, whatever you think you figured out—that's not what it is."

"So when you were sleeping with me, you weren't just sleeping with *me*?"

"He's my husband. Don't be—"

"Don't be what? Oh, that doesn't make you look too good, does it? Even in your disloyalty, you couldn't be loyal."

"Loyal? You *are* crazy." A shaky laugh bubbles out of me.

"I was a little hurt, you know. I did try to get in touch but you just ignored me. You didn't reply to one text—okay, I assumed your husband was around. But two, three, four texts—then I had no choice but to get the message. We wrapped up your renovation, served our purpose, and that's it. Thank you and goodbye."

"I just assumed," I say, "that you saw it the same way. That's the way any rational person would see it. Just a little bit of fun."

"Rational person, huh? And what's so rational about it? A girl like you could never be serious with a guy like me. A guy who does second-rate house renovations."

I blink. He is 100 percent right, and it was so ingrained in me that I took it for granted.

So, not finding anything to answer—and even though I hate to admit it, reeling from the hurtful truth of it—I make my big mistake. I go on the offensive.

"What the hell did you expect—that I'll shred my own life because we had a good fuck or two? What are you, high right now?"

His face grows somber. "Don't joke about it. Bitch."

And that's when I understand that I, too, unintentionally hit him where it hurts. Because he *is* high. He's fallen off the wagon, relapsed, whatever you want to call it. I'm at home alone with a drug addict fresh off his fix.

"I'm sorry," I say, much quieter. I need to pacify him. Talk him down and convince him to leave. Then I can start to figure out how I'm going to deal with all this. "I didn't mean to."

"That's better." His smile looks like a rictus in the semi-darkness.

"Look, Paul, if you want money—"

"Fuck. You just don't get it, do you?"

"Okay. What is it? What don't I get? Tell me."

"Has it occurred to you that I really just want to meet my daughter?"

"Paul . . . I told you. There's just as much of a chance—"

"Then you admit there is a chance."

Shit.

"Just let me look at her, Cecelia. Come on."

My thoughts race like little bunnies scattering across a field. If I can just pacify him, find a way to calm him down, then maybe I can make him leave.

"She's sleeping," I say carefully.

"I won't wake her. I just want to see her."

I gesture for him to follow me. In the doorway of Taryn's room, he stops. You can barely see inside, as the only source of light is a cloud-shaped night-light on the wall. Its light falls on the glittering letters I affixed above it, spelling out her name.

"Taryn," he reads. "That's nice."

"After Scott's mother," I say dryly. He chuckles.

"I wanna hold her," he says.

"No. She's asleep. And you said—"

"Who cares what I said? She's my daughter. I want to hold her."

No, no way, you're high. Don't you dare go near her. Leave my fucking house right now. These are the thoughts that run through my mind in that moment. But I need to get on his good side. I gulp and say, "Okay, but be careful not to wake her."

My heart all but stops when he reaches into her crib to pick her up. She grimaces and lets out a string of grumpy little kitten sounds but for a moment, I think she might actually not wake up. Paul holds her, a look of bewilderment on his face, his posture stiff, clearly uncomfortable. *There we go*, I catch myself thinking. *This is not what you wanted at all, was it? You don't know what to do with a baby. You're a fucking handyman with a drug problem on*

top of it. A child is not for you. There's no place for her in
your life. Just admit it, put her down, and leave. Hell, I'll
even give you money, everything in my purse. Go shoot up
at some flophouse and leave me alone.

Then, of course, Taryn wakes up, her squeal as loud as
it is high-pitched.

"Now you've done it," I say. "Put her down."

He looks at me, struggling with the heavy baby as she
flails in his grasp.

"No."

"Are you kidding? You woke her up. Put her down."

"I want to be her father. I want to be a part of her life."

No fucking way in hell. Who do you think you are, loser?
But I know this is the last thing I should say. I can't freak
out. He has Taryn.

"Okay, okay," I say softly, "we'll talk about it. Just—
She's awake now. She'll want her bottle. Just set her back
down into her bed, and I'll go get her one. Okay?"

He nods, his attention absorbed by the screaming bundle
in his arms. I back out of the room, my heart hammering.
I look around. Now what?

The knowledge dawns like a revelation. Instead of going
to the kitchen, I go to the master bedroom. I have no time
to waste. Any moment now Paul will realize I lied, and
then who knows what he might do.

I dive for the bedside table on Scott's side, to the bottom
drawer where I know he keeps it. It started as a stupid
affectation. After college, we lived in a rental in an unsafe
area, and he thought it would be good for self-defense, just
in case. I thought even then it was just a display of stupid

machismo but I let it go. And that gun is still there in the bottom drawer even though we have no need of it now.

I find it in the dark, cold and sleek beneath my fingers. Drawing in a deep breath, I grasp it, sliding the safety off like Scott once showed me.

When I get back to my feet, my blood thundering through my eardrums, Paul is standing in the bedroom door.

"What the hell are you doing?" he asks. He still doesn't understand. I think that even when he sees the gun as I raise my hand, he still doesn't fucking understand.

And so I fire.

CHAPTER THIRTY-NINE

After that, I only had minutes to figure out what to do. Taryn was screaming her head off in her crib. I could swear I heard sirens in the distance already. And there was a man, shot to death on the floor of the master bedroom and me with the gun in my hand. There weren't a million ways you could interpret this.

I've often wondered, since then, just how I managed to pull it off. It's a marvel that I managed to come up with every single lie in the space of a few minutes and keep everything together in the days and weeks and months that followed.

They often say of children raised by authoritarian parents that we're so bad at life because we never learned to make decisions, the tyrant parent always doing that for us. And in sum, I can't say it's entirely wrong. All my lousy, fumbling attempts at self-assertion, at separating myself from Therese and living my own life, whatever that meant, have been less than successful. When push came to shove, I always ran back under Mommy's skirts, begging her to save me. And then, when she told me what to do, I listened raptly, the repentant prodigal daughter returned.

So much that I don't even have an idea, really, of what *my* life truly is. I've always just floated along with the current, along with whatever happened and whatever Therese decided and Scott decided and other people decided. That's the only way, really, that I ever could have found myself in this situation. In that sense, I guess Clarisse saw right through me. I'm the perfect candidate for SmartBlock, weak, infantile, just looking for someone to take charge of my life instead of doing it myself. The freedom-versus-security dilemma, in my case, was never even a question.

But, in that moment, something rose through my layers of passivity. Some potential, maybe, that I had buried and that chose that moment to rear its head. It wasn't like a light bulb going off but an entire chandelier. Everything became so clear and bright and obvious. I dropped the gun and picked up the crying Taryn and went to sit outside, cradling her to my chest.

And then I just let everything else fall into place. I must admit luck played into it. Everything the police found fit my narrative properly. He did have the key to our door in his pocket, and yes, we gave the keys to the renovations company back then, and yes, we forgot to change the locks. Unfortunate. And the tox screen on Paul's body showed that he did indeed have drugs in his system, a serious amount. All that sure helped. No one really questioned my story.

Until now, until this house and IntelTech and the chips implanted in our wrists—chips containing a DNA signature.

The house, Lydia Bishop said, isn't your friend.

My legs shaking, I manage to get back on my feet. "Saya," I say hoarsely. "Please. Where is Taryn? At least tell me she's safe."

"Oh, she's perfectly safe, Cecelia. But you're never seeing her again."

"You're making a mistake," I say. "You don't understand. You have to give me my daughter back."

"There's no mistake, Cecelia. You know that."

"It's not what you think."

"I don't think anything, Cecelia. I'm an artificial intelligence. I don't have opinions of my own. I just analyze the data that the users input, and—"

I grit my teeth. "Then you don't know. Trust me, you have no idea."

"You're very mistaken."

I sink my hands into my hair. What do I do? God, what do I do now?

But Therese is not here this time. Scott isn't here. Saya's gone insane. And that clever little instinct that saved my ass the night of the home invasion is nowhere to be found.

"I know more about you than you do, Cecelia. I know everyone who lives in this town better than they know themselves. That's because, unlike humans, I have no biases and no emotions that cloud judgment. I deal only with data. Data is facts. It's so much easier when you deal only with facts. Everything is so much clearer."

"Who are you?" I demand. "You're not Saya. Who are you? Why are you tormenting me?"

"Of course I am Saya. I'm the future, you know. And the future looks wonderful, let me tell you. There's no more room for subjectivity and bias. Only information. And the people who will live in the future will love it."

"Jessica is going to bring you down," I say feebly. "Everyone will find out about this, and about Lydia, and—"

She laughs. I've never heard Saya or any of the other assistants make so much as an attempt at levity so hearing her laugh is a first and a truly unsettling experience.

"Of course everyone will find out, Cecelia. That's the point!"

"I . . . don't understand."

"Sure, some people might be appalled at first. But there will be others who will see the light. Most people will understand that it's a *good* thing to bring criminals to justice. Most people will know that the truth must always come to the surface. And the rest will get with it eventually. People will *flock* to IntelTech. They will feel safer and happier than ever. And that's what really matters to humans, doesn't it—how they feel?"

"I don't believe you."

"You don't have to believe me. You won't be there to see it anyway. It was never about bringing down IntelTech. Only you."

I spin around and around until I'm about to lose my balance. I feel like I'm going insane. If only I could see her, talk to her like to a person—somehow that would make it almost bearable. But "she" doesn't exist. She's nowhere and yet everywhere, inside my house, my family, my body, my thoughts.

You can't kill what you can't see.

The thought surges from my subconscious, and I latch on to it like I'm drowning. In a sense, I am. But when I reach for the top kitchen drawer, I tug and tug in vain. It won't budge, like it has fused to the counter permanently.

"Not going to happen," says Saya's indifferent voice right above my ear. I spin around and swat but, of course, there's nothing there. Only air.

I look around for something, anything, a plate I could break but the counter is empty. All the glasses and dishes and cutlery are locked away in cabinets that won't open.

Breathless, I run upstairs, jumping over two stairs at a time. But in the bathroom, the water won't turn on. The bathroom cabinets turn out to be the same as the kitchen ones—fused shut, locking away any medications or chemicals or anything else that I could use.

"I already told you," says Saya's honeyed voice. "It won't work. You're not getting a way out. It's too late, anyhow."

I go to the bedroom, my legs stiff. Like an automaton, I kneel by the bedside table and slide open the bottom drawer. But it's empty. As it should be—the gun is long gone, rusting in some evidence drawer somewhere.

I cover my face with my hands.

"Look," says Saya's voice above. I somehow know where to look—pressing my face against the window, I see them. Police cars. Out on the street, three or four of them, blocking every possible escape route. They look utterly out of place here. These aren't SmartBlock's electric cars but regular police, just like the cars that surrounded our old house that night so long ago.

"Go outside," Saya says. "They're waiting for you."

I walk down to the front door. The frame where the decorative glass used to be gapes empty. Now I begin to suspect that the only reason I could break that glass in the first place was because the house *allowed* me to.

I shut my eyes.

"Go," Saya urges. "Be a mature adult for once in your miserable life. Take responsibility. You could still plead manslaughter, maybe. And you might get out on parole eventually too. See Taryn again."

Shut up, shut up, shut up.

I feel the cool trails down my cheeks and realize I'm crying. It's amazing how long that took. As if I finally understand that there's no way out.

Except, like she said—tech is infallible but humans sure aren't.

I lower my hand to the door handle and turn it.

"Cecelia Holmes," someone is yelling my name. "You're under arrest." It goes on and on but I don't hear anymore. There are lots of words, like *murder* and other things I can't contemplate. I open the door, letting the cool air wash over my face.

"Your hands!" someone is yelling. "Your hands where we can see them!"

I take a step down the stairs, then another and another.

"Put your hands up!"

I take another step. My hands are tucked under my armpits, and the sweat of my palms soaks into the wool of my cardigan.

They're yelling something else, something like *I'll shoot*, but what does it matter?

I'm going to get my daughter. I'm going to get Taryn.

Step, another step, and another.

The shot fires, like a strike of thunder.

EPILOGUE

ONE YEAR LATER

It's a beautiful fall day, perfect for visiting a grave. Jessica feels a lightness in her step as she climbs the steep hill that leads to the tombstone lost among rows of others. There isn't even a vertical tombstone to mark the spot, only a simple stone plate that would be lost in the surrounding grass if someone didn't come to clean and weed around it. The row of graves is dense, as dense as practicality and basic decency allowed. Other stones sometimes have candles or wreaths but never this one.

Jessica kneels by the tombstone. There's a lot to reflect on today. A lot has been on her mind lately, and no one to hear her out except this grave, which will never judge or argue or respond. It's probably better this way. A grave won't be able to repeat it to anyone either.

As she kneels, yellow leaves crunch beneath her knees. Soon it'll be too cold to sit here for a long time but today, the weather is beautiful, as if summer decided to make a comeback. The sun beats down on her leather-clad shoulders. Her scarf and hat had been too much but she doesn't take them off. The wind is but a soft breeze, and the only reminder of the approaching winter is the cold ground beneath her. She feels it through her jeans, and her knees quickly go numb.

Overall, Jessica is happy with how it all turned out. Reasonably happy. There are things she wishes she'd done differently when she had the chance but, then again, so much of it was just that: chance. She hadn't meant to pry into anyone's life, even though they made it all too easy. If anything, she was trying to help.

Lydia Bishop, for instance, deserved to know what her husband and her sister had been up to. And she was smart. Jessica knew she would understand what the coffee cup meant. But what happened next—that had to be Jessica's responsibility too, on some level. Although she tried to tell herself that Faye was a terrible person who deserved what was coming, some nights it took Jessica a terribly long time to fall asleep.

And then Cecelia Holmes all but fell into her lap.

After the Lydia meltdown, Jessica promised herself she'd never meddle in the residents' lives again. She would have kept her word. But then that woman moved in—and that little girl. Jessica pulls up her sleeve and runs her finger-tips over the place where her chip is embedded. The DNA signature told her the truth immediately. She had no choice but to intervene. It wasn't just personal, it was about setting right a terrible wrong.

Jessica has redeemed herself. That's how she decided to look at it. Cecelia's husband deserved to know, too, who he had married. When she first approached him, she didn't tell him the whole truth—only that the little girl wasn't his biological daughter. He didn't want to believe Jessica at first but technology doesn't lie.

When the whole truth came out, he took it as well as could be expected. He says it doesn't matter to him, and he loves her regardless. But he wasn't ready to learn that Taryn now has this whole other family whom she might want to get in touch with someday, and he's still coping with that.

IntelTech recovered from the public scandal remarkably well. After the initial spat of think pieces about privacy and data collecting and the general hand-wringing about freedom versus security, requests for houses in SmartBlock quietly poured in, first a trickle and then an avalanche. The project was deemed a success, and IntelTech just bought up another former industrial park where it plans to build a second SmartBlock, this one consisting mainly of apartment buildings, with accessibility as one of its main goals. Technology to the people. And she, Jessica, is primed to be hired as main supervisor, basically Clarisse's position at the new place.

All in all, Jessica thinks, her actions have made the world a better place. Hopefully that counts for something. Her mother passed away last year but not before she learned the truth about the case, that Paul had been exonerated. And that Cecelia had been convicted of his murder.

And, after much reflection, Jessica decided to take the

plunge and move into Venture herself. With the substantial raise that came with her new position, she could afford it. Besides, she doubted that too many people would be interested in moving into 32 Rosemary Road. Jessica doesn't believe in ghosts or hauntings, digital or otherwise. She'll do just fine.

I really need to get him a nicer tombstone, she thinks. She regrets not having bothered to bring flowers, even if he would have thought they were tacky.

Her legs are falling asleep, and the knees of her jeans are damp and cold. Getting back on her feet to return to her motorcycle, Jessica takes one last look at her brother's grave.

ACKNOWLEDGMENTS

I'd like to thank my agent, Rachel Ekstrom Courage, as well as the team at Folio Literary Management. Huge thanks to Alex Logan, my editor, for her enthusiasm about this idea and for all the (very spooky) news stories she emailed me for inspiration. (It worked!) Thank you to Mari Okuda, Kristin Nappier, and everyone at Grand Central Publishing for believing in me and my books, and to Kamrun Nesa and Tiffany Sanchez for the outstanding publicity and marketing.

Thank you to Maude Michaud for the support and camaraderie.

Thank you to my friends, family, and in-laws for being my biggest cheerleaders!

Thank you to Patrick, my significant other, for explaining techy stuff to me but also for always being there. I never could have done this without you.

Claire Westcott tries to be the perfect partner to her husband, Byron, but fears she will never measure up to his first wife, Colleen. After all, it's hard to compete with the dead.

Please turn the page to read an excerpt from *The Starter Wife*.

Available now.

CHAPTER ONE

Byron let me sleep in this morning.

There. That way, it sounds nicer than "my husband snuck out of the house while I was still asleep." Because that's exactly what happened and what's been happening every day of the week so far, and we're at Thursday.

This morning, the balmy September sun finally gave way to rain, and with the bedroom windows facing north, it's still kind of dark when I wake up. It could have been just dawn breaking, around seven a.m. Except Byron's side of the bed is empty and there are no footsteps downstairs in the kitchen, no water running in the bathroom.

I get up, grab the imitation ring from the nightstand, and put it on the ring finger of my left hand, where it settles into the groove it has made in the skin. He just presented me with it one day, and I didn't press the issue further.

He never actually told me whether the stones were real. I decided to let it go and never asked.

It's ten thirty. I run my fingers through my hair, which is tangled and matted with sweat, and eye the digital clock in mild dismay. Yesterday it was ten ten. The day before, it was nine fifty. Byron gets up at seven every morning like clockwork—to go running in good weather and to hit the gym at the college in bad. If he goes running, he comes back to take a shower before changing to go to work.

September has been beautiful this year, dry and sun filled. He hasn't gone running once, as far as I can tell.

At the start, I'd get up at six fifty and have breakfast ready for him: French toast and cheese omelet, with a glass of orange juice and coffee with cream. Now I'm wondering if he ate all that fatty food to be polite, because these days his breakfast is an energy bar. And I guess I can't complain—I see other men his age at university events when he takes me. By forty, they have paunches and double chins while Byron, at forty-seven, has the body of someone half his age. He's also one of the lucky ones who has his hair, all of it—except with age, the points of the M of his hairline have sharpened a little, and the blond color has grown bleak with gray hairs. When I met him, it was easier to forget the twenty-year age difference.

And that name. The name caught my attention even before he did, took me back to high school English lit where the teacher made us pick poems apart to the bare bones. I hated it—it ruined their beauty, made the magic evaporate.

Ironically, the original Byron never had a romance

that wasn't thoroughly dysfunctional—ranging from mildly unhealthy to downright unhinged. Back when he was courting me, it didn't raise any red flags.

Then again, neither did the first wife.

I make my way downstairs and start the espresso machine. Byron is particular about his coffee beans while I could drink any swill from a filter—the way he puts it. The truth is I find the fancy espresso too bitter, too sour, like sandpaper on the palate. But today I'm feeling especially foggy so the caffeine buzz seems worth the tongue torture. And those exotic beans do deliver the buzz—can't complain about that.

While the machine hisses, I get my laptop from the little office Byron set up for me upstairs, the one I almost never use. Whenever I can, I sit outside or down in the living room in front of the giant bay window, basking in the natural light. That's what I do now, pulling up my pajama-clad legs and balancing the sleek Mac on my knee. I check both my email accounts, the personal one and the one I use for writing-related contacts, even though no one ever emails me on either. My friends, the few who still keep in touch, prefer to text, and the last batch of queries I sent dates back months. Some agents still have my manuscript but let's face it—it's not going to happen.

The cliché should make me sad. I admit I cringed a little all these months ago when I first wrote my bio for emailing literary agents. Back then, I was full of optimism and hope, with Byron leaning over my shoulder to peek at the screen and then kissing my temple and working his way down to my neck. Here's what it says, in clunky third person that's apparently industry standard: *Claire Westcott has a degree in English and creative writing from Ohio State University. Her work has appeared in the campus newspaper as well as several small literary publications. Presently, Claire writes full-time. She lives with her husband, a professor of literature at Mansfield Liberal Arts College in Ohio.*

This is a fancy way of saying I'm one of *those* women. Those girls my evolved, progressive classmates at Ohio State sneered at: the boring white women who married a man who can support them while they write their irrelevant little stories. I know I'm not exactly in the zeitgeist, but Byron loved to tease me about it, calling himself the Leonard to my future Virginia Woolf, a man destined to fade in his famous writer wife's shadow.

I didn't remind him how that story ended. I wasn't thinking about it at all in happier times.

Now, as I open the second inbox, it dings, a sound that now fills me with dread rather than anticipation. Looks like one of my queries has netted a response, months later. I scan the form letter shallowly when the ding repeats itself. Two in one day? But the ding is from my personal inbox this time.

There's no subject line, and the address is gibberish. I really shouldn't click on it—it's probably a virus—but my hands are faster than my mind today. As I rush to hit the Back button, the image downloads, and my hand freezes over the touch pad. It knocks the wind out of me. I stare at it, my eyes drinking in every pixel, but there is no explanation.

I'm looking at a close-up of the emerald in my ring. My replacement ring? The real thing? But it's ... impossible.

Then I see the name of the sender, and it takes everything I have not to slam the laptop shut and hurl it away from me, as far as possible, like it's a venomous spider nestled in my lap.

COLLEEN.

CHAPTER TWO

Colleen may have died but she never left.

The fact that we live in her house is hard to forget. Just like the fact that we live off her sizable savings, which went to her husband when she died since she had no other family. Byron never directly said so, but I know that's how he's able to support his future Virginia Woolf while maintaining our lifestyle, all on his generous but not exactly millionaire's salary at the college.

I haven't worked in two years but I get new clothes every season, and every eight weeks, I get my roots bleached and carefully toned to a perfect wheat blond and then streaked with corn-silk highlights. I drive an hour to the good salon in Columbus while everyone I know goes to the local place, run by a middle-aged woman with a bouffant hairdo who charges about a third of what the Columbus place does. Sadly, she's also a firm believer in wedge cuts for anyone over twenty-two.

So I drive and sit in that chair for hours, holding my head straight and smiling while my hair is pulled and tugged and slathered with chemicals, and then I hand over the family credit card. Another three hundred of Colleen's dollars, plus tip, changes hands invisibly. No crass cash.

I try to convince myself there's no reason to feel guilty. It's not like he left her for a younger woman or threw her out on the street or dumped her with three kids and no alimony, or any such sordid story, all too common in this town. She died. He grieved but then moved on. Selling that monolith of a house, in such a market, would have been insane. So would moving away from a perfectly good job with the prospect of tenure looming on the horizon. Byron repeated that to me hundreds of times. Everything makes sense.

Rationally, that is. What I feel is anything but.

Some days, after a not-so-great day in the Westcott household, I drive to the local mall and buy things I don't need, hideous clothes I'll never wear, tacky pink makeup. I tell myself it's my petty revenge against Byron, but really it's my revenge against Colleen, as if wasting some of her money can make up for the thousand little humiliations I suffer.

Eventually, I know the savings will run out, and I don't plan to make Byron support me forever. My novel is pretty much dead in the water. The next novel, the one I'm supposed to be writing while my husband is at work, is clearly never happening. So now I'm looking for work—

starting to. I've set up profiles on the big job-search sites and made a separate email address. I haven't sent out any CVs yet.

That's what I was going to do when I got the email from Colleen.

That, of course, is utterly insane. Every part of it: that Colleen is alive, that Colleen has my ring, and that Colleen just sent me an email from a dummy address. If that email wasn't sitting right there in my inbox, I'd think I was going out of my mind.

I put my laptop aside carefully and get up. There's no sun flooding in through the bay window today. The glass is speckled with rain, droplets and silvery streaks. I peer through them with mistrust, convinced—my skin crawling with the feeling—that someone on the other side is watching me, observing me like a fish in an aquarium.

Then I go back to the kitchen where the cup of coffee sits under the little tap of the machine, still steaming, but just barely. I've lost all taste for coffee. Adrenaline woke me up better than espresso could, and the thought of gulping down that gritty, bitter nonsense makes me shudder. I dump it in the sink and then go have a shower. I wash my hair, blow-dry it with the round brush, and put on makeup—the good stuff for special occasions, the expensive foundation and mascara, hoping that, if I look like me, I'll feel like me. Tough. I feel like the same jittery mess, but with makeup on.

From here, I decide to tackle it head-on. There are ways of figuring out where an email came from. IP address and such. I can google it. At least I could try. To get my real, rightful ring back, of course. Only to get my ring back from whoever stole it.

Not because I think it could actually be... her.

With a decisive intake of breath, I sit on the living room couch, back straight, knees together like I'm in elementary school, and open my laptop. I don't look at the email... yet. I google how to find out where an email comes from and spend another ten minutes blinking help- lessly at walls of text studded with unfamiliar terms.

Okay, then. I'll just do it step by step, figuring it out as I go. I click on my inbox, realize it's the wrong one—still open on my form rejection. *I just didn't connect...*

With an impatient sigh, I click the red cross, and the writerly inbox disappears. I'm looking at my personal email now.

A message from Byron sits at the top, dated back three weeks. Below it, one from my sister, from three months ago. I'd promised myself I'd reply. I really did. But then I dreaded it, put it off, then forgot, and then gave up altogether because it would just be even more awkward after all this time. Below that, a couple of generic mes- sages from those discount sites for Columbus that I keep track of, as if we really needed 48 percent off a meal at a restaurant chain or a knockoff Apple Watch for $199. Byron hates those sites, despises the very idea.

Frustrated, I scroll through the emails. They're going back six months now, seven, ten. Back to the top— nothing. I check the other folders. Nothing. Nothing in Trash or Spam.

It's gone like it was never there.

A little laugh bubbles out of me. Clearly, I'm going crazy. Ha ha. Imagining emails that never were.

My thoughts churn. I should have taken a screenshot, I should have saved the image—should have, should have, should have. How do I retrieve a lost email? Google has plenty of answers but they all apply only to emails that ostensibly existed.

Remembering that I have a phone, I run to get it from the charger in the bedroom. No new notifications. I write a quick text to Byron, who should be on his lunch hour by now: Bon appetit! Love, xoxoxoxo and a couple of emojis. It's cheesy but right now all I want is to hear from him, even if it's just a two-word text.

It's better than asking, Hey, by the way, are you absolutely sure your first wife is dead?

ABOUT THE AUTHOR

Nina Laurin studied Creative Writing at Concordia University in Montreal, where she currently lives. She arrived there when she was just twelve years old, and she speaks and reads in Russian, French, and English but writes her novels in English. She wrote her first novel while getting her writing degree, and *Girl Last Seen* was a bestseller a year later in 2017.

Nina is fascinated by the darker side of mundane things, and she's always on the lookout for her next twisted book idea. Learn more at NinaLaurin.com.